The Devil's Bedroom

The Devil's Bedroom

BREAKING FREE FROM THE CHAINS OF GUILT & SHAME
AN URBAN NOVEL

MESTANNA

Incite Change Publishing LLC.
Atlanta, GA

ISBN 978-0-578-88299-4

Editor: Shonell Bacon
Design: Mayflydesign.com
Front & Back Book Cover Design: Junriel Boquecosa (baki.com)
Front Cover Original Photograph: Marion Designs

1 0 2 6 2 2

For those who are pioneering with no example to follow, but know that from darkness emerges light and there must be a way to create a better life.

For those who have a burning desire to release their past and heal and begin the journey of spiritual awakening. I say to you, "Rise Phonenix, rise from the ashes and fly high!"

About the Author

Mestanna found her passion for writing through poetry. It was in 1991, shortly after the Rodney King beating that she was watching the Oprah Winfrey talk show. Oprah had people of many different ethnicities on her show to discuss the devastating effects of the LA riots and racism. Overcome with many emotions, Mestanna picked up her pen and discovered poetry as an outlet to express her pain and frustration.

In 1999, Mestanna published her first poem "Able" and received the Published Poet: Editor's Choice Award for Outstanding Poetry. In 2000, Her poem "The African-American Woman Survivor of All Times" was written and used in a state-wide Beauty Pageant.

She started writing her prayers as a supplication to God to heal her immense pain caused by childhood traumas, abusive and dysfunctional relationships. Mestanna turned her pain into her passion and in 2019, Mestanna completed her first manuscript titled, *The Devil's Bedroom – Breaking Free from The Chains of Guilt & Shame*. The poems and prayers in this book were written in real time while the author was experiencing adversity.

Mestanna is an intuitive empath that uses universal truth and spiritual wisdom to teach others how to transform their lives. Her mission is to inspire and teach others how to let go of the chains of guilt and shame by learning unconditional self-love, forgiveness and how to discover their true calling by examining their traumas, experiences, and decisions. In 2021, Mestanna formed her own publishing company, Incite Change Publishing LLC. with the plan to make The Devil's Bedroom a trilogy and to write and publish many non-fiction books. For more information visit her website at www.mestanna.com

Acknowledgments

This book would have never been completed without the Divine instruction and guidance from My Creator, My Source, My Holy Father / Mother / God – Yahweh!!! I am so grateful for your unwavering love and grace.

Thank you to my beautiful children who have been one of my greatest inspirations to win at this game called life. To be a living example that dreams do come true and what you believe, you can achieve. I am grateful for you four beautiful souls joining me on this journey.

Thank you to my Mother & Father for being the vessel in which I emerged into this lifetime. Thank you Mom for being my task partner and I love you unconditionally.

Thank you to my Sista Gurl, for being there for me in my darkest hours and my greatest joys!!! Thank you for encouraging me to keep fighting for my dreams during those times when I felt I had no fight left in me. I love you always.

Thank you to all my Angels, family and friends that have supported and encouraged me on my journey. I will always be grateful.

Last but not least, thank you to the readers! Thank you to the wounded, beautiful soul who reads this book and it helps you discover your passion from your pain. MAY GOD BLESS YOU WITH DIVINE HEALING – YOU ARE THE REASON WHY I WROTE THIS BOOK!!!

Contents

"God is Spirit, and those who worship
Him must worship in spirit and in truth."

John 4:24

"Then God said, 'Let Us make man
in Our image, according to Our likeness.'"

Genesis 1:26

Introduction

We are spiritual beings having a physical experience. Our spirit dwells within our physical bodies; however, our bodies are only a temporary dwelling place for our spirits. Our spirit is energy; we were created by Divine Source Energy—God. Just as a father passes his DNA to his son, God has given his children divinity and the power to create. Everything God created He created with a purpose, including us as spiritual beings first and physical beings second. Human beings have a mission and a divine purpose to fulfill on Earth while living in this physical dimension. Souls come to this planet in the physical realm to learn, expand in consciousness, heal, discover self-love, and assist other souls to do the same.

This spiritual mission was never designed to be easy, and the learning lessons for many souls are very difficult and heart-wrenching. Sometimes, the experiences we suffer here on Earth are unbearable, and the soul is engulfed in so much hopelessness that they end their own life. There can be a sense of feeling lost and empty inside, and the soul begins seeking to be fulfilled through the physical senses, and begins to indulge in superficial pleasures, hoping to reach a feeling of gratification but unfortunately always remaining empty. It isn't until that being realizes that pleasure seeking is an illusion and begin asking questions like "Who am I?" or "Why am I here?" that their lives begin to change, and the unveiling begins.

This is a story of how one young lady discovered her divine purpose through the traumatic events that happened to her in her life. God is the creator of all things, good and bad, including the Devil. If there is no darkness, one cannot appreciate light.

"And war broke out in heaven: Michael and his angels fought against the dragon; and the dragon and his angels fought, but they did not prevail, nor was a place found for them in heaven any longer. So, the great dragon was cast out, that the serpent of old, called the Devil and Satan, who deceives the whole world; he was cast to the earth, and his angels were cast out with him" (Revelation 12:7-9).

While we are on our spiritual journey here on Earth, we will face challenges and obstacles. Whatever your spiritual or religious beliefs are, it cannot be denied that there is good and evil in this world. "The eyes of the LORD are in every place, keeping watch on the evil and the good" (Proverbs 15:3).

God and goodness are synonymous with positive energy, and the Devil and evil are synonymous with negative energy. Humans utilize both these energies, negative and positive, through the power of our thoughts. What do you fear most? What do you choose to focus on in your daily life, the good things or bad? What are you silently suffering from that's haunting you and crippling your progression in life? What thoughts are popping into your mind that are holding you back, preventing you from reaching your full potential? Do you ever wonder why is it is usually a negative thought that pops into our mind before a positive thought? Why is it so easy to believe the negative thoughts and difficult to believe the positive ones?

Negative emotions and actions will attract more negativity. Fear, anger, hate, guilt, shame, unforgiveness, depression, poverty mindset, drug addiction, sexual/physical/mental abuse, low self-esteem, doubt, and procrastination are all synonymous to the Devil. The Devil is a symbolic representation of one or all of these negative attributes that are shackles, preventing human beings from manifesting their divine purpose and their true heart's desires in life. It is the Devil's job to deceive humans into believing that they don't even have a divine purpose for living. As powerful as the Devil may seem, he only has limited dominion based on the authority that we give him in our lives because God created us with free will, the power to choose. The Devil is any adversary, tempter, negative thought or deed, or obstacle that is put in your path to destroy your dreams, desires, and will to become the Christ self, your higher divine self that you are sent here on earth to become.

In this book, the Devil is not an external being that is haunting the main character, Monee Green. The Devil is the negative internal thoughts and feelings that Monee had adapted about herself because of the negative traumatic things that she had suffered through in her life. Monee encountered and battled many Devils, but God also sends her some of His Angels along to assist her on her journey. Most of her trauma and pain occurred in the Devil's Bedroom. The easiest and most venerable place where the Devil can attack a female or an innocent child through their virtue and chastity.

Who am I?

I am the innocent little girl scarred by her deceiver,
locked inside of herself afraid to reveal her molester.

I am the budding teenage girl who hasn't discovered herself,
fighting peer pressure, pimples, and being introduced to esteem.

I am the young woman stripping in the club,
thinking "Mr. Captain Save a Hoe" will be rolling in on dubs.

Who Am I?

I am the frustrated single mother,
raising children without the other.

I am the divorcee who used to be a wife,
now trying to pick up the pieces and create a new life.

I am the corporate executive that wants to do more than just live;
she wants success and happiness.

I am the independent woman that doesn't need anyone or anybody,
but rocks herself to sleep at night wishing she had Mr. Right.

I am the Great Nurturer of all living things,
just as fertile as Mother Earth and yet has no protector to prevent
pollution and destruction

I am spirit, free as the air yet captured in this physical body,
which causes all kinds of stares.

I am a creation of the Most High, the most powerful force of the Universe.
I am not a mistake; I am one of His most prized possessions,
placed here to learn valuable lessons.

I am beauty, love, and joy but I am also anger, hate, and confusion,
living within this thing called life to learn through evolution.

DEAR HEAVENLY FATHER,

I COME TO YOU THIS MORNING FEELING A BIT NUMB. I COME TO YOU THIS MORNING FEELING A BIT DUMB BECAUSE SOMEHOW ALONG THE WAY OF MY LIFE'S JOURNEY, I HAVE MANAGED TO CONVINCE MYSELF THAT YOU HAVE FORSAKEN ME.

I HAVE BLAMED YOU FOR MY TRIALS AND TRIBULATIONS AND SIMULTANEOUSLY LOST THE DRIVE OF DEDICATION AND MOTIVATION TO RIGHTEOUSNESS. WHAT WILL IT BENEFIT ME TO BEGIN TO REGRET MY PAST ACTIONS AND DESTRUCTIVE BEHAVIOR BECAUSE KNOWLEDGE IS THE KEY TO ESTABLISH A FOUNDATION WITH THE CREATOR? I HAVE MANAGED TO ISOLATE MY DIVINE SPIRIT FROM THE HOLY SPIRIT, BUT NEVER CAN I PREVENT THE HOLY SPIRIT FROM MANIFESTING YAHWEH'S MERCIFUL GRACE.

YAHWEH, PLEASE, FATHER, REVEAL TO ME MY LIFE'S PURPOSE AND DIVINE WILL. PLEASE MAKE MY SOLUTION TO MYSELF DESTRUCTIVE BEHAVIOR PLAIN AND GIVE ME THE STRENGTH TO CONQUER MY DEMONS AND RENEW MY FAITH.

GOD, BLESS THOSE WHO GENUINELY LOVE THE GOODNESS AND LIGHT WITHIN ME. KEEP THEM SAFE AND WELL. SHARE YOUR MERCY, GRACE, AND LOVING KINDNESS WITH THEM AND THEIR FAMILIES. GOD, BLESS YOUR CHILDREN WHO ARE PURE-HEARTED AND LOST. HELP THEM FIND THEIR WAY TO THE PATH THAT WILL LEAD THEM TO YOUR HOLY KINGDOM. SELAH

YAHWEH, FORGIVE ME FOR MY SINS, FLAWS, AND REBELLIOUS WAYS. HELP ME TO OVERCOME AND CONQUER MY SELFISH DESTRUCTIVE BEHAVIOR. HELP ME TO BECOME THE CHILD/DAUGHTER OF LIGHT THAT I TRULY AM. BRING FORTH MY GIFTS THAT ARE SUPPRESSED DEEP DOWN TO THE SURFACE. SO THAT THEY CAN EMANATE AND MANIFEST YOUR WILL.

SELAH

CHAPTER 1

The Beginning of the End

(The Wake-Up Call)

The sun was gleaming brightly through Monee's bedroom blinds. The brilliant rays of sun were her silent alarm clock, notifying her that it was time to rise from her warm and comfortable bed. She rolled over and saw that Nefarius was no longer lying beside her. Then she heard the shower shut off and the bathroom door opened.

"Hey, babe, did you sleep good?" Nefarius asked with a bright welcoming smile.

"Yes, I did, and you?" Monee smiled back.

"Sure did."

Monee took a deep breath and exhaled, then she abruptly jumped out of bed and stretched. She looked over at Nefarius with hope in her eyes and said, "I have a big day today!"

"Oh yeah," Nefarius replied in a low voice filled with curiosity. "What do you have planned?"

"Well, you know we have to pay the gas bill and the car insurance today, and I must go to the bank and cash the check from Mrs. Hampton," Monee replied without taking a breath.

Mrs. Hampton was one of their clients that was disgruntled and displeased with the interior renovation services they had provided her. Mrs. Hampton was reluctant to pay Nefarius and Monee even though they provided her with the services she requested. However, Monee negotiated with her, and they came to an agreement that she would pay them 75% of the balance that was owed. Nefarius was not in agreement with Monee's negotiation and clearly expressed this to Monee the previous evening. He wanted Mrs. Hampton to pay all the money.

Monee continued with her to-do list: "I am also going to go and submit a few applications for some bartending positions."

"Boy, you never can tell where you are coming from!" Nefarius gasped in frustration. He didn't want Monee bartending, nor did he want her making any money independently of him. When Monee met Nefarius, he was fixing up a dilapidated house that he bought with money he had made selling drugs; however, it was Monee who helped him take his fix-n-flip business to a professional level. When her father died, she took the money she inherited and invested into the business. She was the office administrator, and Nefarius did the marketing and was the operations manager. However, the flourishing family business suffered a major blow when Nefarius won a bid to renovate fifteen properties for a builder and discovered that his bid was too low, and he could not afford to complete that project.

"You work for us, the children and I!" Nefarius would always tell her. Monee knew that Nefarius wouldn't be pleased with her looking for a part-time job, but it didn't matter to her. Business was slow, and several bills were already past due, including the payment for the minivan. Monee was always a "go-getter," and she felt like she had to make something happen financially for her family. She and Nefarius had been separated off and on for over six years after the big project with the builder flopped. They had only been back together for three months, and although the children were thrilled to have Daddy back at home, it was difficult for Monee to adjust after living the independent lifestyle that she had gotten so used to.

She had been an active participant of living the lifestyle of a Hip-Hop industry model. It was easy for her to be an industry model as she was a stunning beauty — five-foot-seven with glowing skin the color of a caramel candy. Her sexy brown bedroom eyes and her welcoming bright smile were her standout features in her photographs. Monee was not the one who wore her hair in the same style for years. No, that was too boring for her. She always expressed herself through the array of hair textures and lengths although she did prefer honey blonde and light and dark brown contrast. Her style was sexy and classy, never outrageous. Monee's soda bottle shape with full DD breast didn't make it any easier; no man could resist her beauty.

She was always working at album release parties for rappers as a promotional model, which didn't pay much but came with certain perks. Monee was always in VIP at the parties and had the opportunity to rub elbows with many artists and producers. Her goal was to become an entertainment journalist, and Monee saw modeling as a door into the Hip Hop industry. Despite her goal, she grew tired of the fake photoshoots that cost her more to pay for hairstylists, makeup artists, and costumes than the photographers actually paid. Not to mention, she never saw one photo in a legitimate magazine. She got tired of the photographers, artists, and producers making false promises to boost her career and "put her in touch with the right person" if only she would show her loyalty to them by sleeping with them. The lines at the music video castings were always too long, filled with young girls that cared nothing about getting paid as a professional model but just wanted to be seen on television. Monee hated the way the girls were treated at the castings; it was modern-day slavery. The girls were standing on the auction block naked, but now they were selling themselves. She decided that if she was going to be a part of the party scene, she should be making some serious money and went to bartending school. Soon after she finished school, Monee was working part-time at a very popular Atlanta nightclub until she and Nefarius reconciled, and he asked her to quit.

Nefarius was fifteen years older than Monee and was very grounded in his spiritual beliefs. Monee considered some of them to be unorthodox, because he had been dealing drugs for many years and found it difficult to accept some of the contradictions in his lifestyle. However, she understood that no one is perfect and her experiences in the streets helped her understand that everyone has flaws. She believed that she and Nefarius did share the same values when it came to family, and nothing was more important to them than their children. Nefarius made it very clear that she needed to dedicate more of her time to their children and getting reconnected with God and let go of all the worldly habits she had picked up during their separation— even though they both had worldly habits when they met years ago.

"Well, what the hell do you mean by that, Nefarius?" Monee fired back. "You vacillate! One minute you have faith that God is going to answer our prayers, then the next minute you got to go fix everything yourself because you can't wait on me!"

Nefarius was irritated by Monee's ambition while Monee, on the other hand, couldn't understand how he could be so content with not doing anything. Nefarius had a double standard when it came to the ambition of a woman and a man. Women were supposed to be servants to men, be seen not heard. Nefarius resented Monee's strength and her hustler spirit when she wasn't using it to benefit him.

"I'm going to try to borrow the money to get my phone turned on," Monee said, thinking out loud so that Nefarius would know her plans. "Maybe my sister will loan it to me. My cell phone needs to be on so that potential employers will be able to contact me."

Nefarius didn't say a word; he just sat in his easy chair and stared at Monee in disbelief of what he was hearing. He had been telling her for weeks that he was waiting for his former drug connection to contact him regarding a huge drug deal that they were lining up. But Monee was never one to wait on anybody and knew she had to do something fast.

Monee didn't care about Nefarius' disapproval; she was focused and was on a mission to get a job and pay some bills. She went to her closet and pulled out her pretty turquoise halter top with her black Capri pants with bright turquoise and yellow flowers going down the sides of her legs. To keep things modest and professional, she pulled out a short turquoise-sleeve button-down blouse and her three-inch black peep-toe pumps. Satisfied with her selection, Monee went to take her shower. When she came out of the shower, Nefarius was lying on the bed with his face in the pillow.

There he goes again in his damn cave! Monee thought while taking a deep breath and exhaling. "Are you going to give me any money so I can pay the gas bill?" Now, she was irritated with Nefarius' nonchalant attitude, but maybe, she thought, he just might do the right thing and give her some money for the bills.

"Borrow the money like you said!" Nefarius replied coldly.

His response irritated Monee. She knew that even with cashing the check that she was getting from Mrs. Hampton, she would still need at least 65 more dollars to pay the gas bill. Monee turned and left, not saying a word in response to Nefarius' callous bark.

On the way to pick up the payment from Mrs. Hampton, Monee became very frustrated because she couldn't find Mrs. Hampton's office and without her cell phone on and no cash in her pocket, it was close to impossible for her to get any directions. Pulling over at a gas station, she poured all the contents out of her purse on the passenger seat of her van. She found fifty cents and silently cursed Nefarius for always allowing her to leave without giving her any cash.

"He always does this!" she thought. *"This is exactly why I am going to get me a damn job!"*

Determined, Monee thought about her options. She only had enough money for one phone call. She forgot Mrs. Hampton's office number at home on her desk. Even though she was sure she remembered it correctly, if she took that chance and it was the wrong number, she would have to drive back home to get the number. Monee thought about who she could call and visit to use the phone and possibly borrow some money from. She had called her sister before she had left home and was disappointed when her sister told her that she had just spent all her money the previous day on a down payment for new plasma TV. Her sister was always buying new things and then working her ass off pulling doubles at the hospital to make up the money she had spent. If only she would have finished school and become the RN she always wanted to be. However, Monee's sister Lisa settled for being an orderly that helped change hospital beds and kept the rooms clean.

"Hmm," Monee thought, *"I can't call any of my past acquaintances. They would want to see me, wine and dine me, and all that. I need to call a neutral friend, someone who understands my situation."*

"Reggie," she yelled, "that's who I can call!" She smiled, proud of herself for thinking of him. Reggie was an auto broker whom she had met two years ago when she was purchasing a car at a "buy here, pay here" car lot in Jonesboro. The deal had soured, and Monee was not able to keep the car she had purchased. To her surprise, Reggie had predicted that she wasn't going to buy the car the same day they had met.

Both Monee and Reggie were going through relationship drama with their spouses. Although Monee and Nefarius were already officially divorced and separated, Reggie was still unhappily married. It was their spirituality that pulled them very close together. He was always there for her, and she was there for him when he finally was fed up with his wife and filed for divorce. However, timing was always bad for Monee and Reggie to begin a serious relationship; either she was dating, or he was; neither was ever single at the same time.

"Hello," Reggie said with curiosity because he didn't recognize the phone number in his caller ID.

"Hey, Reg, it's me, Monee. Are you busy?"

"No, girl, how you've been? I have been thinking a lot about you lately. Are you ok?" Reggie said in a cheerful yet concerned tone.

"I'm hanging in there, are you at home?"

"Yeah, are you gonna stop by?" Reggie always loved Monee and regretted that things didn't turn out better between the two of them. If he would have had it his way, he would have divorced his bitter wife sooner, during the time that he and Monee were dating. Then he would have taken Monee for his keeping. But he was in denial and didn't want to accept that his marriage was over, and that caused him to be reluctant to file for a divorce. Monee didn't have to wait for any man to make up his mind since she always had a waiting list of men fighting for the opportunity to prove themselves worthy to be a part of her life. So, she moved on, and they remained friends.

"I am on my way, Reg." Monee hung up the pay phone and headed to Reggie's house.

Monee stayed at Reggie's for over two hours. They chatted and updated each other on the statuses of their situations with their ex's since now they were both officially divorced. However, Reggie was fully aware that Monee had gotten back with Nefarius a few months ago, and he had kept his disappointment to himself. Monee took the opportunity to vent her frustration and anger that she was feeling about her relationship with Nefarius and sought Reggie's advice. Monee thought she could trust Reggie and he would be objective since he was a spiritual man. She confided in Reggie, telling him that it was God who instructed her to go back to Nefarius and 'help him.'" But every time Monee and Nefarius had a disagreement or an argument, she would lose faith in God's commandment and began to doubt that reconciling with her ex-husband had been the right decision.

Monee knew it would be easier to go back to the life she recently gave up and pick up right where she had left off. All her men were waiting to be taken off the back burner and to once again be sizzling hot, getting all her attention. The intriguing thing was they didn't even know they were on simmer; all they knew was Monee needed time to get herself together and figure out what she was going to do with her life. How easy it was to be deceptive when you've been doing it for so long. Monee was a pro at it now, not realizing that she had gotten so good at it that she had begun to deceive herself.

"I just don't know, Reggie," she said, sighing, "do you think I don't have enough faith or was I fooling myself thinking that God told me to help Nefarius?"

She looked to him, sincerely hoping that he could shed some light on her dark situation.

"Hmm," Reggie said, grabbing her hand and squeezing it real tight. When he closed his eyes and sat very still, Monee could barely breathe as she watched him and prayed that God would use him to tell her what to do. It seemed like eternity had passed before Reggie opened his eyes. He took a deep breath and then exhaled slowly.

Slowly shaking his head, he said in a prophetic tone, "Sorry, Monee, the spirit tells me that God is not the author of confusion, and even if God did tell you to help Nefarius, you weren't in the right state of mind to receive instruction from Him."

Monee's heart dropped, and her mouth opened. "Humph" was all she could say. She didn't want to believe Reggie, but there was no way he could have known that she was high as a kite when she had her revelation that she needed to help Nefarius. "So, you think I was just being emotional when I decided to reach out to him?"

"Yup, sorry, hun, I know you wanted it to work out between the two of you, but you are like an eagle that needs to soar with the wind. You love your freedom, you are a free spirit, and he can't fly with you at your level." Continuing his consoling tone, he added, "Whether it's me or someone else, you need to be with someone who will allow you to be the eagle that you are."

There was a brief silence before Monee nodded and said, "You are right, Reg, thank you for clarity."

After a big hug, Reggie gave her sixty dollars and told her to get her cell phone turned back on. Monee had gotten the directions to Mrs. Hampton's office and left to pick up the check and head to the bank. Although Reggie's prophetic advice seemed on point, she still wasn't sure that she was just being emotional, and her revelation wasn't truly from God. After all, some of the most talented artists had their best music born from them being in an altered state of mind.

Monee went back in her mind to a few events that happened before she and Nefarius had totally reconciled. First, she went back to the two weeks of dreams she had continually about Nefarius. In one of the dreams Nefarius was hugging her from behind, and she could feel his erection through his pants pressing against her buttocks. This turned her on, and then he suddenly pushed her away and told her to leave before he made passionate love to her. The dream took her by surprise because every time they had talked on the phone it wasn't talking but more like a verbal boxing match between Tyson and Holyfield.

The cursing and name calling that Nefarius spewed at her literally did bite at her ears. But the dreams were all positive and made Monee begin to wonder was Nefarius subliminally vibrating to her through his thoughts. Monee believed that the power of thought was the most powerful tool used in the universe because thoughts were in fact manifested in words, and words are what God used to create the universe and His Son.

> *"In the beginning was the Word, and the Word was with God,*
> *and the Word was God."*
>
> —John 1:1

Monee was fully aware that her dreams had meaning. After them, she called Nefarius' closest friend Que several times to see how Nefarius was doing.

Que would always say the same thing: "He is missing you. He's not doing too good, Monee." And because she knew he wasn't doing well, Monee avoided calling Nefarius directly and called Que instead. Monee knew there was some truth to Que's words because deep down inside she knew even though he was so mean and cruel to her that Nefarius still loved her.

Finally, Monee thought about the night she had her revelation. Nefarius had been on her mind constantly, and they had been conversing peacefully for a couple of weeks before. Monee had called him on her way to bartending school to ask if he would keep the children for the weekend. She had a business trip out of town to attend. Although he had been planning to travel that same weekend, the conversation went exceptionally well, and they continued to talk on a regular basis. They had even taken the children to dinner together on a few occasions.

Then, Monee was doing her usual one night, hanging out with her closest friend Dillion. Dillion was the one guy Monee could talk to about anything, and she would also encourage him to seek God. Although they got high together, Monee wanted better for them both. Dillion would always listen and would offer Monee advice from time to time. This night, they were riding in Dillion's huge suburban, drinking and snorting cocaine while discussing Monee's dreams she was having about Nefarius.

It was then that it hit her: "I know… I am supposed to help him! That's what I am supposed to do!"

"Yep!" Dillion agreed, nodding as if he was going to tell her to do the same thing.

"I remember when Louis told me that Nefarius would never be right until he had his 'rib' back. I knew it was me he was talking about, but I was amazed that he would tell me that, and we were still dating at the time!" For almost a year while she and Nefarius were separated before their divorce, Louis had been Monee's only serious boyfriend.

"Hey, watch it, lady!" Monee had heard a man angrily shout at her as she slowed down to turn into the Sprint PCS parking lot. His yelling pulled her out of her thoughts of the past and snapped her back into reality. Quickly, she paid her cell phone bill and headed home. Monee decided on the way home that once she got there, she would get the directions to the night club that was hiring bartenders and leave back out. Maybe Nefarius would give her the extra money she needed to pay the gas bill.

"I could have used the money that Reggie gave me," she had thought, "but then Nefarius would find out. Besides, I need my cell phone, especially if I am going to seriously start looking for a job, and with all these bills due, a job is top priority."

When Monee walked into the house, the children were all sitting in front of the television watching a movie. They barely looked up when they said, "Hi, Mom," simultaneously.

"Hey, my babies," she said, "where's your dad?" She smiled, admiring how well behaved her three children were.

"Upstairs," her eldest son Nathan replied.

Monee headed upstairs and found Nefarius still lying in the bed. Monee hated when he went into his "cave" mode. It was like he wasn't even alive, just deep in a cave full of his male testosterone and his thoughts. She decided not to let it bother her and told herself not to react to his obvious withdrawal from reality—even though she thought that he should be trying to make something happen just like she was doing to get the bills paid. She would never admit it to him, but in a strange way, she admired his ability not to panic over mundane things.

Monee jumped when Nefarius sat up quickly. "So, are you done with your errands now?" he asked her in a low and stern voice.

"No," Monee replied softly.

"Where do you have to go now?"

Although she heard the irritation in his voice, Monee smiled and replied, "I am going to put in a job application, and then I will be back."

"Well, can you drop me off?" Nefarius snapped while putting on his shoes.

"Sure," Monee replied as she went to the mirror to put on a little lipstick and check her hair. Nefarius stormed out of the bedroom and headed downstairs. By the time Monee had gotten downstairs, Nefarius was nowhere in sight. "Where is your father?"

"He went outside, Mommy," her daughter Eternity sweetly replied. Eternity was the youngest of her three children; she was six and sweet as pie. Monee loved all her children dearly. Eternity, Gideon, 12, and Nathan, 14, were beautiful jewels that she cherished with all her heart. She would do anything for her children even if that meant remaining in an abusive relationship because it was with their father.

Monee went outside and wasn't surprised that Nefarius wasn't in the van. They had only one vehicle, and Nefarius' license had been suspended because he refused to pay her child support when Monee sought a divorce—even though there was a court order for him to do so. Nefarius told Monee that he wanted to make her life miserable and refusing to help her financially was part of his rebellion. Ironically, his refusal to pay child support was not just hurting his family; it hurt him, too. Despite it all, Monee ignored his selfish and abusive tendencies and tried to make their dysfunctional relationship functional.

Monee knew Nefarius had left her condo and was angrily walking down the street. *Why is he so upset with me?* she thought. "No matter what I do, it is never the right thing to do!" She wondered if he detected that she was reconsidering their reconciliation. Suddenly, her phone rang, it was Nefarius. He was always very calculating—he wanted to see if she had paid her bill and gotten her cell phone service restored.

Monee knew that he would know her service was on even if she didn't answer, but in a calm, peaceful voice, she answered, "Yes."

"I am sick and tired of you always thinking of your damn self!" Nefarius yelled. "I am going to show you that you cannot continue to use people for your benefit then kick them to the damn curb!" Nefarius was enraged, and Monee stared at her phone like it was possessed. She had no idea what spawned such anger.

"What are you talking about, Nefarius?" Before she could continue, Nefarius yelled, "I must be a damn fool!" and hung up on her.

Over the next hour, Monee was frantic. Nefarius was calling her cell phone continuously. He was furious with her. After he had told her he was going to go back home and bleach all her clothes, Monee had stop answering his calls. She was very nervous, smoking cigarette after cigarette. Her heart was in her stomach, and her mind was racing with thoughts. She was trying hard to stay focused while driving to find the night club she was going to for her bartender interview, but now fear had set in her mind. Thoughts of all the previous times that Nefarius had gotten angry with her and would do sinister things to her, kept popping into her mind. She knew he was very capable of bleaching her clothes and even worst.

"Reggie was right," she shouted, "God is not the author of confusion! Why can't we resolve our problems like civil human beings? Why does it always end in drama?" Grabbing her cellphone, Monee called Reggie. As soon as he answered, she said, "Hey, Reg, well, I guess you were right! He's threatening to bleach my clothes. I don't even want to go back home while he's there. He always creates drama and it's not good for our kids to always see us arguing! I just want him to leave. You think I should call the police?" Monee asked like a confused, frustrated, helpless child.

"I would," Reggie said without hesitation. "Call me if you need me."

"Ok, thanks for everything, Reg."

Deep inside, Monee was hurting; her stomach was in knots. Her heart was beating fast, and her head was pounding. "I wish this was a bad dream. We were doing good! Damn!" She took a huge deep breath and exhaled while dialing Nefarius' cell. "Look, I don't know what's wrong with you, but I just want you to leave! I called the police, and they are on their way there. So, whatever you are going to do to my clothes, you need to do it and leave before they get there!" Monee was calm and firm; she didn't want Nefarius to really go to jail, but she didn't want him there when she got home either. Nefarius could be very irrational when he was very angry with her.

"Oh, you called the police on me? Well, let them come! If I lose my family, I have nothing to lose anyway!"

He had given her no choice, so she hung up on Nefarius and called the police. She had pulled over in a gas station because there was no use for her to continue to drive around Buckhead in the state of mind she was in.

She told the police what Nefarius had threatened to do with her clothes and that she just wanted him to leave her home. When the police arrived at Monee's home, the children were there, but Nefarius was gone. Nathan had called Monee and told her that the police had come, but Nefarius had already left. She was grateful that Nathan was very responsible and that her children were well behaved. The last thing she needed was to have additional stress of rebellious children. She was carrying enough on her shoulders already and unruly children probably would have been her breaking point.

Monee took a deep sigh of relief and headed to the liquor store. She bought a pint of tequila and a fresh pack of cigarettes and called "sell you anything" Sam. Sam could sell you anything you wanted from weed to a plasma TV, but Monee wasn't going to buy any weed or a TV. She wanted to feel numb. She wanted to try to forget, if she could forget, just for a few hours the terrible events that just had taken place. She didn't want to think about how the man she loved and the father of her children was emotionally withdrawn, and he didn't even realize it or just didn't care. He was always right and would refuse to compromise or communicate. Monee discovered years ago there was such a thing as mental and verbal abuse, and Nefarius always made her think that something was wrong with her. The way she spoke, behaved, and even the clothes she wore was never good enough. This constant pressure of feeling not good enough caused Monee to question herself; she never felt confident about anything. This dysfunctional saga had been going on for way too many years, and yet Monee didn't want a broken family and she still believed she could fix it.

But first she had to get high to escape it all for a while.

Cocaine had become Monee's best friend, the one thing she was sure wouldn't let her down, and Sam was where she could pick her friend up.

By the time Monee had walked through the front door of her home, she had already began drinking to have her a bit relaxed when she faced her children. She was ready to go to her room and have that conversation with her "best friend," but first she had to talk to her children, especially since Eternity had called her on the phone while she was still parked at the gas station, wanting to know why Monee had called the police on Daddy.

Monee sat down and explained to her children how sometimes adults make mistakes and get angry at each other, and it becomes very difficult for them to get along. She could hear herself saying these oh so common words to her children and hated the fact that this wasn't the first time that she had to explain their dysfunctional behavior. Her stomach was still in knots, and her head was still pounding.

"However, I will always be here for you all, and your father and I love you very, very much. No matter how old you get, in life you will still have lessons to learn but always remember to follow your heart." Monee kissed her children and headed upstairs to her bedroom. She tried to read her Bible but couldn't concentrate on a single verse. Too many things were going through her mind. "Just don't think about it!" she told her herself and grabbed her "best friend" she did a couple of lines and realized that the children hadn't had dinner yet.

Monee was in no condition to cook. She was barely in a condition to walk, but she smiled at her children and said, "I'll be back. I am going to get you all something to eat."

Monee stopped back by the liquor store before she headed to McDonald's. While perusing the aisles, Monee heard a familiar voice say, "What's up, girl?"

Turning around, she found Dillion smiling at her. "Hey, Dillion, what's up with you?" Monee asked, already knowing the answer to her own question.

Dillion, although Monee considered him to be a friend, was always very peculiar to her. He was in a relationship with a woman, but they had no children together, and they had absolutely nothing in common. Dillion was always either in the streets getting high or at work high. He always kept cocaine for company and was always looking for a female to get high with. He told Monee that his girlfriend didn't get high or like to party. Monee also thought it would be close to impossible for his woman not to know about Dillion's recreational pastimes either. Monee always felt that Dillion was like herself—trying to escape his demons, but his demons seemed to constantly have him where he had to stay high all of the time.

"Not much," he replied, "same ole, same ole… what you doing out of the house? And it's Friday night! You and your dude must have had a fight."

"Yeah," Monee replied, responding to his sarcastic statement. Opening the passenger door to Dillion's suburban and hopping inside, Monee engaged in a brief exchange of the most recent events going on in their lives, and of course, Dillion had a nice bag of their "friend." After about ten minutes of small talk, Monee said she was getting ready to go.

"Hey, you gonna come back out later? I know a kat who got some good cush," Dillion said enticingly.

"Uh, I doubt it although some cush would be nice, but I think I am going to chill at home. I don't want to be out too late tonight." Monee felt her energy getting low.

"Oh, ok hit me up if you change your mind." Dillion pulled out of the liquor store parking lot, and Monee headed to get food.

Once she arrived home, Monee gave her children their dinner and put the beer she had bought in the freezer and headed back to her room. Her children knew that Mommy was upset and didn't mind giving her some time to herself. Monee saw the huge garbage bag full of her clothes that she hadn't even noticed before. She sniffed the bag of clothes, but it didn't smell of bleach. She was relieved but wanted to be sure, so she dumped the clothes on to the floor. Monee shook her head in disbelief when she saw all her purses, dresses, halter tops, underwear, lingerie, wigs, and makeup fall to the floor.

"Damn" was all that came out of her mouth. She grabbed her cell phone and sent Nefarius a text message: *You hate who I have become!* Monee tossed the cell phone to the bed. She knew had it not been for the alcohol and coke in her blood stream she probably would have cried because deep down inside she hated who she had become, too.

Monee grabbed her cheeseburger and plopped down in her chair. She took two small bites and frowned. She had no appetite. Monee knew she should eat because she hadn't eaten a morsel of food all day, but who could eat at a time like this? She was high but not enough to pass out.

"Just eat the burger and go to sleep!" She heard a small voice say to her from inside her head. "Naw, I'll go smoke a blunt. Then, I will be able to sleep," she convinced herself.

Monee grabbed her cell phone and called Tank, an old acquaintance that she was involved with before reconciling with Nefarius. She cared a lot about Tank, but she knew there would never be anything long term or serious between them. Tank was good with his hands, could fix anything, and loved children, even had a son of his own, but he was in the streets and was too possessive when it came to Monee. He was in love with her and made it known by his constant phone calls and unannounced visits, which annoyed Monee to the upmost. But she knew he would be happy to see her, and there would be no strings attached.

"Hey, Tank, it's Monee. Whatcha doin'?" She knew the call would take him by surprise. Monee hadn't talked to Tank since she changed her cell phone number months ago and got back with Nefarius.

"On my way to drop off a package. Where you at?"

Monee could tell he was smiling from ear to ear. "Home, wanted to come out and smoke one with you. How long are you going to be tied up?"

"Not long, maybe fifteen minutes, but I would love to tie you up!"

Tank and Monee both laughed. "You are so silly! I will call you back in twenty minutes," Monee replied.

"Ok, make sure you do—for real!" Tank shouted over Tupac's "Blasphemy" resonating from his car.

After hanging up, Monee sat back in the chair and thought for a minute. "I wish I would have just got a bit from Sam, then I could just stay home."

Stay home anyway and eat the burger and go to sleep! The still small voice in her head would not leave her alone, but Monee just ignored the wisdom.

Monee got up, put on her sandals, grabbed her purse, and headed downstairs. "I'm going out for a while," she told her children who had just finished their meal. "I'll be back shortly."

"Ok, Mommy, make good choices," her son Gideon shouted lovingly. He was very intelligent and very analytical like Monee. Monee looked at her children who were playing their PlayStation 2 and quickly snatched a Corona out the freezer.

Leave it here until you get back. You won't be gone long. It was that damn small voice again.

"Nah, I might want to drink while I'm out." Monee locked the door behind her and left with the beer. As soon as she jumped into the minivan, Monee started the minivan and began backing out of her driveway while calling Tank back. "Where you at?"

She could tell he was at a club somewhere by all the noise and music in the background. "I'm at J.R. Crickets, come here! All the drinks are on me! A buddy of mines begged me to stop in here for a few drinks. Come on, it will be fun!"

"Naw, I'm not in the mood to go inside a club. Don't feel like socializing much." Monee sighed.

"Well, come get me from here. We can go somewhere quiet and smoke."

"Uh naw, maybe I better just go back home." Monee was beginning to feel that her smoke mission wasn't such a good idea after all. Even still, all the anxiety of her very stressful day was still with her. She just couldn't shake her melancholy mood.

"Come on," Tank said. "I rode with my boy, come get me! I would like to see you!" Tank persistently slurred his words. Monee could tell by his voice that he really didn't need another drink either.

"Ok, I'm on my way." Monee reluctantly drove to the bar. Fifteen minutes later, she was in the parking lot waiting for Tank to come out. The parking lot was packed with cars and more were pulling in by the minute. Funny, Monee thought. Several months ago, the upbeat atmosphere would have charged her "party battery," and she would have been eager to go into the bar and watch heads turn as she walked in. She always considered herself to be a "Ghetto Supa star," all the fame with no money. But things had changed, and the club scene had gotten the best of her. She was no longer curious about the Atlanta nightlife. She had been there, done that and no longer desired to be a part of it.

"Maybe I should just head home," she muttered. "What the hell is taking him so long?" Monee had been sitting there for twenty minutes before she realized he hadn't come out yet. "Nah, I'm out of coke, and I know he has some. Let me call him again."

It's strange how the law of attraction works; people connect, *vibrate* with others who have similar levels of consciousness. When all Monee did was drink and smoke weed, those were the kinds of people she associated with. When she started to use cocaine, she discovered so many others who snorted coke, too. If only she knew that the law of attraction could work to vibrate more positivity in her life, too.

When Monee had arrived, she called Tank, and he answered on the second ring and said he was going to finish his double of Hennessy and then would come right out. When she called the second time, twenty minutes later, the phone rang three times before Tank said, "I'm coming out now, baby!" and hung up before Monee had a chance to say anything.

Tank was smiling from ear to ear when he hopped into the van. To him, she always made him smile. Monee was the only woman that Tank really loved. It tore him up inside when she told him she was going back to her ex.

"Hey," Monee said with a sigh of relief that the waiting was over. She looked at Tank's eyes and then at the rest of him. His eyes looked weary, but he still had a nice physique, and she loved how he always looked crisp, clean, and smelled good. They headed to his mother's home; she didn't live too far from the club. Tank suggested they go there and chill out in front of her house, sit in the van, and get high. Monee was tired, she knew it was time to leave but convinced herself to stay long enough to smoke a few puffs of the blunt, then she would leave.

"Are you staying here at your mom's?" Monee asked while putting the van in park.

"Naw, you know Ray… he's coming to get me. I'm going back to the bar after we smoke." Tank was still smiling at her. "You don't look too good, everything ok?"

"Naw, but I don't want to talk about it now," Monee said, taking another snort, hoping that it would perk her up a bit.

"Dude isn't putting his hands on you, is he? You know all you got to do is call me and I will be there in a heartbeat!" Tank said, hyping himself up.

"No, nothing physical this time. I called the police on him earlier, and I've got to make some decisions," Monee said sadly. Tank didn't say a word. Monee thought that was odd and then went back to the time she had called the police on Tank.

Tank probably empathized with Nefarius when it came to her calling the law. Monee really didn't believe in calling the police for anything, especially when it came to domestic relations with black men. She knew that the system was set up to destroy the black family, and the mission was to separate and destroy by incarcerating the black man and isolating him from his family. Calling the police was only if it was a matter of life and death. However, Monee had broken that self-created code on both occasions, and she blamed herself for betraying both men. She took another snort and the hit the blunt once more.

"Well, listen, it was good seeing you, Tank," Monee said, her voice slow and sad. "Appreciate you taking some time out for me, but I'm not feeling like myself. I need to lay it down." She winced as her stomach churned.

"Monee, you know you can call me more," Tank whispered. "I was missing you."

"I know." Eyeing him, she added, "I will."

Ray slowly-rolled past them and parked at the curb.

"Here, you keep the rest of the blunt. You want some of this for the road?" Tank waved the small plastic bag.

"Yeah, not much though. I'm going to finish this Corona when I get home and go to bed." Tank gave her the rest of what was in the bag and a long tight hug. Then, he jumped into the car with Ray. They pulled off, headed down the street and took a the left in the direction back to the bar. Monee turned right and headed home.

Take route 314, go the back-way home. It was that small voice in Monee's head again, but she ignored it.

"Nah, I want to see if the Frozen Place is jumping tonight." Although Monee had lost the desire to go inside, she still enjoyed riding by the clubs she used to party at. Just to see if she could recognize any of the cars as it gave her an idea of who was in the club. She used to always circulate the parking lot before going inside any club that she would frequent to prevent any surprises when she got inside. She always wanted to know if any of the men she was dating were in the club ahead of time.

Some habits die hard.

She was pulled from her thoughts when she noticed police lights flashing ahead. Monee could see two officers waving flashlights, but she couldn't tell if they were letting cars through.

Monee's heart started pounding. "Shit!" she yelled. The Corona sat between her legs. She saw the car in front of her turn left down a side street. "Maybe I should turn off, too?" She hesitated and passed the side street; it was too late.

As she got closer to the police, she remembered that the van still reeked of weed smoke. She quickly turned in a residential driveway, backed out, and headed back the way she came. She looked through the rearview mirror to make sure she was safe.

"Damn!"

The police cruiser was on her like white on rice with their patrol lights flashing. Monee immediately pulled over to the side of the road. She quickly dug into her purse, grabbed her perfume, and sprayed it on herself before the cop could get out of his cruiser. She could see him walking toward her. He was brown skinned, bald, and with a fat stomach—the typical look of a cop.

Monee quickly rolled down her car window before the cop got close, hoping that would let the weed smell dissipate.

"Can I ask why you turned around, ma'am?" the police officer asked in a firm tone.

"It looked like you all had the road blocked off. I thought you all were turning people around, Officer." Monee was sure that the cop could see her heart beating through her chest, she was trying to stay calm, but she was shaking like it was freezing below zero in the van. She tried to keep the beer steady now in between her feet so that it would not spill.

"I see," the officer said, not convinced. "Can you pull into the park parking lot for me, ma'am?" He turned and pointed behind him to the left side of the street. Monee nodded and turned left into the park. Once she was in the lot, the officer was right on her. She didn't have a chance to move the beer or put the van in park before the officer was already tapping on the window.

Monee lowered the window.

"Can I see your driver's license and insurance?"

Monee was shaking but managed to lift the beer bottle up high enough to grab it and quickly drop it in the rear on the floor behind the passenger seat. Then, she smoothly reached in the glove compartment for her insurance card. She looked through the white envelope that contained all of the paperwork to her minivan, but the card was nowhere in sight.

"Where the hell is it?" Monee whispered. Panicking, frantic, and severely shaking, Monee reached up to turn on the light and then hesitated. She was fearful that the officer would be able to see the beer bottle with the light on. She grabbed her license and turned to the window to see that there was now another officer talking to the officer who initially pulled her over. He was telling the new officer that he could smell the marijuana over the smell of Monee's perfume.

"Damn! I can't believe this is happening," Monee said, feeling defeated and numb.

"Ma'am, can I see your driver's license please?" The new officer had big eyes and a big hairy mustache; he was bald too and kinda resembled and old ugly version of Nicolas Cage. He was getting impatient. Monee handed him her license. "Have you been drinking tonight, Miss?" the officer asked in a very firm and intimidating tone.

"Yes, sir," Monee timidly replied.

"How long ago?"

"Thirty minutes, sir," Monee replied humbly.

"And what were you drinking tonight, Miss?" the officer fired back, annoyed.

"Tequila and beer, sir."

"I see." The officer pointed the flashlight into her eyes. Monee could imagine how she looked. "Could you step out of your vehicle but first turn it off and put it in park."

Monee obeyed and stepped out of the van. She could hear her cell phone ringing continuously. When the officer asked her if she had anything illegal on her or in the van, and she replied, "No."

"Would you be willing to take a breathalyzer test?"

"Officer, please, I was just trying to get home, back to my children!" Monee pleading.

"How many children do you have?"

"Three!"

"And how old are they, Miss?"

"Sir, they are 14, 12, and 6."

"Are they home with someone?"

"No, sir."

"Ma'am, do you have anyone who can come and drive you home because you are not driving away from here alone."

"Yes, my sister can come get me."

"Well, you better call her now."

Monee reached into the van for her cell phone which had fallen between the seat and the console. She was trying to grab it as quick as possible before the officer had a chance to look inside the van. Monee grabbed the phone and closed the door.

"Ok, Miss, I am going to ask you one more time, do you have any open containers inside your vehicle?" He was getting angry now, but Monee stuck to her lie and said, "No, officer."

He grabbed her, spun her around, and put handcuffs on her. "You are under arrest."

"What, why?" He held the bottle of beer up to her. "Officer, wait, I can explain!"

"It's too late! You already lied to me once! You don't get another chance to lie to me again!"

He grabbed Monee and read her Miranda rights as he placed her in the back of his police car. After what seemed like eternity, the officers had found the empty bottle of tequila.

"Damn! I forgot to throw that away!" Monee prayed that they wouldn't find the cocaine in her purse. The officer who initially pulled her over walked toward the police cruiser and opened the door.

"Miss, is there anyone that you can call to check on your kids?" Monee knew they had found everything. She didn't want to call Nefarius, but she knew that he was really the only person she could call. She sighed. "Yes, call their father." Monee knew that the grim reality of what was happening had not completely sunk in her mind. How could it, she was too high to even begin to feel the cold hard truth that she was going to jail.

Reflections

Life Changing Events

A wake-up call is usually an event, experience or crisis that forces one to make a major life change. This usually happens when it is time spiritually to transition to a higher level of consciousness. We attract these situations into our lives to show us ourselves and to have the opportunity to love, forgive, and heal those parts of self that are no longer serving our highest good.

What is your most impactful, life-changing moment?

_____

_____

_____

_____

_____

_____

_____

_____

_____

_____

_____

_____

How did this moment change your life?

_____
_____
_____
_____
_____
_____
_____
_____
_____
_____
_____

What were the lesson(s) you learned and how did they cause you to change?

_____
_____
_____
_____
_____
_____
_____
_____
_____
_____

The **Law of Attraction** is one of the Spiritual Universal Laws that governs our lives. Everything is energy. Thoughts, feelings, and emotions are energy that is sent out into the universe and comes back to the sender in energetic form.

During your wake-up call, how did the law of attraction work in that situation?

_____

_____

_____

_____

_____

_____

_____

_____

_____

What do you still need clarity about?

_____

_____

_____

_____

_____

_____

_____

_____

_____

_____

_____

Affirmations to Read during a Wake-up Call or Crisis

I am Divinely protected, and no harm can come to me. God loves me, and I am safe.

I am grateful, and I welcome this opportunity to grow.

I am getting better and better every day.

I am confident.

I am opening up my heart to receive my highest good, and all is well.

I am a spiritual warrior that knows surrendering the desire to control the outcome of this situation is faith and trusting God.

I am inner peace, and I know I am living a harmonious life.

Scriptures to Read during a Wake-up Call or Crisis

Psalm 27:1 "The Lord is my light and salvation; of whom shall, I fear? The Lord is the strength of my life, of whom shall I be afraid?"

Psalm 25:20 "Oh keep my soul and deliver me; Let me not be ashamed, for I put my trust in You. Let integrity and uprightness preserve me, for I wait on you."

Psalm 31:1-2 "In You, O LORD, I put my trust; Let me never be ashamed; Deliver me in Your righteousness. Bow down Your ear to me. Deliver me speedily; Be my rock of refuge, A fortress of defense to save me.

Psalm 27:13-14 "I would have lost heart, unless I had believed, that I will see the goodness of the LORD, in the land of the living. Wait on the LORD, be of good courage and He shall strengthen your heart; Wait I say, on the LORD!"

When Prey Becomes Predator

Young,
Innocent and Pure.

Bloodthirsty,
Ravenous wolf...
Lurking for the unprotected.

The Beautiful Butterfly
that is still in the cocoon,
clueless and empty,
not yet violated with hurt and pain.
Only the Light of Love,
Divinity dwelling within.

The predator smells the Aura of Virtue,
sinks his venomous fangs into the angelic flesh
to purge innocence with death.
Where there was once joy and wonder...
evil struck...
now only guilt and shame remain.
A domineering invasion of power
and manipulation
becomes a life changing humiliation.

Because the molester was once
the molested,
left alone and unprotected...

force of perverted power usurped
over the powerless.
No one was there to protest this violation.

Victim filled with shame and humiliation...
confused how from perversion emerged
sick pleasure and sexual stimulation.
Envious of the power of his manipulator,
vows to never be the victim again...
becomes infected with illusion and sin,
accepts his infestation and slithers to the dirt
to seek victims to infiltrate with his
poison of perversion...
this is now his truth.

Wears the masks of father, brother, uncle, homie, lover, and friend.
While simultaneously spreading his poison over and over again.

Able to do so,
because Shame and Guilt is holding the
Prey captive...
However,
Justice speaks and
Truth has set the Captive free!

Truth has exposed the enemy,
Light shines on darkness...
The Prey...
the predator...
Healing steps in and
behold a new day!

Chapter 2

The Devil's Bedroom

As Monee sat in the back of the police cruiser she twisted and turned to try to get comfortable with those tight handcuffs on. It was pointless, the more she struggled the more painful the cuffs became. The feeling of helplessness overwhelmed Monee with fear. Monee knew these feelings and her mind took her back to when she was five years old.

○ ○ ○

"Stop moving or it will hurt more!"

"If you make a sound, I am going to kill your momma!"

Monee could hear the deep, rough, intimidating voice of the demon that had been hunting her for years.

What is that noise, Monee asked herself. *It sounded like water running from the bathroom faucet. But why would someone leave the water on for such a long time?* She knew her mother and some other relatives were in the bedroom adjacent from the bathroom. There were always people living with them; either a relative was having financial problems, or her mom's boyfriend at the time had a needy relative that needed somewhere to live to get themselves together. Whatever the situation might have been, it was never just Monee and her immediate family living in their house.

Monee had three sisters and two brothers. They all were watching *Family Feud* when she got up and went to the bathroom. She saw some man standing over the sink with a hanger and the water running.

What was he doing? Monee had thought.

"Monee! Leave him alone, let him be," called her mother from her bedroom.

"Oh, it's all right, Virginia, I'm just unclogging the sink," replied the strange man in the bathroom. He was tall, dark skinned with a big thick mustache and dark mysterious eyes. He smiled at Monee and opened the door wide. She began to investigate and interrogate him about the wire hanger and why the water was running. He politely answered her questions while he dug deeper into the faucet. After a couple of minutes, Monee could hear footsteps going downstairs. The man heard them, too, because he slid down the side of the wall and slowly closed the bathroom door.

Grabbed Monee's waist, he said, "Come to your Uncle Luke."

"I didn't know you was my uncle."

"Yeah, I'm with your Auntie Thelma, now pull your pants down," he commanded.

"I'm not going to pull my pants down," Monee replied, not understanding why he wanted her to pull down her pants.

"Yes, you are, or else I'm going to take my belt off and whip you." Luke was getting a little impatient, and it was reflecting in his tone.

"Then I will tell my Mama," Monee proudly replied in a sassy tone.

"And then your mama will whip you, too!" Luke didn't wait for Monee to oblige to his request; he simply pulled her pants down himself. He laid her on the ground. "Don't move and don't make a sound. If you do, I'm gonna have to kill yo' mama!"

Monee wasn't feeling very brave anymore. As young as she was, she could tell that this man was serious, and she was afraid. She was afraid to move, afraid to cry even as this grown man grabbed her legs and folded them Indian style while she was still lying on her back and forced his large penis inside her small, tight five-year-old vagina.

The pain Monee felt was indescribable. She felt like he was killing her, but she was too afraid to scream, thinking that he would kill her even more and then kill her momma. As tears rolled down her cheeks, Monee closed her eyes tightly. She could see Uncle Luke in her mind, but he was even scarier with her eyes closed. He had horns coming out of his head and a long tail coming out his rear, raised and waving in the air. His eyes were black like coals, and he had an evil grin on his face. Monee quickly opened her eyes and realized that whatever the reason, the Devil had stopped killing her and was now standing over her.

"You bet not tell anyone about this, or you will be in a lot of trouble," Uncle Luke snapped coldly. Then, he reached down and pulled Monee to her feet, pulled up her panties and then her pants. Then, he turned and walked out the bathroom as if nothing happened.

Monee didn't completely realize what had happened to her until a couple years later.

The curiosity that provoked Monee to watch a stranger unclog a faucet was the same curiosity that caused Eve to eat from the Tree of Good & Evil in the garden with Lucifer. It is in a woman's nature to seek. It is the mother's job to teach her daughter what exactly it is in life she should pursue. It is not the lion who hunts but the lioness that is the predator. She searches out her kill and shares it with her family. If the lioness fails to teach her young cub how to hunt successfully, this can mean death because now the predator becomes prey.

Monee's legs were shaking; she felt as if she would collapse at any minute as she walked out the bathroom and down the hall slowly back to the family room. She slowly sat down silently in front of the television. She was cold, and her legs felt weak, but she just sat there in a daze and didn't say a word. Monee began to have a strange sensation as if she had to urinate. She went back to the crime scene but was unable to pee. Monee was scared and confused but something inside of her wouldn't allow her to reveal the serpent. In her shame and guilt, even though innocent, she would carry that burden of concealing a gross injustice of theft and perversion.

Why didn't Eve confess to Adam that Cain was not from his righteous seed? Eve allowed her righteous son Abel to be slain by Lucifer's evil son Cain; truth had to reveal itself through murder.

This was the first encounter Monee had with the Devil, and it was also the most crucial one. By Monee suppressing what had happened to her, she also prevented receiving help to overcome the severe damage that was caused more psychologically than physically. Throughout the years, Uncle Luke haunted her in the form of nightmares. Monee had a reoccurring nightmare that the same devil she had seen when Uncle Luke was raping her would always torment her while she slept. He would call her name and then laugh at her in a deep, evil laugh. Full of fear and dread, she would wake up in a panic. She began sleeping with her mother at times to feel safe.

As she got older, the realization that this demon was probably raping other young girls began to make carrying the guilt of secrecy like a huge infected sore inside of her oozing with pus and blood. As she tried to do the things regular adolescent girls did, there was still this sickness inside of her. She began to look at men differently. Now aware what the bulge in his pants was, she would always look and wonder did the man in front of her want to penetrate her, too.

It wasn't until Monee was eight that she felt she was forced to tell her mother her dark secret. One night Monee had nightmare that she was being raped by her Uncle Luke. In the dream, Uncle Luke was violently choking her it seemed so real that Monee began screaming and choking in her sleep. Her mother tried frantically to wake Monee from her nightmare. Monee woke up hysterical and in tears.

"Mommy, there is something I have got to tell you." Monee sat up on the bed still crying.

"What is it, baby?" Her mother asked

"Well, you remember when Auntie Thelma and Uncle Luke came to stay with us?"

"Monee that was a few years ago, what are getting at?"

"Well, Un-Unc-Uncle Luke had p-pu-put his penis inside of me!" Monee began to cry hysterically.

"What!" Virginia, eyes wide, whipped her head to Monee. "What, when baby!?" Standing, Virginia stomped around her room as if prowling for her next prey. "I am going to kill that bastard!" Virginia was losing control, the anger she was feeling was tremendous, and the feelings of rage and anger were so intense she felt like she was going to explode! She forced herself to calm down enough to sit beside Monee on the bed.

As Monee revealed the dark deep hidden secret to her mother, all the shame and embarrassment she had felt when Uncle Luke raped her had now resurfaced.

"Monee, why are you just now telling me this?" Virginia asked her daughter in a voice filled with pain and confusion.

"I was scared that he was going to hurt you! He told me that he was going to kill you!" Monee winced in between the tears.

"He said he was going to kill me? No! I am going to kill his ass! Get your coat, let's go!" Virginia yelled as tears fell from her face.

Virginia had taken Monee to the doctor. The doctor examined Monee and taken several tests.

"Well Ms. Brown," he had told her, "It is obvious that her hymen has been broken, and her uterus is tilted abnormally toward the back of her spine. This should not cause her any problems. It's just positioned abnormally." In a more solemn voice, he added, "Because of the time span, there is no way you can get a conviction or build a case against this person. Unfortunately, all the physical evidence is gone. What is important now is to get counseling for Monee."

The doctor looked over at Monee, who stared lifelessly out the window.

"Thank you, Dr. Randall, I'll do just that."

Virginia was not giving up yet. She and Monee drove over to Uncle Nate's house. Uncle Nate was Virginia's older brother. He had just gotten out of prison a couple a months ago for carrying a concealed weapon.

Virginia jumped out of the car. "Stay in the car, Monee."

Monee watched as her mother raced up to the porch where Uncle Nate and some family friends were on the porch talking.

"Are you sure that it was Luke, Virginia? "Uncle Nate asked in shock.

"I know for a fact it was that no good son of a bitch!" Virginia yelled.

The adults continued to discuss what actions they should take against Uncle Luke. The angry roaring settled down into a calm hum, so Monee could tell that the conversation was coming to some closure. Several of Monee's teenage cousins approached the car, including Uncle Luke's daughter Unis.

"What's all this about you and my daddy?" Cousin Unis yelled angrily. Monee didn't know what to say, feeling ashamed and embarrassed. She just stared at Unis with no expression.

"Why are you telling these lies on my daddy?" Unis was almost into tears. Unis who was fourteen at the time was Monee's older first cousin. Virginia's younger sister Thelma and Luke were her parents. Thelma and Luke's relationship was explosive and very abusive. They were always fighting but managed to conceive four children in between the fighting. After Aunt Thelma had Unis, she couldn't take the fighting with Uncle Luke anymore and left him. "He didn't do nothing to you!" Unis loudly screamed in disbelief, refusing to believe that her daddy would do something that terrible to her cousin.

"I ain't lying!" was all Monee could get out before she burst into tears, feeling defeated. Unis and the crowd of children left when they saw Virginia coming. Monee quickly wiped her face. Her mother drove off and announced that Uncle Nate was going to handle Luke. Monee was silent the rest of the way home, feeling regret about ever opening her mouth. She didn't think about how the truth might affect her whole family, especially her cousin Unis. Monee wished that she was a turtle and could crawl into her shell.

Trying to forget everything that was going on, Monee focused in on the song that was playing on the car radio. Al Green's "Love and Happiness" vibrated across the radio waves, and Monee hoped that one day she could know what it felt to feel love and happiness.

"Monee, Monee!" Virginia was annoyed; she had been talking to Monee for the past three minutes. "Monee, honey, haven't you been listening to me?"

"Huh, oh, what did you say, Mommy?"

"I asked you do you think you need to go talk to someone, get some counseling." Virginia pulled out a joint from her cigarette box of Benson Hedges and lit it with her lighter. Virginia was never much of an alcohol drinker, but she loved smoking marijuana. The smell didn't bother Monee; she always thought the smoke smelled good.

"No, I'm all right." Monee couldn't imagine lying on some shrink's couch spilling her guts out to a total stranger.

"Are you sure, honey?"

"Yes, I am sure."

That was the last time Monee and her mother talked about the whole ordeal. Nothing ever happened to Uncle Luke either. The last the family knew was that he moved out of state and got sent to prison shortly thereafter. Monee buried all her feelings about the rape and the feelings of rejection and shame. She pretended it never happened and went on with her childhood. What Monee didn't realize was that being raped opened her eyes to the fruits of good and evil. The seed of evil had been planted within her soul, tormenting her and taking root. This was her first encounter with Lucifer and most certainly would not be the last.

"Ok, Ms. Greene, step out of the car."

Monee jumped, startled, realizing that it was the officer's authoritative voice that had brought her back to the present and out of her dreary past. The police officer was helping Monee exit the cruiser and escorting Monee inside the police station. Inside the jail, she was put into a holding cell. The cell was concrete and cold, and contained one metal bench and a metal sink that was attached to a stainless-steel toilet. The cell was like an ice box, freezing cold, but Monee managed to block out the cold and drifted off to sleep.

After being interviewed by the jail nurse and being searched, the booking clerk counted her money and listed all of her property to be stored away until she was released. Then the clerk told Monee her charges: DUI, open container, possession of less than an ounce of marijuana and possession of an illegal substance. All were misdemeanors except the possession of an illegal substance, which was a felony charge. The booking agent advised Monee of her bond and then told her that she had no bond for the "felony charge," and that she had to go before a judge in order to get a bond. Monee's day to appear before the judge was Sunday. The officer moved her into another cold empty holding cell, only this time there were two stainless steel benches along both sides of the walls. Monee flopped down on one of the cold hard benches and pulled her arms inside her new green inmate shirt to keep warm.

She sat there, waiting to be fingerprinted and photographed; she couldn't help thinking about how the press praised Paris Hilton's mug shot and how she managed to still look great with numbers underneath her mug shot.

Damn! If only I was rich! Monee thought. To her, it seemed she had waited in that cold, desolate jail cell forever for someone to come and take her upstairs to her temporary new living quarters. Monee would drift in and out of sleep while trying to keep warm. All the alcohol and drugs she had consumed the day before was still flowing through her blood stream and was still preventing her from realizing the hardcore reality that what was happening to her was going to change her life forever. She had nothing but time on her hands right now. But would time become her best friend or her worst nightmare?

She began to think about why she had experienced so much hurt and pain in her life.

"So much darkness. I thought Nefarius was going to be my eternal sunshine that God had blessed me with to erase all the storms that I have been tossed to and fro in. But it seems as if the dark cloud is like a halo of doom that is a crown I must wear." Her self-loathing was interrupted by the loud resonating sound of the steel jail door unlocking and then slowly sliding left to open. Monee, startled by the external break of silence that had accompanied her for so long, sighed with relief as she welcomed the interruption. She knew it was time to relocate. She quickly raised her head to meet her rescuer.

"All right, it's time to take you upstairs. Once you get upstairs, you will be introduced to Officer Blight. She will brief you on the rules and regulations and place you in the orientation pod. This is where you will stay for the next three days until you are moved to common population. Follow me and stay to the right side of the wall, there is no talking. Do you understand?" the Officer asked with a firm tone.

"I do," Monee replied. She was thinking that none of what the officer had just explained to her really mattered because she knew once she went to court and the judge set a bond, that her mother would be there to get her. Monee knew with assurance that her mother had her back, even though she knew that her reasons for being arrested were because of making stupid and careless decisions. Just because she and Nefarius had broken up once again did not justify her reckless behavior. Nevertheless, Monee found comfort in knowing that her incarceration would be short lived.

Disconnected

I don't know the ways of
the Divine
I always say I am doing fine
but thoughts of hopelessness
confuse my mind
Feeling disconnected from
the Divine
Everyone is on the outside
looking in
I often wonder
do I have a genuine friend
or does everyone
look and judge and grin
and pretend
No one knows when this
earth will end
I would do things different
if I had a chance to
do it all again
Maybe I would have
tried to be an unconditional
friend
Now lost again

Reflections

Healing Our Inner Child

Our childhood is the foundation of our beliefs, core values, and perspective of the world. It is our childhood experiences that set our course for our destiny and divine purpose in this lifetime. We choose our parents, geographical location, race, economic conditions, and sex before we enter into our human bodies. Our soul mission is discussed and pre-determined with our spirit guides before arriving in the third dimensional world on planet Earth. This is all designed for us to learn, grow, and expand our consciousness on a soul level. The traumas and challenges that we experience in our childhood become clues to help us discover why we are here and our divine purpose. Our life mission is not just for us to expand as individual souls but for us to expand in consciousness as a collective.

What challenges and trauma did you experience in your childhood?

_____

_____

_____

_____

_____

_____

_____

_____

How are those experiences affecting you now?

_____

_____

_____

_____

_____

_____

_____

_____

_____

When we can identify that we have not healed from past traumas and abuse, the healing work can begin. First, we must forgive ourselves and forgive others for any guilt, resentment, and anger that you are still feeling about the experience.

Write down the negative feelings that you feel about yourself.

_____

_____

_____

_____

_____

_____

_____

_____

_____

_____

Now look at those negative feelings you have about yourself and the trauma or pain you experienced and write a positive statement that reverses the negative statements above.

_____

_____

_____

_____

_____

_____

_____

_____

_____

The Power of Forgiveness and the Universal Law of Cause & Effect

This law is also called the law of Karma. Most are familiar with this law by the biblical scripture in Galatians 6:7, "whatsoever a man sows, that he will also reap." This means that our thoughts, actions, and deeds will boomerang back to us in due time. If we think negative thoughts and/or negative deeds, the Universe will send back negativity back to us. It works the same way for our positive thoughts, deeds, and actions. Positivity given out will ensure positivity will return. It may not be instantaneously, but it will return.

Now with understanding the law of cause and effect, when someone does wrong to us, it is not our responsibility to wrong that person. It is our responsibility to forgive and in doing so allow healing to happen in our mind, body, and soul. If we hold on to the pain and hurt of the wrong that was done, it will create more hurt and pain to manifest in our lives. Why? Because those negative emotions create negative thoughts, which will produce negative actions and thus reap negative results. The faster we can release the negativity and pain, the faster we can begin to heal. The power of trusting God and allowing Him and His universal law to deal with the person that wronged us is liberation of no longer being that person's victim. Once forgiven, true personal power reigns supreme, and life takes on a more positive meaning.

Now take those positive statements that you wrote about yourself and say, "I forgive myself because..." before each statement and then take three deep breaths and say, "I release and let go and let God do His great work in me."

Write down the negative feelings that you feel about someone who hurt you.

_____

_____

_____

_____

_____

_____

_____

_____

_____

Now look at those negative feelings you feel about that person(s) and write a positive statement that reverses the negative statements above.

_____

_____

_____

_____

_____

_____

_____

_____

_____

Now take those positive statements that you wrote about that person and say, "I forgive (person's name) because (insert positive statement)" before each statement and then take three deep breaths and say, "I release (person's name) and send you back into the Universe from which you came and let God do His great work in you."

_____

_____

_____

_____

_____

_____

_____

Affirmations for Healing & Forgiveness

I am opening my heart and mind to the healing power of Spirit.

I know that God has gifted me with the power to heal myself, and I am releasing all doubt and fear. I am healed now.

I release all negative emotions that are lodged in my energetic body, and I am healed now.

I am divine love, and I call on all Angels of Healing to cover me now.

I am thankful for a healthy body, sound mind, and strong, vibrant spirit.

I love, respect, and accept myself.

I call upon Source Energy to guide me through the healing process, and I am trusting that I healed.

I am responsible for my healing, and today, I am taking action and making the necessary changes in my life that are no longer serving me.

I am healed.

Scriptures to Read for Healing

Jeremiah 17:14 "Heal me, O LORD, and I shall be healed; save me, and I shall be saved. For You are my praise."

Psalm 147:3-6 "He heals the brokenhearted and binds up their wounds. He counts the number of stars; He calls them by name. Great is our Lord, and mighty in power; His understanding is infinite. The LORD lifts up the humble; He casts the wicked down to the ground."

Proverbs 17-22 "A merry heart does good, like medicine, But a broken spirit dries the bones."

Psalm 54, "The Lord Is Our Helper" "Save me, O God, by Your name, and vindicate me by Your strength. Hear my prayer, O God; Give ear to the words of my mouth. For strangers have risen up against me, and oppressors have sought after my life; they have not set God before them. Selah

Behold, God is my helper; The Lord is with those who uphold my life. He will repay my enemies for their evil. Cut them off in Your truth. I will freely sacrifice to You; I will praise Your name, O LORD, for it is good. For He has delivered me out of all trouble; And my eye has seen its desire upon my enemies."

Romans 12: 21 "Do not be overcome by evil but overcome evil with good."

Mass Confusion

I look at you every day.
An image so clear,
inside our son,
I begin to believe that you're really here.

I can't believe how easy it was to conceive
such a beautiful, perfect thing.
The love shared between two
makes one believe it will always remain true.
But reality always lingers in and
distressful separation happens...
once again.

Now the perfect being that was conceived
walks in his daddy's invisible shadow,
Left without his father's knowledge.
Vulnerable to believe
false misconceptions
that manhood can conceive.
Now playing hooky,
was that the right thing to do?
Leaving our child to never get to know you?
Now there's a part of him missing.

Mass confusion,
No excuse will suffice,
for a young innocent boy
whose daddy is absent
for his entire life.

Chapter 3

Fear: False Evidence Appearing Real

The corrections officer led Monee down a long cold hall. Once arriving at the end of the hall, Monee found herself at two thick glass doors that were the only way inside the women's jail. The first glass door slid open, and the officer instructed Monee to continue forward on her own. Monee stepped inside the glass door and was trapped with the first door behind her and facing the second, waiting for it to open so that she could enter the jail. Anxiety tried to take Monee as a prisoner, but then she took a deep breath and exhaled as she accepted that there was no escaping this situation. She would have to go through incarceration to see freedom once again.

There was a loud click, the sound so invading that it caused Monee to flinch. The click was the sound of the lock releasing the second glass door for it to open. The glass door slid to the right and Monee entered the jail. In front of her was the control center that was enclosed with glass. She could see three women correction officers inside the glass booth, looking at cameras and talking among one another. While Monee was standing there, she could see one of the correction officers turn and walk toward the door that led to the open area of the jail. The correction officer was tall and thin. She had her hair pinned into a bun, and she appeared to be in her mid-thirties. Monee looked expressionless because she had no clue what to expect next. Monee looked around before her. She could see four individual cells; each called a pod. Each pod was enclosed by glass walls that were soundproof. Each pod also had one glass door in the center of the glass walls, which was the only way into the pod.

Inside, each pod was two floors; on the bottom floor were steel tables in the center of the room. Behind the steel tables were three shower stalls in the back of the pod on the lower level. Behind the shower stalls were more steel doors that enclosed individual jail cells that ran along the back wall of the bottom floor of the jail. On the left side of the room were steel stairs, the only way to the top level of the jail. At the top of the steel stairs were nothing except individual steel doors across the wall all leading to individual cells.

The officer was now standing in front of Monee. "I am Officer Tate; you will be staying inside of pod one which is the orientation cell. You are required to stay in this cell for your first three days, and then you can move into common population. Follow me." Officer Tate escorted Monee into the first cell on the left. They stood there silently waiting for the glass door to open. With a click, the door slowly slid open, and Monee followed the officer into the pod.

There was a young girl sitting at the first steel table on the far-right side of the of the pod. She appeared to be in her early twenties. She was tall at least five-foot-eight and slender, her skin was milk chocolate, and she had the face of an innocent China doll. The girl had both her arms and legs crossed, looking out through the thick glass wall at the officers in the glass control center in the center of the jail, as if to be waiting for something to happen.

The glass door slid shut, and Monee was alone with the girl. Monee sat at the table closest to the stairs which left one table in between them.

"Whatcha in here for?" The girl turned to Monee and asked with a thick southern accent.

"Ugh, DUI... how 'bout you?" Monee replied in a low ancient voice as if she hadn't spoken in centuries.

"They said I was soliciting at the strip club I work at. Talkin' 'bout I was trying to get this dude to pay me money for sex. All bullshit, that dude was begging me to leave with him! They ain't got nuthin' on me!" the girl yelled angrily. I am tired of these nuthin' ass cops always harassin' me! And this stupid bitch officer better let me make my phone call to my boyfriend! I need to get up out of here!"

"Oh, you strip, at what club? I used to strip a few years back." Monee didn't think she would know the club but was trying to make small talk. She was happy to have someone to talk to.

"I work at the Lion's Den, I been there for three years. It's all right. The money is good. It pays the bills." The girl abruptly jumped up and began pounding her fists on the glass wall. "Can I get my damn phone call?"

Monee could no longer hear the girl screaming. The girl's voice faded as Monee's mind drifted back to when she first made the decision to start stripping.

○ ○ ○

"Ok, class make sure that you complete your practice problems every evening! Midterms are in three weeks!" Mr. Oshea shouted as he slammed Monee's graded quiz on her desk. She flipped it over… the letter F- was circled at the top of her paper.

"Damn! I might have to drop this class. I thought I did good on this quiz," Monee whined to herself.

"Class dismissed, see you all on Thursday."

This was Monee's first semester as a freshman in college, and she had been struggling with passing Mr. Oshea's weekly geometry quizzes for the past three weeks.

Looking down at her watch, she noted it was 11:45 a.m.; she had two hours to kill before her psychology class. "Oh well might as well get something to eat." She sighed and left her class feeling defeated. Upon entering the student center, she sat at her favorite table closest to the Chinese restaurant and ordered what she always did: General Tso Chicken. The student center was always crowded with college students socializing, eating, and studying. The place was huge and was filled with every fast-food restaurant a student could possibly desire.

After graduating from high school and giving birth to Nathan, she enrolled at a community college back home. Monee had decided that she wanted to be a forensic psychiatrist, and after one semester of college and achieving a 3.0 grade point average, she transferred to a university over 350 miles away from her hometown. Monee had gotten pregnant by her boyfriend Guy when she was a senior in high school. Guy was a high school dropout and a drug dealer. Monee was a party girl and liked the fact the Guy had his own car and apartment, and he loved to party, too. Monee had been going to nightclubs since she was fifteen. She never had any problems getting in because she was built like a grown woman and knew what to say and who to say it to. She and her friends would go to the local nightclubs and hangout with Guy and his friends.

Monee was just living life and didn't put much thought into how her behavior and actions could cause lasting effects on her life. Monee was always very intelligent, so getting good grades in high school was easy for her. However, Monee had no discipline, and with very little parental supervision, she did what she wanted to do. Her mother Virginia was preoccupied with the heartaches of broken marriages, low self-worth, and her own childhood demons that were still haunting her, while simultaneously struggling to raise Monee and her siblings. Virginia had been self-medicating with marijuana for as long as Monee could remember.

Monee's home was considered the "party house," and alcohol, marijuana, card playing, and eating plenty of good soul food were her family's culture. This was the way Monee's family celebrated life and bonded during times of tragedy, and tragedy they knew very well. So partying was in Monee's blood. She had her first taste of alcohol when she was twelve and started smoking marijuana the summer before her senior year of high school.

By the time she moved to Columbus, she was smoking weed almost every day. Even though Monee left her hometown and moved into an apartment off campus with her son Nathan and did not know anyone in this new city, she managed to meet Carter, one of the biggest marijuana dealers on the college campus. But even with this new weed connect, she didn't smoke often because she always had Nathan with her unless she was in class.

"Hey! How you doin'?" Monee looked up from her geometry book to see this very tall, slim, brown skinned guy standing in front of her table, smiling at her. The guy didn't give Monee a chance to answer. "I'm Dabir, what's your name?" Dabir was staring at Monee with an intense look of interest and wonder.

"My name is Monee." She smiled, startled by his intrusion but intrigued by his confidence.

"You're fresh! I've never seen you around the student center before. This is your first quarter here, isn't it?" Dabir already knew the answer to his own question.

Monee laughed. "Yes, this is my first quarter here. You seem surprised as if you're supposed to know everyone on campus!"

"I do know everyone on campus just about. You never seen me around campus before?" Dabir said, now perplexed.

Monee laughed even harder; she found it amusing that Dabir really expected her to know who he was. "No, sorry, can't say that I have," she answered, still smiling.

"We have history class together. What's your major?"

"Forensic psychiatry, you?"

"Engineering. I am a sophomore," Dabir replied in his deep, debonair voice.

"Engineering!" Monee's brain was spinning now. "Doesn't that mean you are great in math?" She felt a great sense of hope.

"Yes, I am great at math, why?"

"I just failed my third geometry quiz! This stuff is like a foreign language to me. Do you think you could tutor me pleeeasse?" Monee batted her eyes and smiled as big as she could to make sure her dimples were beaming from her cheeks.

"Sure, I can tutor you." Dabir wrote his phone number and address on her notebook that was on the table. "You can come over tomorrow evening. Just call me before you come."

"Thank you so much, Dabir!"

"Nice meeting you, sexy, see you tomorrow," Dabir said and quickly disappeared.

Monee was so happy. She met a nice guy, and he could help her pass geometry.

For the next few weeks, Monee and Dabir' s friendship blossomed. She was at his house more than she was at home. She would even bring Nathan with her in the evenings. Dabir and his roommate Ben loved Nathan, and everyone that came around all seemed to enjoy having a toddler around the frat house. She learned a lot about Dabir; he was from the same hometown and was vice president of a well-known Greek fraternity on campus. Dabir's house was the frat house as well. So, Monee met plenty of students just by being at Dabir's house getting help with math. Monee really began to care about Dabir, and even though he wasn't the most attractive guy physically, his bubbly outgoing personality and crazy sense of humor made him appealing. Dabir was tall, slim and very inquisitive. People were drawn to his magnetism.

One Friday evening, Monee and Dabir decided to go to Monee's house to study for midterm exams they had coming up on Monday. There were also parties going that weekend, and they knew they wouldn't get any studying done at Dabir's house with his frat brothers and their girlfriends there getting drunk. Monee and Dabir had their own alcohol with them but decided to study first before indulging. That lasted the first thirty minutes after putting Nathan to sleep when Monee cracked open a bottle of vodka and got two glasses.

"I'm ready for a drink. How 'bout you?" Monee looked at Dabir with a sneaky grin on her face.

"Hell yeah! Add some cranberry to mine though."

Monee and Dabir sat at the dining room table talking and laughing for hours. "So, Dabir, why don't you have a girlfriend?" Monee asked.

"I don't know. I'm talking to a few chicks but nothing serious. I think females can be very demanding of a man's time, and I'm too busy to be trying to cater to some chick. I got too much going on right now for a relationship. How 'bout you? Why your sexy ass ain't got a man?"

"Well, I was dating this guy from back home who was supposed to move here a few months ago, but he ended up going to jail. We had a very strong connection both mentally and sexually, but I don't understand why sometimes guys get sidetracked and think that the fastest way to wealth is taking it from someone else! I believe what you do will eventually come back to you." Monee seemed to grow sad as she shook her head. "I don't know… every guy that I have fallen in love with ended up going to jail. No more drug dealers or gang bangers for me!" Monee took another sip of her drink.

"Yeah, unfortunately, a black man doesn't have to be a drug dealer or a gang banger to end up going to jail! I know plenty of brothers who were just at the wrong place at the wrong time or was racially profiled and charged with a crime they didn't even commit! It's grimy out here!" Dabir said with frustration in his voice.

Both Monee and Dabir nodded in agreement and took another sip of their vodka and cranberry. As they sat their glasses on the table, their eyes met, and for what seemed to be an eternity, they gazed at each other, and a sweet smile turned into a sensual long-lasting kiss. One thing led to another, and clothes were flying off their bodies and onto the floor. The piles of clothes became a mattress that cushioned their bodies as they began to have hot passionate sex.

The next morning, Monee woke up to Nathan calling for her to set him free from his crib. Monee got up off the living room floor and could hear Dabir talking on the phone in the bathroom. As she walked past the bathroom after getting Nathan from his room, Dabir was walking out. He was done with his phone call.

"Private phone conversation, huh?" Monee asked with sarcasm in her voice.

"Oh yeah, just a business call I had to make," Dabir said.

"You are always making 'business calls.' What kinda business you running that is such a secret?" Monee had witnessed Dabir making calls, and sometimes, their tutoring session was cancelled due to Dabir having to attend a business meeting, but he would never let on to any details.

"Nothing special, baby! Damn mind ya business!" Dabir began to laugh and then grabbed Monee and kissed her on her cheek. "I gotta go, let's hook up later." He gathered his books from the dining room table.

"Ok cool, see ya later, Dabir," Monee replied as she closed the door behind him.

"What just happened?" Monee thought as she prepared Nathan's breakfast. Monee was really liking Dabir, but she didn't have any intentions on starting a relationship right now. She was trying to stay focused on getting good grades and successfully finishing college. However, Dabir intrigued her; he was very smart, ambitious, and was very focused. She knew he was going places and could see them being a young power couple on campus and then possibly marriage. But Monee decided to play it cool and go with the flow; she was a bit uneasy about him not sharing some things about his life with her. Especially something as simple about what type of business he was involved in, so she decided to play safe and not tell him how strong her feelings were for him.

Later that evening, Dabir called Monee and asked her and Nathan to come over. She obliged, and when she got there, Dabir decided to share with Monee more about the business he was running. He had a white dry erase board on a tripod and began asking Monee where she would like to be financially within the next five years.

Monee replied, "Rich, of course!"

Dabir laughed, and then the smile quickly changed to a very stern look. He began sharing wealth principles and how having his own business through network marketing was his vehicle to financial and time freedom. "You don't have to trade time for dollars and work for the next 60 years on the same job giving 30% of your income to the government for taxes! You can't leave a job to Nathan, but you can leave a legacy to him through residual and passive income!"

Monee could tell by the way Dabir was speaking that he was serious and passionate about this business. The foundation of the network marketing business was getting customers to order household products online instead of going to the grocery store to buy them. Due to the distributors and their customers ordering household products consistently on a monthly basis, large profits and residual income were supposed to be generated. Monee was excited and wanted in. She invested a little over $500 to start her own business and began attending the network marketing meetings with Dabir. Personal development was the culture of this business, and for the first time in her life, she was surrounded by successful business minded people, young and old, that wanted to help her succeed!

As a young girl, Monee always loved reading books, so it was perfect that her colleagues had a book list with titles like *Think and Grow Rich*, *Seven Principles of Highly Successful People*, and *As A Man Thinketh So Is He*. Monee was fired up, and things seemed to be going great in her life. Although she was now on academic probation due to her declining grade point average, Monee was still determined to pull up her grade point average and build her business with her soon-to-be boyfriend and possible future husband.

One day while Monee was over Dabir's house, there was a knock at the door. Dabir's roommate opened the door, and two girls walked in. Dabir went over to greet the girls, one of which he embraced and rubbed his hands down her back. He then turned to Monee and introduced the girls to her.

"Monee, this is my girlfriend Leah and Tina, her best friend," Dabir said with a matter-of-fact tone with no conscious at all. "Y'all, this is my friend Monee. She's from Cleveland like me, and she's cool as fuck!"

Monee was in shock. She sat there frozen for what seemed like hours, but in reality, it was only a minute that had passed before she mustered up the poise to smile and say hi to the girls.

"Oh my God! He is so cute," Leah said. "Is he your son?"

"Yes, he is my son. This is Nathan. Nathan, say hello." Nathan was being bashful and buried his head in Monee's lap. "I think he's tired. We are going to go ahead and leave." She tried not to sound choked up and quickly grabbed her and Nathan's bags and proceeded to the door.

Dabir got up and opened the door for her and followed her outside.

"You told me you didn't have a girlfriend!" Monee exclaimed. "Why did you lie to me?"

"I didn't have a girlfriend. We just made it official two weeks ago," Dabir said, trying to sound sincere even though he knew he was being deceptive.

"Two weeks ago? You just spent the night with me last week!" Monee was almost yelling now. She was hurt and angry. Monee didn't wait to hear Dabir's response. She put Nathan in his car seat and pulled off with tears rolling down her face. She was devastated. "How could he have been such a shallow asshole? Why didn't he just tell me when he started seeing someone else? That selfish bastard! I can't stand to look at him. How am I going to be in business with this fool?" Monee began crying so hard that Nathan could feel her pain and began crying, too.

Hole of Blues

Wishful thinking,
reaching for a dream,
then every time I lay eyes on you,
I always want to scream.

You see it's like
insanity married intimacy.

There was a time that all I asked for
was for you to feel me.
But then you'd say,
"I'm not feeling you."
Then we'd be through,
but were we really through?

I love you always, but should I stay?
Hell no!
I want to get away cause all I ask is for you to step up!

Then I reminisce about the finesse,
the energies of two brilliant lights,
vibrating on an universal ride.
Then we somehow
collide into a chaotic
hole of the blues.

Monee decided to continue to be a part of the networking business even though she knew she would still have to interact with Dabir. He introduced her to the business, and therefore was Monee's direct upline, and he was obligated to train her and help expand her business. Monee knew that it would be hard not to express her hurt and anger toward him. However, she vowed that nothing would prevent her from accomplishing her dreams, and being wealthy was what she always desired since childhood.

The fraternity that Dabir was a part of had started their annual indoctrination. It was thirteen guys on the line and five of them Monee knew very well—either from back home or from hanging out with Dabir. Four of the guys that were on the indoctrination line lived in a house together close to campus. Dave, Jaylan, and Bruce were all from Beachwood, Ohio, and were freshmans like Monee. Beachwood was a suburb not too far from Cleveland Heights where Monee grew up, so they knew a lot of the same people from back home although Monee met the guys through Dabir. Their fourth roommate was from Akron, Ohio, and his name was Marlon. Marlon was a sophomore and was a bit more reserved than the other three guys. He was a pre-med major and spent most his time studying at the library. Dave, Jaylan, and Bruce were live wires and loved to have a great time. Back home in Beachwood and Cleveland Heights, these suburbs were middle- and upper-class economic status and mixed communities with great educational school systems. Dave, Jaylan, and Bruce were all considered to be "preps."

In high school, there were many different categories you could get boxed into, and "Preps or Preppie" kids were the ones that wore all name brand clothing and shoes. Everything matched and was coordinated with careful consideration. Females had to have name brand handbags and real gold and silver jewelry, no costume jewelry allowed. Every preppy guy owned several pair of khakis, loafers, cardigans, and Polo shirts. However, these guys were very down to earth, and Monee liked them a lot. They were so cool, their house off campus became known as the "Prep House."

Since Dabir was now always with Leah when they were not attending network marketing meetings or class, Monee was often hanging out at the Prep House. She even would buy the food for some of the barbeques. It reminded her of being back home with her family. It was pretty much the same scenario: good food, music, alcohol, and all the marijuana you could smoke. The only difference was that everyone there was under twenty-five, not a parent to be found anywhere. Except Monee of course who always had Nathan with her if it was after 6 p.m. and childcare was closed.

One Friday afternoon, Monee decided to go over to the Prep House and see what plans everyone had for the weekend. When Monee got there, she walked right into a party. Music was playing loud, people were everywhere, and the house reeked of cigarettes, alcohol, and weed.

"*Wow,*" Monee thought, "*this is the life!*"

"Hey, sexy, what's up with you?" asked a guy who was approaching Monee as she was bending over, digging through the cooler to get a beer bottle that was closest to the bottom. She knew that beer would be the coldest. Monee could feel the guy walking toward her from behind, so she quickly stood up and turned toward him to prevent him from brushing up against her from behind. The guy was a little bit taller than Monee with heels on, around five-foot-eight or nine. He was dark skinned with dreds and a goatee beard. Monee smiled because she was happy with what she was looking at.

"I'm good, Mr. Sexy, how are you?" Monee said, smiling from ear to ear.

"Here let me help you with that." The guy grabbed the beer out of Monee's hand and popped the cap off with his teeth.

"Gee, thanks!" Monee said, laughing as she grabbed the beer from the guy and took a swallow.

"I'm Red, I just moved here from Dayton. What is your name?" Red asked while eyeballing her from head to toe.

"Monee," she replied smoothly. "So, you went to school in Dayton and transferred here?"

"Nah, I left school, and I came here to make some money. I know Bruce, Jaylan, and Dave from back home. We all graduated from Beachwood together. They told me to fall through, plenty of bread to be made here with these rich college kids on this campus. So, I decided to grab a few pounds and check it out. You smoke?" Red's left eye lifted higher than the right one, and the corners of his mouth raised, giving him this cute little smirk.

Monee began to laugh and nodded, and then said, "Yes, I do."

"Awe hell nawl! What are you doing here, nigga?" It was Dabir. He walked into the kitchen and gave Red a handshake then grabbed him and gave him a half-hug. Then Dabir looked at Monee.

"I been here for about a week now, nigga, what's up, why you just now falling through?" Red responded.

"Well, I see you two know each other," Monee said, "so I will let y'all catch up." Monee proceeded to leave the kitchen because she really didn't want to be around Dabir any longer than she had to.

"Monee, can I holla at you outside for a moment? Matter of fact, I was about to go to the store and get some more beer. Would you ride with me?" Dabir said in his smooth apologetic voice.

"Ugh nawl, I don't feel like going to the store," Monee said, still heading out the kitchen. At this time, more people funneled into the kitchen and began asking Red for beer and smoke. Dabir followed Monee out of the kitchen and into the dining room where the music was playing so loud that you couldn't hear yourself speak let alone someone else. Dabir grabbed Monee's hand and pulled her out of the dining room through the living room and outside on to the porch. There were other people on the porch as well, two of which were Bruce and Jaylan.

"Man, Dabir, I thought you were going on a beer run. What's up?" Bruce blurted as he chugged his can of beer down his throat.

"Monee, come on and go with me. I wanna talk to you, please!" Dabir did not take no for an answer and grabbed Monee's hand again, leading her down the porch steps. Monee obliged him, and they got into Dabir's car and pulled off.

"Why I haven't I heard from you? You haven't called me nor came by the frat house in over two weeks," Dabir asked as if he had no clue as to what could possibly be wrong with Monee.

"Why should I? I think you made things very clear when you introduced me to your girlfriend!" Monee stated angrily.

"What does that have to do with our friendship?" Dabir asked, still playing dumb.

"You are in denial, what friendship? Is that what you call all the women you sleep with and then introduce them to your girlfriends? Monee asked sarcastically.

"Lies, I didn't lie to you about anything, girl! What are you talking about?" Dabir yelled as he sped down the street.

"You told me that you didn't want a girlfriend because you have too much going on with school, business, and the fraternity! But we are having sex every other day, and then you introduce me to your so-called girlfriend two days after the last time we slept together! What kinda bullshit is that?" Monee turned completely in her seat to face him and watch his response.

Dabir wildly pulled into a gas station next to a pump and slammed on the breaks and threw the car into park.

"Look," he said, "at the time I told you that, that was how I felt, but when I met Leah, I changed my mind."

"Really? When you met Leah, you changed your mind, but you still were sleeping with me! I guess I missed the memo, huh?" Monee's heart was aching. She couldn't believe what she was hearing.

"I have feelings for you, too, Monee, I can't deny that, but I don't know. I just feel differently toward Leah."

"Oh, so you thought you could have your cake and eat it, too, huh? You got me fucked up, nigga! Oh, I know what it is. You don't want a ready-made family, huh?" Monee's heart was pounding through her chest; she was too angry to cry and wouldn't give the satisfaction to Dabir to see her cry.

"Hold on, baby, now that's a low blow! You know I love Nathan and would do anything for that lil guy! What is wrong with you?" Dabir was now getting emotional and was getting very close to Monee in the car. They were now looking each other face to face and less than a foot away from each other even though Dabir was still in the driver's seat.

"I know what I feel, and I know in my heart the reason you decided to get into a relationship with Leah over me is because of an image! You are worried about what people would say if we got serious, and you're afraid of the responsibility. Well, you don't have to worry about that because I don't want you anymore!"

As soon as Monee said that, Dabir grabbed her and began to passionately tongue kiss her while embracing her. Monee couldn't resist the emotions, and the passion she felt at that time would not allow her to push him away. She realized that she did love Dabir, but he had hurt her. The kiss lasted for a few minutes, but when Dabir finally turned Monee lose, it seemed like they were kissing for eternity. They both were looking into each other's eyes and were speechless. Neither had anything to say.

"I will be right back," Dabir said calmly. "I am going to go get the beer. Do you need anything?"

"Naw, I'm good. Thanks," Monee said in a slow calm voice. Dabir got out of his car and walked into the store. Monee began shaking her head. *"This shit is crazy."*

Dabir came back carrying two cases of beer. He put them in the back seat on his side of the car and got back into the car, started it, and pulled off. He looked over at Monee, who was now looking straight ahead.

"I never meant to hurt you, Monee," Dabir sincerely said.

"Well, you did, and being in love alone isn't a good feeling! But don't worry, I wish you the best. We're cool. I won't tell your lil girlfriend that you've been sleeping with the both of us." Monee meant it, too. Although she still cared for Dabir, she felt that it was time to let go and move on. The fact that he chose to commit to someone else and still strung her along was selfish and deceptive. That showed Monee that he didn't know the true meaning of loyalty.

They got back to the party to discover there was double the amount of people there than it had been before they left. It was Memorial Day weekend and also the end of the second semester of school, and summer break was right around the corner, so everyone was celebrating that finals were over and the holiday. Monee quickly got out the car and went back into the house. In the dining room, there was about nine guys and seven girls sitting around taking shots of Tanqueray as a part of some drinking game where everyone sang a song, and at the end, everyone drank a shot of liquor.

"Hey, Monee, here is a shot glass, come on!" It was Jaylan waving for her to come get the shot glass.

"Yeah, I could use a shot or two right now!" Monee said as she grabbed the shot glass. Jaylan and Monee laughed at each other and tapped their shot glasses together and started singing.

The party went on all day, people came and left. Some left and came back, but all day, there was a constant flow of drinking, smoking, and music. By the time the sun went down, things were beginning to taper off. Everyone was mainly in the house, sitting around laughing and talking. A few couples were in the dining room dancing. Monee was on the porch sitting with a few girls from her African-American History class talking about the final. Her mind had drifted off to thinking about how happy she was that Nathan was spending the night with one of the teachers from his day-care, who also took care of the children on weekends when the daycare was closed. So, Monee was able to relax and not have to rush home. Her train of thought was broken when the porch screen door swung loudly open. Monee looked up to see Jaylan stumbling out of the door.

"Hey, what y'all sexy ladies doing out here when all the fellas are in the house?" Jaylan was feeling good, but he wasn't intoxicated yet. Jaylan was a big guy. He stood about six-five and over 200 pounds. He was dark skinned and had jet black hair. Monee always thought Jaylan was a nice-looking guy, but she wasn't attracted to him.

"Hey, Monee, can I talk to you for a sec? Come walk with me for a minute." Jaylan waved for her to come down the stairs while holding a beer can in his other hand. Monee got up from her chair and went down the stairs, curious to see what Jaylan wants.

"Hey, Jay, what's up? Something wrong?" Monee asked, trying to hurry up to get to the point.

"Ugh, I just need to talk to you about something. I got something on my mind that's been bothering me, and I need your advice. Can we sit in my car for a minute and talk?" Jaylan asked, now sounding a bit stressed.

"Sure, Jay, that's cool." Monee wondered what he was so stressed about. They got into Jaylan's car, and he rolled down all the windows. It was around 9 in the evening, so the sun had gone completely down, and there was a nice breeze blowing even though the temperature hadn't dropped much and was still around 82 degrees. Jaylan was in the driver's seat, and Monee was in the passenger seat.

"What is it with me and cars today?" she thought.

"Well, you know we have been pledging for over two months now, right?" Jaylan said, trying to gather his thoughts.

"Yes, I know," Monee replied.

"And I love my line bros and I got much respect for my upline, including Dabir. I mean we was cool before I actually pledged, but now that he's my upline, we kinda been a bit distant, you know since he is the upper echelon and really shouldn't be fraternizing with his line."

Monee realized that she had managed to completely forget about all that drama that had occurred earlier that day between her and Dabir. She was glad when she saw him leave the party shortly after they had returned from the store. Red had found her sitting out on the back patio, and they stayed out there for hours talking and getting to know each other. Red shared that he was from Beachwood and that is how he know the Prep boys. She liked Red; he was a year older than Monee and very smart. He also made her laugh.

Now Jaylan managed to bring up Dabir, and it brought all the drama right back to the forefront of her mind. But she was trying to stay focused on what Jaylan was saying, so she responded, "Yes, Jaylan, I think it's very cool that soon all of y'all will be frat brothers and y'all were already friends."

"Yeah, I know. But the problem is you see, recently there has been some new developments that is making things a bit complexed," Jaylan stated, sounding tense. "You know Dabir is in a relationship with Leah. You know Leah, right?" He nodded. "Oh, hell yeah, you know Leah because you and Dabir are business partners, right?"

"Yeah, I know who you are talking about. I met her, she seems cool." Monee now wondered if he was about to ask her something about Dabir and her messing around.

"Well, just recently, Leah and I hooked up, and the feelings are very strong between us. She even told me—"

"Wait, wait, hold up! What you mean y'all hooked up? Like hooked up like went on a date or hooked up like really hoookkked up?!" Monee looked Jaylan straight in the face.

Jaylan pulled the blunt he already had rolled and lodged behind his right ear, reached down into his pocket to pull out his lighter, and lit the blunt and took a long pull and then proceeded to talk, all the while holding the smoke in his lungs. "Both, Mo." Then he slowly exhaled, blowing all the smoke out of his lungs.

"What? You mean you smashed you upline's girlfriend? Awe shit, Jay, what are you thinking? He could throw you off the line if he finds out!" Monee's mouth was hanging wide open. She was in disbelief, but at the same time she was smiling on the inside.

"Look at karma," she thought. *"This dude stringing me along, gets a girlfriend and deceiving the both of us only to find out that she is playing him, too! Wow! What you do definitely is going to come back to you sooner or later!"*

"I know, Mo, it's all bad, but the connection we have is crazy! I think I love this girl already. She really wants to break up with Dabir, but she is afraid of hurting him and then how he will respond when he sees us together. I mean like you said he can make things very difficult for me while I am pledging, or he could try to get me kicked off the line completely." Jaylan shook his head, pulling the blunt again and then handed it to Monee. Monee took the blunt, pulled long, and blew out the smoke slowly.

"Yeah, Jay, you in a tight space. The only advice I can give you is whatever decision you make be prepared for the consequences. What means more to you, Leah or the fraternity? Because you might lose one while gaining the other."

"True. Aye, Mo, I know you cool with Dabir, but you gotta promise me that you won't tell that nigga what's going on! I think we may just keep it a secret until I cross over, and then he can't do shit. She can break up with his ass now, but we won't let anyone know about us until later. Ya feel me?" Jaylan said proudly.

"Yeah, Jay, I think that will be best. I won't say anything I promise," Monee said convincingly. But deep-down, she hadn't completely convinced herself that she wouldn't leak the information that was shared with her by Jaylan at some time in the future. Could you blame her, she was still hurt by the way Dabir treated her and to have the opportunity to hurt him sounded really good to her.

"Nah, I ain't gonna give him no payback," she thought. *"I will be the bigger person."*

A week later, Dabir called Monee, upset because Leah had broken up with him, and he didn't understand why. Monee was on the phone with Dabir for almost an hour. She would tell him she had to go, but he would call her back ten minutes later, asking her opinion and creating scenarios trying to figure out why his girlfriend dumped him.

"Look, Dabir, put it this way, maybe the way you treated me just came back on you. Did you not think that your actions were not going to have any consequences?" Monee asked, feeling like he left her no choice but to tell him the truth. *"Hell, why should you spare his feelings he didn't spare mine?"* Monee thought.

"You heard something, didn't you? What do you know, Monee? I feel like she cheated on me! Is there someone else?" Dabir was livid. His ego was bruised, and he could not keep his composure.

"All I am going to tell you is yes, she found someone with a deeper connection than what the two of you had. She's moved on, and you should, too. Good bye, Dabir."

Monee could hear him screaming while she hung up the phone, but she didn't care anymore. She had moved on, too.

Over the next couple of weeks, Monee was feeling like she was on an emotional rollercoaster. She was happy because she and Red had become inseparable. Either Monee and Nathan were at the Prep House where he was living, or he was at her apartment with them. But Monee had found out that she hadn't did as well on her finals as she had hoped for and failed two of her classes. Now, she was on academic probation and had lost all her scholarship money. She had to pay her rent, car note, insurance, childcare, and the list went on. Nathan's father was now in jail, and he never paid any child support anyway, so that wasn't even an option for financial help. It was now summer break, and since most of the students went home for the summer, Red's marijuana sells dropped tremendously, and his money was low.

But the fact that Red wasn't working and didn't have much money didn't matter that much to Monee. She was happy that he genuinely loved her for her, and he also loved Nathan.

"What am I gonna do now, I don't have any money nor a job?" Monee was in tears talking to her then boyfriend Red. It was 1995, and she was struggling to stay in college.

"You will make it, you're smart and beautiful. You can do whatever you put your mind to, Monee." Red was very convincing, and although he didn't complete college, he was Monee's biggest cheerleader. He admired how she was able to go to college with a two-year-old son. He knew she had potential.

"I should have managed my money better!" Monee managed to go to college with a full scholarship, and because she had her son, she also received public assistance. When she first arrived at school, the financial aid advisor told her that she wouldn't receive her scholarship money in time to buy her books and recommended that she apply for student loans. Monee became a college freshman with an ample amount of money and no guidance or direction. She had a one-year-old car that she purchased on her own when she was still living with her mother, working full time, and going to community college.

"Hell, with yo' fine ass, you might as well be a stripper! You got the body for it, and you love takin yo' clothes off anyway when you drunk!" Red said, laughing.

Monee came back from her celebratory daydream. "Shut up, Red yo' ass always talkin' shit!" Monee couldn't help but chuckle because she did have a habit of getting drunk and taking her clothes off, whether it was because she was hot or just intoxicated; somehow, her shirt would always end up coming off.

"Nah, but seriously, I have a few friends that strip back home, and they make damn good money doing it, and they can't even dance," Red said. "You can shake that ass, and with that pretty ass smile, you can't go wrong, girl!" Red brushed her cheek and smiled at Monee while he undressed her with his eyes.

"You really think I can make money doing that?" Monee asked with her eyes getting big as she realized that stripping just might be the solution to her money troubles. Her mind began to see nothing but dollars signs. Monee was too bold to be fearful of anything and too naive to even consider the danger and risks that she would be putting herself in, in that kind of negative environment. She was too blinded by her problems to see that the spiritual damage caused by self-degradation was not worth the physical money she would get from taking off her clothes in front of many strangers.

The next day, Monee began to look in the help wanted section of the newspaper to see if there were any job postings for exotic dancers. She saw an ad that caught her attention: *Massage parlor seeking attractive ladies to be massage therapists. No skills needed—will train!*

"I can give massages!" she thought *"This just might be the job I am looking for."* She picked up the phone and called the number listed in the ad.

"Ease Your Mind Massages," a woman answered the phone with a soft inviting voice.

"HI, I saw your ad in the newspaper that you are looking to hire a massage therapist?" Monee asked.

"Oh, yes, are you over 18?" the woman asked as if she could hear the youthfulness in Monee's voice.

"Yes, I am."

"Ok, be here tomorrow at 1 p.m. for an interview with Eva the manager," the woman replied quickly.

Monee thanked that woman and hung up the phone. She was excited. "This could be better than dancing. All I have to do is massages and have the potential to make $500 to $1,500 a week in cash. This is great!"

At 12:55 p.m. the next day, Monee arrived at the massage parlor. She was proud of herself because she was usually late to everything.

The massage parlor wasn't too far from the college campus and was in a small brick building that looked like it could have once been someone's home. When she went inside, it was small as well. When Monee walked through the door, she heard a doorbell ring as if to notify someone that there was a guest in the waiting area. Monee stood by the wooden podium that was to the left of her, close to the door. As she stood there waiting, she could smell the aroma of incense and candles burning. She contemplated on the smell trying to guess the scent while she scanned the room. There was a door with a curtain draped to prevent seeing what was on the other side of the door. To her far left was a staircase leading upstairs. Clearly, this was once someone's home. A woman walks into the room from behind the curtains.

"Hi, I am Amanda, are you Monee?"

"Yes, I am, nice to meet you." Monee smiled and grabbed the young lady's hand that was extended to her. Amanda was an average looking girl maybe a few years older than Monee. She had pale white skin and was very tall and thin. Her hair was short and trimmed into a bob cut. She didn't look very happy to Monee; her eyes had wrinkles that made her look tired.

"I spoke with you on the phone yesterday. Eva will be out to get you shortly." Amanda didn't wait for Monee to respond; she turned and went up the staircase. Monee sat down on the antique couch that was up against the right wall. She was a little nervous because she really needed this job and wanted to impress the manager. As she was contemplating to herself if she should lie and say she had previous experience working in a massage parlor, an older woman emerged from between the curtains that were hiding what was through the doorway. The woman was tall and of an average weight with more meat on her bones than Amanda; her figure was more pear shaped than hourglass. She had brown eyes and very long dark brown hair that almost swept the top of her buttock. Monee got the feeling that she probably was a hippie back in the '70s.

"Hi, Monee, I'm Eva, you can follow me." Eve turned and disappeared back behind the curtains, and Monee quickly jumped up to follow her. When Monee separated the curtains to walk through, it was like she entered a totally different environment. In front of her was a long hallway with doors on both sides of the hall. To her right was another small waiting area with two red leather couches facing each other and a small glass coffee table between the couches. Instrumental jazz was coming from the speakers mounted in the corners where the ceilings and the walls met. The aroma of sandalwood was more intense. As Monee stood there, she could see a woman wearing a thick white terry cloth bathrobe leave one of the rooms and cross the hallway and go into another room with a glass and cigarette in her hands.

"*Wow, they get to drink on the job,*" she thought. "*I know this is the job for me!*"

"Monee, come have a seat on the couch next to me so that I can learn more about you," Eva said as she motioned for Monee to have a seat. Monee sat on the couch facing Eva, and she noticed behind Eva was a large mirror hanging on the wall above her. Eva grabbed a black leather cigarette case from off the coffee table and pulled a cigarette from it and lit it. Crossing her legs and sliding deeply into the back of the couch, she forcefully blew the cigarette smoke up into the air. "So, Monee, have you ever worked in a massage parlor before?"

The question caught Monee of guard, and before she knew it, she quickly said, "No, ma'am."

"Please call me Eva. Calling me ma'am makes me feel old and withered!" Eva burst into a boisterous laugh and then quickly regained her composure.

"Eva, can you tell me what I have to do?" Monee asked.

"I have a special clientele that come here to relax and receive special VIP treatment from beautiful young girls such as yourself. You will be responsible for making these men feel special and giving them full body massages. You will get paid $75.00 per massage plus tips. Do you think you can handle that?" Eva asked in a firm voice.

"Oh yes, I can handle that," Monee replied.

"Ok, good, you look like you have a nice body, but I have to make sure you look just as good with your clothes off." Eva was sizing Monee up like she had X-ray vision. Her eyes examined Monee so intensely it made Monee very uncomfortable.

"Why do I have to look good naked?" Monee was now feeling uncomfortable and confused.

Eve again broke into her boisterous laugh and then took another long drag of her cigarette. "Because we give massages in the nude, silly! Amanda didn't tell you that over the phone?" Eva still chuckled a bit as she blew the smoke out of her mouth. Before Monee could respond, one of the doors down the hallway swung open and then loudly shut. Monee could see an older Caucasian man walking toward her tucking his shirt into his slacks. He appeared to be in his late fifties, tall, and overweight.

He was having trouble tucking his shirt into his pants because he was struggling with getting the shirt over his large stomach. He had black hair slicked over his bald spot in the center of his head. He was also sweating and appeared to be disoriented. By the time he finally got his shirt tucked in, he was approaching the sitting area where Monee and Eva were. The man, now realizing that Monee was sitting a few feet in front of him, revealed a large devilish grin as if he was a hungry dog drooling over a nice juicy bone.

"Well, well, well," he said, "Eva, tell me, who is this sexy piece of brown suga you got here?" By this time, the man was standing in front of the coffee table facing Monee and Eva.

"Mr. Harris, this is Monee. She is here to possibly become one of my girls. Isn't she lovely?" Eva said as she took one last drag of her cigarette. She stood to her feet while simultaneously smashing the cigarette in the ashtray that was beside her leather cigarette case until there was no longer any smoke escaping from the cigarette bud. Eva slid from in between the couch and the coffee table until she was standing next to Mr. Harris. She then caressed his wide back and patted him.

"Did Theresa take good care of you back there, Paul?" Eva smiled as she walked him through the curtains and into the front waiting area. Monee could hear Mr. Harris say, "Oh, she always does! I call her magic hands!" Monee began to wonder if this was a good idea.

When Eva reentered, she said, "Ok, Monee, Mr. Harris is one of our biggest tipping clients, so you are lucky that he has the hots for you already!" A huge smile grew on Eva's face. "So, what you are going to do is go into the room directly behind this wall. This mirror is a double mirror. I will be able to see you, but you won't be able to see me. You are to take off all your clothes and face the mirror in the room so that I can determine if your body is nice enough for me to hire you."

Eva walked to the first door that was closest to the waiting area. She opened the door and turned the light on in the room. Monee was still sitting on the couch, feeling dazed.

"Monee, what are you waiting for, suga?" Eva waved for her to walk into the room. Monee got up and walked past Eva who was still standing in the doorway and entered the room. "This will only be a minute. It doesn't take long for me to make a decision. Just take off all your clothes including your bra and panties and face the mirror. I will knock on the door, and this will be your signal for you to get dressed. Got it?"

"Yes, I got it," Monee responded slowly in a soft unsure voice. Eva closed the door, and Monee reached behind her and unzipped her long full-length skirt until the skirt fell to the floor. She looked around the room and realized that the room must specifically be for "auditions" because there was only one-armed chair in the far corner and behind her on the wall were clothing hooks as if it was an undressing room. She stared blankly at the mirror in front of her, intrigued by the reality that the woman on the other side could see her. Monee took off her soft pink short sleeve sweater and then unhooked her bra and let her firm, plump 36 D breasts free, and then removed her panties. Now, completely naked with nothing but her heels on, Monee realized it was cold as death in there. Her cold silence was broken from the sound of the knock on the door. She quickly began to redress herself.

Once Monee finished dressing, she opened the door and saw Eva standing by the coffee table lighting another cigarette. "You have a beautiful body, Monee, can you start tomorrow?" Eva exhaled the smoke that filled her lungs.

"Thank you, Eva, yes, I can start tomorrow!" Monee pretended to be excited.

"Ok, be here at 3 p.m. sharp ready for training!" Eva said as she separated the curtains to allow Monee to walk into the front waiting area.

"Ok," Monee said as she walked to the front door. After turning to look at Eva and smile, she quickly walked to her car.

As soon as she pulled off and was down the street, she burst into tears. She felt so uncomfortable, so violated. She now knew the truth; the massage parlor was a front for prostitution! As tears streamed down her face, she heard a still small voice inside of her say, *This is not the answer.* Monee drove home knowing that Eva would never see her again.

Monee came home to find Red and Nathan outside at the playground that was inside Monee's apartment complex. Because the daycare wasn't open on Saturdays, Red agreed to keep Nathan while Monee went on her interview. It didn't hurt that Red enjoyed playing with Nathan—and money was tight, and she couldn't afford to pay a sitter.

When Monee went to kiss Red, he didn't look to be his normal jovial self. "What's wrong, Red?" she asked, very concerned.

"My pops is sick. He just got released from the hospital back home, and I need to leave and go see about him. I'm worried about him, Monee. He didn't sound too good over the phone. Jaylan, Dave, and I are getting on the road in a few hours."

"I am sorry to hear that. Listen to me, your father is going to be fine. When are you coming back?" Monee asked in an encouraging tone.

"I am not sure. It depends on how he is doing. If he is ok, I will come back next weekend. I'm gonna miss y'all." Red reached over to kiss Monee and then grabbed Nathan off the swing and put him on his shoulders as they walk toward Monee's apartment.

After dropping Red off at the Prep House, Monee returned home to spend a quiet Saturday night with Nathan. While watching *Sesame Street* on television with Nathan, Monee's phone rang. It was her friend Rita who was also from Cleveland, and they were in the same Ethics class together. Rita was real cool. Her and Monee got along very well, neither thrived off drama and negativity, and both carried themselves as ladies with class even though they were only 19 years old.

"Hey, Monee, what are you doing?" Rita sounded very excited over the phone.

"Nothing much, girl, sitting here watching *Sesame Street* with Nathan before I put him in the tub. What's going on with you? What you so excited about?" Monee began laughing.

"I just got invited to this party given by this NBA player! It's tonight at Club Emerald. You wanna go?"

"I would, but my money tight right now, and plus I don't have a sitter tonight. But damn I need an NBA player in my life right now. That would make everything right!" Monee and Rita both started laughing hysterically.

"Girl, I feel ya, Where is Red at? He can't keep Nathan?"

"No, he went back home for about a week. His father is sick. I miss my baby though. I just wish he was able to help more financially. You know how it is, it's hard to find someone with all the qualities you need." Monee sighed.

"Yeah, I know, girl, that is why I am single. You know my roommate Mary. She has kept Nathan before, and she doesn't have any plans tonight. You want me to see if she would keep Nathan?" Rita was excited again.

"Sure, why not ask her," Monee said. "I wouldn't mind getting out and having a few drinks."

"Ok, hold on, Monee. Let me go ask her." After a couple minutes, Rita came back to the phone. "Ok, girl, we good to go. She said she would love to keep Nathan with his handsome self! So, get dressed and let me know when you are on your way."

"Ok, Rita. Tell Mary I said thanks. See you soon, bye." Monee hung up and got her and Nathan ready for their overnight outing. Monee would just sleep over at Rita and Mary's apartment to prevent having to take Nathan out at night, especially since she would be having a few drinks.

Monee and Rita arrived at the NBA player's party at 11:30 p.m. The club was packed with celebrities, NBA players, and a few NFL players. However, Rita's tickets were not VIP, so they didn't get access to mingle with many of the celebrities and athletes. Monee could careless; she and Rita still had a great time, and Monee did what she always did best—dance. She got on that dance floor and had a great time. She didn't need a dance partner to dance as she had no problem dancing by herself.

However, she did end up dancing with the short guy who emerged out of nowhere and began winding and gyrating when a reggae song came on. Monee thought it was funny because he was a great dancer but was so short. He was about five-foot-six with muscles everywhere. Not an ounce of fat on his body. Monee thought he had a nice smile, but he was not attractive at all. He said his name was Prince and asked for her number. Monee agreed to exchange numbers with Prince, but she really didn't have any intention on seeing the guy again.

They next day, Prince called Monee, and they talked on the phone for over an hour. She shared with him that she was looking for a job and what happened at her interview at the massage parlor. He told her that he used to work as a male stripper until a year ago when he began his auto sales business. Prince told Monee how he knew where every strip club in Columbus was located and that it would be no problem for him to take her to the best strip clubs in town so that she could get a job.

Monee wasted no time in taking Prince up on his offer. She made arrangements for Nathan to go to the sitters the next day while Prince took her to different strip clubs for interviews. Prince even paid for Nathan's sitter.

The first strip club was Diamonds, the most upscale club in downtown Columbus. When Monee and Prince got there, Monee was impressed and nervous.

The club had a large marquee over the front entrance that read "DIAMONDS The Most Beautiful Women in the City." As soon as Monee and Prince walked inside, a big, huge, white bouncer stopped them and asked for their IDs. Prince asked if they could speak to the manager, and the bouncer asked him what it was about. When Prince told him that Monee was looking for a job and wanted to audition, the bouncer looked Monee up and down and then told them that he would be right back and walked away.

Prince and Monee walked toward the bar that was across from the stage and sat down. The club was huge. There was one main stage that was in the center of the club. There were chairs all around the center stage so the patrons could order from the bar and sit at the stage or order from one of the waitresses. There were two other small stages in the back of the club as well. Monee had never been inside a strip club and had no idea what to expect. She was in awe. The strippers were beautiful, they were all shapes and sizes with beautiful lingerie, and some even had on costumes. There was one dancer that was on the large center stage with this magnificent cowgirl costume on. The dancer had to be at least five-foot-seven with a very pale complexion and long brown hair. She had an hourglass figure, and the cowgirl pants exposed her butt cheeks and her bikini thong. She had on a vest with no bikini top. She was slowly swaying from side to side to the music with this very alluring smirk on her face. The men surrounding her were drooling, and then they all began to cheer when she grabbed the strip pole on stage and flipped herself upside down and spread her legs wide as she used only her hands to spin completely around the pole, giving all the men surrounding the stage a good view of her jewels.

"Wow! I am going to get me a costume like that," Monee whispered into Prince's ear.

"I know just the place you can go and buy it," Prince said, laughing.

Just then, the big bouncer walked up. "I am sorry. The manager said we are full and are not hiring any girls right now. Check back in few months." The bouncer then walked away.

"Come on, Monee, I know another spot we can check out." Prince grabbed Monee's hand and led her out of the club. "Damn, you would have made plenty of money in that club, girl!" Prince said angrily. Monee could tell Prince was more disappointed than she was.

"It's ok, Prince, I'm sure one of these clubs will be hiring."

The next club they arrived at was Club Khaos. Club Khaos was one of the very few topless strip clubs in Columbus. This club was located on the Eastside of Columbus. The place was not as classy as Diamonds, but it was big and had just as many girls. When Monee and Prince spoke to the manager, he told them he was only looking for girls to work the morning shift during the week. That wasn't going to work for Monee because she was still intended on taking classes in the fall. So, she didn't bother to audition.

After a thirty-minute drive on the highway, Prince and Monee arrived at Foxy's Saloon on the northwest side of town. This club had a western theme, the exterior of the club looked like a saloon, and inside, there were lights everywhere. The chairs and tables were made from barrels, and there was even a mechanical horse for customers and the dancers to ride.

When Prince and Monee walked in, the guy sitting at the end of the bar got up and went over to them to search them.

"I'm good, man," Prince said, "I left my piece in my car. My sister here is looking for a job. Are y'all hiring for dancers?" Prince didn't want to waste any more time and decided it was best to tell the security guard that Monee was his sister to prevent them getting sent away due to them thinking that they were dating. Most club managers didn't like when the dancers had overprotective boyfriends.

"Yeah, I am actually hiring. I just lost two girls. One I had to fire using that stuff, and her looks started to deteriorate. The other got pregnant on me! Damn shame, she was pulling in all the good ol' boys, had them spending plenty of money in here!" The manager shook his head. Then, he took a long drag of his cigarette and smashed it in the ashtray while simultaneously blowing the smoke forcefully out of his mouth. "Come on let me show you the dressing room. Can you dance, pretty lady?"

"Ah yes, I can dance," Monee said, a bit distracted due to watching the dancer who was dancing on the main stage.

"What clubs have you worked at?" He chuckled. "Oh, I'm sorry. My name is Bill. I was so mesmerized by your beauty I forgot to ask you your name."

"My name?" Monee didn't have a stage name picked out. She never thought about that part of the gig. "Nikki," she said quickly.

"Nikki? Is that your real name? We recommend our girls not to use their real names here as a form of protection. You know these guys can get attached…if you know what I am saying?"

"No, Nikki….like 'Darling Nikki' by Prince? That is me… Nikki," Monee stated with confidence. She smiled at Prince, who winked at her.

"Oh, ok, I get it now, well, Darling Nikki, go in here and change so I can see if you're gonna be my next money maker!" Bill opened the dressing room door while undressing Monee with his eyes at the same time. Monee walked into the small dimly lit room with three vanity mirrors lined up against the wall and five old high school lockers lined up against the opposite wall. This was not the type of club Monee thought she would get her first gig at, but hell, beggars can't be choosy, she thought. Monee got undressed and pulled her favorite summer bikini out of her bookbag. She then put on the heels she had worn to her going away party before she moved to Columbus. She looked at herself in the mirror, took a deep breath, and a big swig of vodka that she had stashed in her bookbag and walked out the dressing room.

Monee's heart was beating so fast she could barely hear the music the DJ was playing. There was about six men sitting around the main stage, and there were two other dancers sitting at the bar.

"After this song, Monee, go on up on stage and let me see what you got," Bill said as he signaled to the DJ to change the song. As the song began to fade, the dancer walked off the stage. Monee was standing next to the stage steps, and the dancer was staring at her as she walked down the stage stairs. "Knock 'em dead, sexy girl!" the dancer said and smiled.

Monee's heart was now pounding as if it was going to bust through her chest. She was never afraid to speak in front of crowds. She did great when she gave the graduation speech to her class in the fifth grade and loved mock trial competition and public speaking and debate team in high school but getting up on stage in a bikini in front of total strangers—this was new. Monee could hear the intro music to Prince's "Darling Nikki" playing as she grabbed the stripper pole in the center of the stage.

You got this, Monee, she thought, *you know you can dance. You need this job, girl!*

Monee began to walk around the pole, holding it with one hand and moving her hips to the beat of the song. Spotting a guy sitting at the stage, she leaned forward and looked into his eyes. As she leaned toward him, his eyes grew larger as they beamed on her breasts like a red laser from a gun. Monee smiled then swung around the pole and bent over so that the guy could get a good view of her behind. The guy jumped up out the seat and began to dig in his pocket, pull out a wad of cash, and toss dollar bills on to the stage.

Monee was no longer Monee when she saw that money flying on the stage. She had become Nikki and went into full character. She slowly slid down the pole with her back against it, laid on the floor into a full split, and then rolled over, opened her legs, and grabbed her foot like she had seen the other strippers do at Club Khaos. Two other men began to toss money at Nikki, too.

Before she noticed, the song had stopped, and everyone was clapping. Bill was standing at the bar smoking another cigarette, staring at Monee in amazement. Monee picked up all the money off of the stage and ran down the stage steps into the dressing room to change.

"I can't believe I just did that!" she said. "Wow, what a rush!" She counted the money that she had got off stage. She had made $25 in tips from dancing to one song. "Not bad I guess!" Monee had no idea if that was a good amount of tips for one dance or not. She had no experience and no expectation to have made any money during an audition, so she was happy. Monee got dressed and went over Prince who was sitting at the bar not too far from the manager sipping on a drink.

"How did I do?" Monee asked humbly.

"You did great with your sexy ass! All eyes were on you, babe!" Prince said, smiling from ear to ear. Monee turned to Bill, and before she could say anything, he said, "Be here tomorrow at 6 p.m. sharp and don't be late!"

Monee was officially a stripper.

The Mad Stripper

Growing up, I thought I was crazy
the way all the madness in this world
used to faze me.
All the sickness, disease, and poverty.
So, I gave up on world peace,
started changing my outlook.
Living a carefree life,
hitting them books,
started kicking it with the in crowd,
smoking weed and laughing loud.
Y'all know what I'm talking about.
Feeling like my nigga Pac,
it was me against the world.
Nobody to turn to,
so I had to make all the decisions.
Looking back on it now,
it wasn't nothing but a bunch of illusions.
God works in mysterious ways.
Keep your faith, stay strong, it pays.
Started dancing,
trying to make something happen.
It is a lot of young ladies
still stuck in that trap,
showing their bodies,
disrespecting themselves,
sitting on some nigga's lap.
Y'all know I'm telling the truth in this rap.

If it was your daughter,
she'd have to stop.
Trying to back that thing up,
shaking her butt.
What is it really worth?
Don't y'all thug misses realize
that it's your own soul that gets penalized?
It's just another strategy to be institutionalized.
I'm not trying to criticize.
Just want y'all to open y'all eyes
to what's really going on.
That stripping leads to porn
all because a young girl is scorned.

"Get away from the damn glass!"

The argument between Officer Tate and the young stripper abruptly pulled Monee out of her memory and back to reality of being behind bars. She looked up to realize that Officer Tate was now walking into the glass pod toward the girl who was yelling for her phone call. As Officer Tate walked through the sliding door, the girl rushed toward the door as if she was attempting to run out of the jail pod into the main entrance way.

"Fuck you! I am tired of this bullshit!" the girl screamed while she attempted to run past Officer Tate and out the door. Officer Tate quickly raised her arm and knocked the girl to the floor, jumped on top of her, flipped her over, and handcuffed her. All the while, the girl was screaming, kicking, and crying that she didn't belong in jail. Within seconds, two other women officers ran into the pod to assist Officer Tate, and they lifted the girl to her feet and dragged her out of the orientation pod.

Everything happened so fast; Monee was left in the pod alone, shocked and overwhelmed. She couldn't believe what she had just witnessed. The reality that she was not leaving this jail until she was "released" caused her heart to begin beating extremely fast again. The faces of her three children flashed before her eyes, and she could not breathe. A frightening wave of anxiety rushed all over her.

"How did I get myself into this mess?" she whispered. "I have hit rock bottom, and I am not there for my children. My children." Tears began to roll down Monee's face, and her heart was beating fast as if it was about to burst through her chest. She looked around the jail, feeling as if she wanted to get up and run, but she knew there was nowhere to run to.

As her anxiety steadily rose, Monee found it difficult to catch her breath. She closed her eyes and visualized her children safe at home sitting at the dinner table eating with their father. She took a deep breath, and whispered, "Thank you, Holy Father, for protecting my children and keeping them safe." She slowly exhaled. Her concentration was broken by the loud annoying click of the heavy glass door sliding open. She jumped and opened her eyes to see Officer Tate escorting an older brown skinned woman with salt and pepper hair into the orientation pod. The woman was limping, and her left eye was swollen shut.

"Have a seat, I will be back soon," Officer Tate said to the woman in a calm, cool voice.

"Thank you," the woman said slowly. Monee watched the woman as she went to the silver steel table mounted to the floor opposite the one Monee was sitting at. The woman began slowly rocking and rubbing her arms to warm herself. "Lord, it does no good to complain, I know, but Lawd, I'm gonna freeze to death in this place." Then the mysterious woman began to hum. Monee realized that with the distraction of the arrival of this new inmate, she had calmed down and her breathing had returned to normal.

Monee was listening to the older woman humming; it sounded like an old spiritual hymn of some sort. Monee always loved gospel music and even was a member of the high school gospel choir. She always felt that even through all the drama going on in her life, gospel music would give her spirit peace and her soul assurance that all things work for the glory of God, and everything would eventually be all right.

"Lawd! Lawd! Lawd! Grant me the serenity to accept the things I cannot change; the courage to change the things I can; and the wisdom, knowledge, and understanding to know the difference," the older woman said with a tone that resonated strength and comfort at the same time.

"The Serenity Prayer. I used to say it all the time, and I had the plaque hanging up in my bathroom for years until I moved to Atlanta, and it was thrown away," Monee said as she turned slowly to face the older inmate sitting across from her to her right.

"Child, we got to give our burdens to our Creator. We can't carry them all on our own. What's a beautiful soul like you doing in this dark, cold place?" the older woman asked as she looked directly at Monee through her one good eye that wasn't swollen.

"DUI," Monee answered reluctantly.

"Hmm, well, I ain't one to judge, chile, no reason to be ashamed. God don't make no mistakes just put tests in your path to help you along on your journey." The woman was still rocking back and forth, sitting with her arms crossed, and rubbing them to stay warm.

"I guess so," Monee replied. "So, what happened to you? No offense but you look like someone's sweet grandma that should be home baking cookies. How did you end up in here?" Monee wasn't exaggerating; the older woman was short, a little on the heavy side, and appeared to be in her mid-60s. Her hair was brushed straight back into a bun, but the streaks of gray hair didn't blend with the remaining jet-black hair. The gray hair looked like streaks of lightning flashing through a dark sky during a storm. Her skin looked smooth as butter with a warm glow that radiated comfort. Despite the swollen red eye and the limp when she walked into the pod, the older inmate appeared to be strong and in good health.

"Well, the Lawd blessed me with a beautiful daughter who happened to despise her own beauty. She contaminated her body with that crack cocaine and left me with my grandson years ago. My grandson hates me because I ain't his mama, and he likes to throw things at me and call me names when he sees fit.

"And, baby, I tell you this last time, I just couldn't take it no more! So, I did what the Lawd told me to do!" The older woman was no longer rocking. She was sitting straight up with her feet firmly planted on the floor. She was shaking her head as if in disbelief. "I'm Isis, and what is your name?" the woman asked in a sweet motherly tone.

"Monee. Nice to meet you, Ms. Isis."

Just then their conversation was interrupted by a woman's stern voice over the intercom system. "Wright and Green, time to get your supplies." It was the other officer that was sitting inside the glass booth in the center of the jail. Then there was a loud click of the glass door unlocking and then sliding open for the two new inmates to leave the orientation pod. Monee and Isis walked through the door, and Officer Tate was standing in front of the tall glass control center where the other officer was sitting inside monitoring all three pods.

"Ladies, follow me." Officer Tate led the two inmates into a room that was next to the main exit door that led to the long hall that Monee was escorted down when she first arrived in the women's jail. When they got inside the room, there was a stack of thin mattresses in the corner and shelves of jail supplies for the inmates. Officer Tate instructed both of them to grab a mattress and then she gave them a hard plastic cup with a handle, one spork, one blanket, one sheet, one towel, wash cloth, toothpaste, toothbrush, and a bar of soap. "Ladies, keep up with your supplies. You will only get additional supplies every two weeks during commissary. You both will be in unit 1 of the orientation pod for three days. After that time, you will be moved into common population either in cell block unit 2 or 3 for the remainder of your stay. You will not get commissary until you are moved out of the orientation pod."

Officer Tate escorted the women back to the orientation pod, and both women were put into the same cell with another young lady that was already in the cell. The other young lady in the cell was sleeping on the bottom bed. There were only two beds in the cell.

"One of you will have to put your mattress against the wall. The orientation pod is completely full; therefore, we have three inmates in each pod." Officer Tate stepped out of the cell and yelled into her walkie talkie that was on her shoulder, "Lock up cell 3111!" Just then the heavy steel door to the entrance of the small cell that was now Monee's temporary home slid shut. The jail cell was like every jail that Monee had ever seen in prison movies. There was a toilet close to the door and next to a sink. Bunk beds against one side of the cell and a mirror above the sink that had a small shelf where the inmates could sit their cups and toothbrushes, etc. Everything in the jail cell was steel and secured to the floor. Fortunately, there was a glass block window close to the top of the back-cell wall. The sunlight beaming into the jail cell from that window was the only indication they had to know if it was day or nighttime. Monee was still in disbelief that her freedom was gone.

"I just have to get through this night," Monee thought. *"Court is in the morning, I will get bail, and my mom will get me out of here."* Telling herself this would keep her calm and not completely freak out at the thought that she was trapped in this tiny jail cell with two strangers and no contact with her children or the outside world. Her freedom was gone, and for the first time in a long time, she realized that she had no control over a situation.

"Ms. Isis, you can take the top bunk, and I can sleep on the floor," Monee said as she pulled herself out of deep thought.

"Chile, you're so precious, but there's no way my big butt is climbing on top of that bunk even if Jesus himself would lift me up! I injured my left leg years back when I was in a car accident. Monee, you take that top bunk. I will be just fine over here on this floor. At least they gave us this ole mat to cushion my butt."

Ms. Isis chuckled a little bit as she slid her mattress to the wall across from the bunk beds. She slowly got down on her knees and began to put the sheet over the thin mattress. The inmate that was initially sleeping when they had first entered the cell was now sitting up on the bottom bunk bed silently watching Monee and Ms. Isis talk. Once she saw Ms. Isis begin to put the sheet on her mattress, she laid back down and rolled over on her right side. Her back was now to Ms. Isis and Monee, and her face was to the wall.

Monee looked at the girl, shook her head, and tossed her mattress onto the top bunk. Then, she climbed up onto the top bunk so that she could put the sheet on the mattress.

Reflections

Eliminating Self-Limiting Beliefs

What we feel and think internally about ourselves, others, and our circumstances will reflect in our external world. A person's perception is what creates their reality. This is called the Universal Law of Correspondence. In order to change our external circumstances, we must change our internal thoughts about our circumstances. Monee had the desire to create a better life and improve her financial situation, but what she didn't know was until she made changes to her thinking, nothing in her life was going to change. She thought becoming a stripper was going to generate large sums of money fast and thus fix her life financially. However, Monee failed to realize that the act of making money by degrading herself lowered her vibration and thus could only attract more lower vibrational energies.

Any time we try to make money out of desperation, lack, greed, selfishness, lack of self-love (stripping and prostitution), and manipulation (scams, dishonesty), we are working within a poverty-based mindset. Everything is energy, money is energy, so even if a person manages to generate large sums of money by using lower vibrational actions, it will not last, and eventually, they will end up losing their wealth. When we operate out of fear, we will attract more fear into our lives. If our actions and thoughts are founded by a vibration of frustration and fear of loss and lack, although our desire is to improve, our results will be impoverished. It is the universal law; we can only receive what we perceive.

To change our circumstances, we must change our thought, feelings, and actions to become aligned with what we truly desire and not what we fear. This starts by making a conscious commitment to changing our thoughts and how we feel about our circumstances. That means really looking deep within ourselves and being truly honest about our stinking thinking and what is no longer serving our highest good. Then, we release those habits, vices, and attitudes that we know need to go!

Take a moment and write down what you truly desire in your life. If they were no barriers or obstacles hindering you from getting what you want, what do you want in your life right now?

_____

_____

_____

_____

_____

_____

_____

_____

_____

_____

_____

_____

_____

_____

_____

_____

_____

_____

_____

_____

_____

_____

_____

Now what are the things that you need to change about your thinking? What are the top dominate negative thoughts that are preventing you from achieving the life you desire?

Think on the thought(s) and write down a positive thought that is opposite of the negative thought(s). Then make a commitment to yourself today that when you have a negative or self-limiting thought, you will immediately release it and replace that negative thought with a positive, empowering one.

_____

_____

_____

_____

_____

_____

_____

_____

_____

_____

_____

_____

_____

_____

_____

_____

_____

_____

_____

_____

_____

What habits, people, and vices do you need to let go of that are preventing you from manifesting the life you desire? Be patient and loving with yourself. Understand that this exercise is not to cause shame, guilt, or self-condemnation. This is an opportunity to be honest with yourself in order to begin the journey of self-love and healing. This is a journey not a race. Remember, you developed and practiced the bad habits for years, so don't get discouraged and quit trying. Transforming your life doesn't happen overnight, but it does happen.

Write down strategies to conquer your triggers that might cause you to go back to bad habits, self-medicating, coping mechanisms, and co-dependency.

_____

_____

_____

_____

_____

_____

_____

_____

_____

_____

_____

_____

_____

_____

_____

_____

_____

_____

What healthy, self-empowering, and uplifting new strategies and activities are you going to begin to implement into your life to replace the negative tools you have been using to cope?

Write these strategies and activities below along with a start date for when you will begin to do each.

_____

_____

_____

_____

_____

_____

_____

_____

_____

_____

_____

_____

_____

_____

_____

_____

_____

_____

_____

_____

_____

_____

_____

Affirmations for Creating a Positive Mindset & Self-Love

I am creating the beautiful life I desire, and I am worthy.

My inner strength grows stronger each day, and I am powerful.

I love me, and I am worthy to have goodness in my life.

I am beautiful in all ways, and my inner beauty shines forth.

I respect myself, and I am confident with who I am.

I release negativity, and I fill my mind with positive thoughts.

I am healthy and happy.

I love and accept myself just the way I am.

I am pure positive energy, and I am an expression of love.

I am a unique soul that is part of the universe.

I am creating my wants and needs by feeling good.

Each day, I am getting better and better, and all is well in my life.

I am in the flow of abundance.

I am happy, whole and complete.

I am unlocking and opening up the door to my inner power.

I am patient with myself and others.

I am in control of my thoughts, and I choose to think positive.

Scriptures to read for Self-Love and Positive Thinking

Romans 5:3-5 "We also glory in tribulations, knowing that tribulation produces perseverance: and perseverance, character and character, hope. Now hope does not disappoint, because the love of God has been poured out in our hearts by the Holy Spirit who was given to us."

Psalms 37:3-4 "Trust in the LORD, and do good; Dwell in the land and feed on His faithfulness. Delight yourself also in the LORD and He shall give you the desires of your heart."

I John 4:7-8 "Beloved, let us love one another for love is of God; and everyone who loves is born of God and knows God. He who does not love does not know God, for God is love."

Proverbs 23:7 "For as he thinks in his heart, so is he."

Soul Ties

There is a bet against my soul.
My spirit is troubled
because my sins have doubled.
I don't understand why
the world is so evil.
I know Lucifer is lurking
and I haven't waited on
YAHWEH's blessings.
His saints grow weary
cause our behavior is forsaking
His holy name.
Like our ancestors,
We haven't changed.
A sinful people we are
But our greatest gift
is reaching for the stars.
My life's purpose
seems so far...
I got to find a way out
of Lucifer's nest.

Chapter 4

Wounded Warrior

Monee got very little sleep that night in jail. Sleeping in a small cold cell with two strangers was not easy. Plus, she couldn't stop thinking about the events that happened the night she went to jail.

"How can Nefarius say he loves me so much and treat me like gum stuck to his shoe?" Monee was hurting; she had been through so much drama with her husband. They had been through hell and back. Monee and Nefarius had separated several times before. Every time they got back together; things seemed to get worse. Monee couldn't understand why every time she sought to get employment or do something to assist with their financial situation, Nefarius would become violent and spiteful.

Monee laid in the hard, uncomfortable bed and prayed that she would get out tomorrow so that she could figure out what she was going to do to get her life right.

HEAVENLY FATHER,

I KNOW YOU HEAR MY CRIES, AND I KNOW YOU FEEL THE PAIN WITHIN MY HEART, FOR YOU, LORD, ARE ALL KNOWING. I KNOW THAT YOU, FATHER, KNOW ME BETTER THAN I KNOW MYSELF, BUT I HAVE COME TO REALIZE I AM THE SINNER, AND I AM THE CAUSER OF MY SHORTCOMINGS THROUGH UNCLEAN THOUGHTS AND DEEDS.

HOLY FATHER, I ASK THAT YOU USE YOUR DIVINE POWER AND YOUR HOLY WORD TO HEAL ME FROM ALL MY HURT AND SUFFERING. I ASK THAT YOU FORGIVE ME OF MY INIQUITIES AND WASH ME IN THE BLOOD OF THE LAMB SO I CAN BE FREE OF SHAME AND GUILT.

OMNIPOTENT CREATOR, I ASK THAT YOU COMFORT AND PROTECT MY CHILDREN AND KEEP THEM FAR FROM THE DEVIL'S SNARE. I PRAY THAT THEIR FATHER KEEPS YOU AS THE PRIMARY PRIORITY IN HIS LIFE AND LOOKS TO YOU, OH GOD, FOR GUIDANCE AND LIGHT AND NOT ALLOW HIS EGO TO CLOUD HIS JUDGMENT.

MY MERCIFUL GOD, I ASK THAT YOU HAVE MERCY ON ME AND FREE ME FROM THIS JAIL. I ASK THAT YOU BLESS ME WITH CLARITY AND VISION PERTAINING TO YOUR DIVINE WILL AND PURPOSE FOR MY LIFE. I ASK THAT YOU GRANT ME A CLEAR UNDERSTANDING OF WHERE I SHOULD PUT MY HOPES, DREAMS, GOALS, AND PASSION SO I WILL NOT FALTER AND WASTE ANY MORE TIME CHASING FUTILE THINGS.

THE ONE AND ONLY TRUE AND LIVING GOD; THE GOD OF ABRAHAM, ISAAC, AND JACOB; THE GOD OF MY EARTHLY FATHER, ALL THESE THINGS I ASK AND PLEAD THAT YOU MOVE SWIFTLY SO THAT YOUR DIVINE LIGHT MOVES IN AND THROUGH MY SPIRIT AND SOUL. FOREVER, I WILL ALWAYS PRAY IN THY HOLY NAME AND IN THY SON'S NAME. SO AS IT IS WRITTEN, LET IT BE DONE.

SELAH

Monee was finally able to close her eyes, but as soon as she did, she was awakened to the buzzing of the jail cell door opening. A woman officer stood in the hall out front of the cells calling names of inmates to line up for court.

"Green let's go!" the officer yelled.

Monee jumped up quickly brushed her teeth, washed her face, and got into the line of other inmates outside the cells. There were two female officers instructing the inmates that there was to be no talking, and everyone was to walk along the right side of the walls through the halls of the jail. Once the inmates arrived outside the courts, the inmates were all placed in handcuffs and shackles.

Monee couldn't believe it. "How am I supposed to walk with these shackles on?" she mumbled. "This is crazy."

All the inmates were placed in a holding cell together as they waited for their turn to go before the judge.

Monee sat in that cell, trying to remain calm and fight off the anxiety that was trying to infiltrate her mind. It was about twenty women in the holding cell with her, and the smell confirmed that some of them wasn't that clean. There were three women that continuously talked…complained…the entire time they were in the holding cell. The women were loud and using every curse word that had been created.

Monee began to feel like she was suffocating. "Green!" one of the male officers called out. "Monee Green!"

"I'm here!" Monee yelled, feeling like she had just won money at bingo game. She quickly jumped up and stood at the holding cell door until it unlocked to let her out. The male officer escorted her to the court room where she went and stood behind a podium with a microphone attached to it.

The judge began to read her charges. Monee pled not guilty, and her bond was set at twenty-five thousand dollars. Monee felt relieved; at least she could post bond and be home by tomorrow.

By the time court had adjourned and the inmates were taken back to the women's jail, Monee couldn't wait to call her mother. It seemed like most of the day had gone by; however, it was 5:30 a.m. when they left for court, and by the time they had gotten back, it was just before lunchtime. In the jail pod, the steel lunch tables were on the bottom level in front of the lower cells and showers. Monee stood in line and got her brown bag lunch. Bologna with white bread no cheese, an orange, a choice of coffee or milk, and one chocolate chip cookie. Monee hadn't eaten bologna in years and wasn't about to start now. She traded her sandwich for another inmate's orange.

She was throwing her brown bag away when her name was belted out over the intercom, "Green, Monee! Visit!" The glass door unlocked, and Monee hurried to get in front of it as it slid open. Her heart was beating fast, but she knew it wasn't Nefarius because he owed child support to his first wife, and he was afraid there was a warrant issued for his arrest.

The visitation room was in the main area of the women's jail. There were three glass windows all next to each other with a steel stool to sit on and a phone on the side of the divider wall that was the only form of privacy an inmate would get from the other inmates with visitors. The officer told Monee to go to booth three. When Monee got to booth three, she could see her mother on the other side of the glass window looking as if she was in a daze. Monee picked up the phone on the wall. Her mother Virginia was already holding the phone to her ear on the other side of the glass window.

"Hi, Mom. How are you?" Monee said in a very gentle but sincere voice.

"How do you think I am doing? You are in jail, Monee!" Virginia was frantic. "What the hell is wrong with you? I was in court this morning when the judge said that you were arrested for driving under the influence, open container, and possession of weed and cocaine? I thought you were done with that!"

"Mom, it wasn't as bad as the judge made it seem. The beer wasn't open, and there wasn't any cocaine just an empty bag. I was—"

"What were you trying to do—kill yourself?" Virginia interrupted.

"No! I was depressed and upset! Mom, Nefarius and I had gotten into an argument, and he threatened to bleach all my clothes! I was upset and feeling down. I don't want to die! Mom, I need to get home to my kids."

Virginia shook her head. "I can't believe this! You are trying to kill yourself! I ain't gonna have no part in it! You need to think about your actions, Monee!" Virginia was yelling so loud the other visitor in the booth next to her looked over at Virginia then at Monee.

"Mom, I need to get out of here and get home to my kids, please!"

"Well, you should have thought about that before you got yourself locked up!" Virginia said in a very stern tone.

"Mom, so you're not gonna post my bail?" Monee had tears streaming down her face. She couldn't believe what she was hearing from her mother.

"No, I am not, Monee. You will figure it out. Goodbye!" Virginia slammed the phone on the receiver, turned around, and walked out the visitation room.

Monee was devastated. "What the hell?" she said as she slowly hung up the phone. "How could she leave me in jail? My children? What am I going to do now?" Monee wiped the tears from her face and tried to pull herself together before walking back to her cell. She didn't know much about jail, but one thing she did know was that you couldn't show weakness in jail or the other inmates would try to take advantage of you.

When Monee got back to her cell, Ms. Isis was sitting up with her back against the wall on her mattress. The other inmate was lying on her bed, and they were talking to each other.

"Monee, guess who is talking today?" Ms. Isis said, smiling.

Monee could not speak. She knew if she opened her mouth nothing would come out except for wailing. She pulled herself up quickly onto the top bunk bed and turned toward that wall and began crying profusely.

All she could think of was her children and how she had left that night and told them she would be right back. She never came back. Now, she had no control over when she was going to see her children again, and that devastated her more than anything.

"How could I have been so selfish?" Monee thought while tears still streamed down her face. *"All I was focused on was my own pain and misery. I was on auto pilot, trying so hard to protect them from the truth. Trying to pretend like Mommy was ok and everything was all right. Look at the mess I have made!"* Monee could not stop the tears from flowing.

"Chile, those tears are cleansing you from all that guilt and pain you've been carrying around inside of you. How can you expect for God to heal you if you refuse to let go?" Ms. Isis' words got Monee's attention. She turned toward Ms. Isis and leaned forward so that she could look down at her. She was sitting on her mattress on the opposite wall of the jail cell. Monee stopped crying and wiped her eyes. The inmate below her got up off her bed and grabbed the roll of tissue next to the steel toilet a few feet from Ms. Isis and handed the tissue to Monee.

"Thank you," Monee said, realizing that this was the first time she had the opportunity to see her cell mate.

"You're welcome. I'm Precious." Precious was tall and slim but had very distinct facial features as if she was from Ethiopia or some part of the Middle East. She was a caramel complexion with very smooth skin and a short curly hair.

"Hi, Precious, sad that we have to meet this way," Monee said then blew her nose into some toilet paper.

"Monee, why are you so upset. Your visit didn't go well?" Ms. Isis chimed back in.

"No, it didn't. My mom came to visit me and said that she wasn't going to get me out. Can you believe that!? How dare she leave me in here! I need to get home to my children! Talking 'bout I was trying to kill myself!" Monee was beginning to get worked up again.

"Why would she think you were trying to kill yourself? You are in here for a DUI not attempted murder, right?" Ms. Isis asked.

"Because I was caught with some weed, beer, and a little coke! So, she is thinking that I was trying to kill myself again," Monee said in a shameful tone.

"Again! My Lawd, 'for everyone practicing evil hates the light and does not come to the light, lest his deeds should be exposed. But he who does the truth comes to the light, that his deeds maybe be clearly seen, that they have been done in God.' Chile, that's John 3 19 through 21. You have nothing to be ashamed of, Monee. You are not alone on this journey. God is guiding you, and sometimes, even in the darkness comes forth a bright light!"

Ms. Isis's voice was resonating through that jail cell like church bells ringing on Sunday morning. Monee was speechless.

"Amen," whispered Precious from the lower bunk.

"Everything is going to work out, you just wait and see! Now cheer up! Would you like my chocolate chip cookie I saved from lunch?" Ms. Isis pulled her cookie from underneath her mattress and handed it to Monee.

"No thank you, Ms. Isis, I will pass." All three of the women broke out into laughter.

"Well, chile, take this Bible. Something tells me you can use it more than me right now."

"Thank you." Ms. Isis stood up and handed Monee the Bible.

"Ms. Isis, so you really believe what is written in that bible?" Precious asked cynically.

"Babe, let me tell you something," Ms. Isis replied. "Every book was written by a man, but the good book was written under the inspiration of our Creator. I know that God is real in my heart. You don't believe in God?"

"How can a God allow a man to rape and molest his wife's daughter repeatedly for years? What kind of God would allow so much evil in this damn world when he supposed to be a creator of unconditional love?" Anger resonating in tone. Precious's question to Ms. Isis caused Monee to think of Brown Suga.

Brown Suga was a stripper and one of Monee's closest friends that she had met at Club Illusions. When Monee was working at Foxy's Saloon, she had met Lee who would come there and have a drink before going to work at Club Illusions as the main cook. Lee had told Monee that Club Illusions was looking for some fresh faces and that she should come and meet the owner. Lee recommended Monee to the owner and was hired without completing any paperwork or auditioning. She started working there immediately and was making double what she was making at Foxy's. No one knew that Monee was only nineteen and was under the drinking age limit.

The interesting thing about Club Illusions was that it was on the eastside of Columbus and was owned by Sue Lee, a petite Asian woman who seemed to be fascinated with exotic dancing. Monee always felt that Sue Lee always wanted to be an exotic dancer but because she was so short, and her body was shaped more like a beer can than a coke bottle she never became a stripper. Monee's other theory was that Sue Lee was a prostitute during Vietnam and made enough money to move to the United States and opened her own strip club. However, no one never knew Sue Lee's real story except her brother Gino who would never talk about their family history.

When Monee started working at Club Illusions, there was only one African-American stripper working there, Brown Suga. Monee knew that Brown Suga looked at her as competition because although the club's clientele was diverse, Brown Suga had an advantage by being the only stripper of color working there. Most of the strippers at Club Illusions were European and Asian.

One night at Club Illusions, it was raining very hard, and the club only had a few customers there drinking. Brown Suga had arrived late and sat next to Monee at the bar. They began to talk and drink to pass the time—although Monee usually kept to herself while there. Brown Suga suggested that if Monee wanted to make more

money, she needed to purchase a real stripper costume with a thong and stop dancing in swimsuit bikinis. She even offered to take Monee to the costume boutique
where she bought all of her dance costumes and lingerie. Monee agreed, and her tips
tripled after listening to Brown Suga's suggestion. Monee and Brown Suga were
inseparable after that. Monee was so thankful that she now had a friend who could
relate to her and her new lifestyle. Monee also started spending time with Brown
Suga when they were not working.

One night, Monee was in the dressing room at Club Illusions changing into her
costume when Brown Suga stormed into the dressing room. She slammed the locker
door open and threw her bag and her purse into the locker. Monee, who was looking
in the mirror putting on makeup, was startled by the abrupt noise. She turned around
to see what was going on.

"Damn, Suga! What the hell is wrong with you tonight?" Monee asked, a bit annoyed at her friend's irrational behavior.

"Did you and Butch get into a fight?" Monee asked, trying to figure out what was
wrong with her friend.

"I hate him! I swear I am going to kill him, Nikki! I can't take this shit no more! I
can't take it!" Brown punched the locker.

"Who are you going to kill? What happened?" Monee was now saddened by the
pain she could see in her friend's face.

"My mother's husband! I hate him! I wish he was dead! He has no right to keep
touching me like this! I am too old now, why can't he leave me alone?" Brown Suga
started crying hysterically and fell into Monee's arms. Monee hugged her friend and
told her that everything was going to be all right. Monee was hurting for her friend
because she knew oh too well how it felt to be violated by a perverted old man. Up
until that night, Monee had no idea that Suga's stepfather had been molesting her for
years.

When Brown Suga was five years old, her mother re-married and had twins, a
boy and a girl. Her stepfather started molesting Suga when her mother was pregnant
with her brother and sister. Suga thought that he would stop once her mother had the
twins, but he didn't. After a few years of her stepfather molesting her, Suga finally
got the courage to tell her mother. But her mother got angry at her and told Suga that
she was jealous and was trying to destroy her marriage. Her mother never confronted

Suga's stepfather, and Suga never mentioned it again. She had been suffering in silence ever since.

"I'm moving out, Nikki! I don't have to take this anymore. I am eighteen, I am going to move in with Butch," Brown Suga said as she wiped her tears away and grabbed her dance bag out of the locker.

"I think that would be a good idea as well, Suga. Have you told Butch about your stepfather?" Butch was Brown Suga's boyfriend that she had been dating for the six years.

"Hell no! I don't want him looking at me like I am some weak, weird bitch that enjoyed fucking her stepfather! I would never tell him, and you bet not either!"

"I would never say anything, but you are no weak weird bitch Suga! It wasn't your fault. You were just a young, scared girl! Don't blame yourself for what that sick fuck did to you!" Monee yelled, getting very emotional.

"My mother is such a bitch. How could she not believe me? Well, fuck her I am leaving now! She will just have to put them in an after-school program because I ain't tolerating his shit anymore!" Brown Suga was feeling stronger though still angry as she slipped her panties off and put on a one-piece negligee.

"Nikki! Where the hell is Nikki?" Gino was yelling Monee's stage name as he bust through the dressing room door. "Nikki, what the hell is taking you so long? We got customers out there drinking, and no one is on the damn stage!" Gino yelled in his heavy Asian accent.

"All right, all right, damn it!" Monee grabbed her garter belt off the vanity table, slipped it on, and looked at Brown Suga. "Suga, we will finish this conversation later." Monee darted out of the dressing room and ran on the stage.

Monee and Brown Suga never talked about Brown Suga's stepfather again. After work that night, Monee was driving home and was very sad about what her friend had shared with her. She began to wonder why it was so much pain and misery in this world.

She remembered how she started writing poetry as an outlet when Rodney King was brutally beaten by four police officers in 1991. Since then, Monee had written numerous poem and prayers to quiet her thoughts by using words to exorcise her pain that had been buried deep in her heart for so long. But it seemed to Monee that the more she lived, the more pain she endured. Her friend Suga was a very sweet young lady. When Monee first meet her, she thought that she was mean because her countenance was always so serious. Brown Suga rarely smiled, but when she did, her whole face lit up. She had perfect pretty, white teeth and was always chewing on ice. Monee would always joke with her and say that the ice was her cigarettes. Suga was always trying to encourage Monee to quit smoking, but Monee wasn't hearing it. Monee would just counter Suga's request by trying to take her cup of ice from her.

Monee was surprised to learn earlier that night that Suga was actually a year younger than she was. Neither of them had any business working in a twenty-one and over strip club drinking liquor all night, but who was going to know? Monee and Suga sure weren't going to disclose their real age.

All the way home, Monee ranted about men, women, and life.

"It's a shame how men take advantage of their masculinity and force themselves on women," she yelled. "How can there be a God in a world filled with so much hate and perversion? I swear men are devils themselves, so selfish and stupid! All they want is to bust a nut and move on to the next girl."

"Most of the men that are regulars in the strip clubs are married men that get off on a fake fantasy that their wholesome wives at home won't allow them to fulfil. That's why I tell their dumb asses anything they want to hear and take their money. Really, that's all they are good for is money! Can't trust them worth a damn."

Pulling into her apartment parking lot, she continued, "Well, if there really is a heaven and a hell, God, I guess you should let me know, so I can have enough time to get my act together!"

As Monee walked up to her apartment door, she saw a dark figure standing not too far from her door smoking a cigarette. Monee slowly reached into her purse for a switch blade that Prince gave her a couple of months ago when she started working at Foxy's. She stopped walking when she got to the steps to her apartment door.

"Who's there? Who is that?" Monee yelled in her tough hood voice.

"Baby, it's me!" a familiar voice said.

"Red?" Monee was in complete shock. So much had happened since Red had left to go to Cleveland to check on his sick father, Monee didn't have much time to think about him. After a few weeks, the phone calls stopped completely, so Monee figured he had decided to stay in Cleveland and move on with his life.

"Yes, Monee, it's me! Where the hell have you been? I have been coming to your apartment for the past two weeks, and you are never home. What the fuck is going on, and where the hell is Nathan? What, you moved in with your boyfriend or something?" Red was completely perplexed, and it showed in his voice.

"Whoa, whoa, partna, slow your roll! Who the hell do you think you are? Disappearing for over two months and then popping up at my apartment at 3:30 a.m. with all these questions!" Monee was annoyed but a bit flattered at the same time. She opened the door to her apartment, and they both stepped inside.

"So, you have a boyfriend now, huh?" Red stood directly in front of Monee with a saddened look on his face.

"No, Red, I don't have a boyfriend. I have been working. Why are you acting like you are so concerned about me? Nigga, I haven't heard from you in about five weeks!" Monee went to the fridge and popped open two beers, sat them down on the table, and plopped down on her couch.

"Look, I lost my pager. I have been calling your house phone every chance I got, but you never answered. Your answering machine is full, and I couldn't leave anymore messages." He walked over to the coffee table and picked up the extra beer Monee had opened, chugged down some before sitting down next to Monee.

"Yeah, I guess I have been a bit preoccupied with surviving and all. I ain't in school no more, so I had to do what I had to do to take care of me and my son. Ain't nobody else helping me." Monee rolled her eyes.

"Where is Nathan, and what kinda work are you doing that you are getting home at 4 a.m.? Stripping?" Red started laughing.

"What's so funny?" Monee looked at him with a serious stare.

"You are serious, aren't you? Whoa, Monee, you really are stripping now!" Red took another chug of his beer.

"Yes, Red, I am. Wasn't you the one who told me I had a bad body and could make good money stripping? Well, look, you were right!" Monee grabbed her dance bag, turned it upside down, and let a pile cash fall out on to the table along with three garter belts and two stripping outfits.

"Oh, shit baby! Where the hell are you working? I got to come see you do your thang!" Red began to laugh as Monee unfolded all the dollar bills and began counting them.

"Whatever, I don't need you at my job while I'm telling lies all up in some man's face, taking his money and you get jealous," Monee said not losing count of her bills.

"Where's Nathan when you be out shaking your ass?"

"I got a sitter who lives in this apartment building, so I let him sleep there until the morning. I like her, she's a nice older lady. She has two older daughters but no sons. She spoils Nathan like the son she never had, and he eats it up. It is a blessing because I don't worry. I know he is in good hands and well taken care of. So, how's your father doing?"

"He is better now. That's why I was able to leave. I've been worried about you and Nathan, baby! I been coming here for two weeks. So, I decided to just wait and see how long it would be before you came back to your apartment." Red had turned to Monee and grabbed her hands to stop her from counting her money so she could pay attention to what he was saying. "I love you, Monee. I want to be with you, baby."

"Really? I am not so sure that you know what love is. I feel like you just saying what you think I want to hear!"

○　○　○

Monee was snatched from her memory by the voice of Ms. Isis saying to Precious, "God watches over the good and the evil of this world, and one thing I know for sure is no man is exempt from the wrath of their own doings, good or bad. You see, there are forces at work in this universe that govern the world that we live in. One of those laws is what you do will surely come back to you! It might not happen when you want it to, but trust and believe, it will come back.

"That's the law of karma, baby! That is why God says vengeance is mine and not man's. The Most High has created laws that govern every human being rather you are aware of them or not." Ms. Isis spoke with conviction.

"Well, Ms. Isis, I believe what you are saying to be true," Monee said, "but I can't understand why it seems like the evil men do takes so long for it to come back on them. My cousin's father molested me when I was four years old, and he is still living, and even if I wanted to do something about it now I couldn't because the statute of limitations has run out.

"He a free man, and I feel terrible about not saying anything when it happened to me because in my heart, I know I probably wasn't the first girl he raped and most assuredly not his last victim either! If I could kill him, I would!" Monee said with a fury in her voice that caused both Precious and Ms. Isis to look up at her.

"Monee, that man is physically free, but by no means is he spiritually free. That man is being haunted by his demons every day. You must forgive him so that hatred and anger in your heart don't haunt you and distort your life," Ms. Isis said as she clutched her heart with her hands.

"Well, I guess it is haunting me, Ms. Isis, because most of the men I have fell in love with have all betrayed me. My daddy was hardly ever around after he and my mom divorced. When he did come around, he was always making false promises to me. Hell! It was a miracle when he did keep his promise!" Monee said, shaking her head.

"Ladies, listen to me," Ms. Isis said, her voice strong and deep with fury, "I am in here for shooting my grandson in his leg, so you know I don't take no shit off any man! Now, I didn't have an intention to kill him, but I refuse to let anyone, a friend, family, or foe disrespect me or abuse me!"

"We as children of God must love God and love ourselves enough to not harm ourselves and not allow anyone else to harm us either. Speaking of which, Monee, why were you drinking so much alcohol and driving at the same time to get a DUI?" Ms. Isis asked while raising her left eyebrow.

"Well, I wasn't drunk. I wasn't pulled over for any driving violation. I drove into a roadblock; you know an insurance check point when police are checking to make sure drivers have license and insurance? I wasn't aware that the police did these types of check points here in Georgia, and I honestly thought the road was blocked off due to an accident and the police officer was flagging me to turn around and go back the way I came and so I did. That's when another police car pulled me over." Monee sighed.

"So why did they arrest you?" Precious chimed in.

"Because ten minutes before I drove into the check point, I had just finished smoking half a blunt with my homeboy. Ms. Isis, that's marijuana rolled in cigar paper in case you didn't know."

Monee and Precious began to laugh.

"Chile, I got a twenty-year-old grandson, I know all the slang and lingo when it comes to these streets!" Ms. Isis rolled her head back and belted out this soulful gratifying laugh.

"Oh, ok I was just making sure. Well to answer your question, Precious, when the police officer pulled me over, the weed smoke escaped from my mini-van, and that is what made him suspicious."

"Damn, girl, you were getting to it! You look so square you don't look like you even drink!" Precious said as if she was impressed with Monee's drug use.

"Lawd! God has something special for you to do," Ms. Isis proclaimed. "He loves you more than you love yourself. So sad that you don't even realize how beautiful you are. Don't let your demons destroy you, baby. You got to ward off the devil and know that you are stronger than the trials you are going through. Monee, I know most young folk like to drink them some liquor and smoke them blunts. But, babe, what made you start messing with that other stuff?" Monee could tell Ms. Isis was trying hard not to say the wrong words to offend her.

"It's ok, Ms. Isis, I don't mind talking about it. Hell, I learned years ago the type of life I lived, so I don't give a fuck about what someone thinks of me!" Monee said, throwing up her hands.

"God is the judge not me. I will tell you this; I have a sixth sense about certain things, and the Lord reveals what he wants me to know. I have prophesied to plenty of folk, most of them being strangers. I hear what you are saying and what you don't say. I know how to read between the lines if you know what I mean." Ms. Isis looked at Monee, and Monee looked back at her, wondering what she was really getting at. But she could feel that Ms. Isis was being sincere and not malicious, so she continued.

"I have asked myself that question numerous times, but I still don't really know why I decided to snort coke." Although she said it, Monee remembered the first time she tried cocaine.

Monee was working at Club Illusions, and it was her twenty-first birthday. She was excited that she was finally of age to drink legally. Things were looking up for her; she was making good money at Club Illusions, and she and Brown Suga were still thick as thieves. To keep herself motivated to work in that environment, however, Monee had to drink every night. Although the money was good, the effects of interacting and dancing for so many men, not just the successful attractive men but men from all walks of life, was very draining. Monee was amazed at how some of the girls were able to strip sober. *"Did they really like this job?"* she would wonder. One of Monee's rituals was keeping her own bottle of vodka in her locker. If the evening shift was slow, she could still manage to sit at the bar and dance the whole night, even if the customers weren't there to buy her drinks. That way, she prevented having to ask the bartender Janet to give her free drinks. One thing about Monee was she looked at her job as a business and wasn't going to spend money that she was making to buy alcohol at retail price in the bar.

She witnessed plenty of strippers make one-hundred dollars in their first hour of their shift just to have given it back to Sue Lee paying for drinks because the night turned out to be a bust.

Suga leaned over to Monee while they were sitting at the bar. "Here comes Freddie," she said. "Awl shit, you know it's gonna be a busy night. Janet is about to get her fix!" They both laughed as they watch Freddie who was Janet's boyfriend walk into the bar and sit at the opposite side of the bar. Freddie was a local drug dealer. Suga told Monee months ago that a lot of the girls that worked at Club Illusions did coke, and they all bought drugs from Freddie. Janet and Freddie also did coke.

"I wonder what that high is like?" Monee whispered to Suga.

"Don't wonder Monee! Nothing good can come out of that type of high believe me." Suga looked at Monee with conviction.

"How do you know. Have tried it before?" Monee asked.

"Hell no," Suga snapped, "and I never will. I will stick to alcohol and weed, thank you very much, and you will, too!" She then nudged Monee in her side.

"Hmm, I don't know, Suga. It's my twenty-first birthday! I think I want to celebrate with a blast!" Monee was laughing, but she was serious. It was something about trying something new on her birthday that excited her.

"Don't do it, Monee! Don't do it!" Suga wasn't whispering anymore, but there wasn't anyone sitting close to them anyway to overhear their conversation. Monee put her feet on the bottom bar of her chair and lifted herself up so that she was leaning close to Janet on the opposite side of the bar.

"Hey, Janet, come here for a sec!" Monee yelled. Janet was talking to Freddie. She walked over to Monee.

"What's up, Nikki?" she asked with her words slurring. Janet had sandy brown, stringy hair with very large breasts, but that was about it. She had a very bad over-bite, and her teeth protruded profusely, which caused her words to slur at times. But when she was intoxicated, her slurred speech was worse, and she had a tendency to spit when she spoke. But most of the regular customers loved her and always tipped her good.

"I want to try some of that stuff you and Freddie got," Monee said slyly.

Janet's eyes widened. "No, you don't. Is this a joke? You don't get down, Nikki."

"Seriously, I do! Come on, it's my birthday. Show some love, Janet!"

"Ok, when you see me go into the bathroom, I will leave it on top of the stall. Make sure you go in as soon as I come out! Don't let one of these slick bitches get my shit!" Janet said.

"I won't." Monee sat back down in her seat. She looked over at Suga and smiled.

"One day, that daredevil in you is going to catch up with you! Don't you have any inhibitions?" Suga was upset with her friend.

"Yes, I do! You will never have to worry about me doing crack, heroine, or any other type of drug that is known to kill you," Monee said confidently and then laughed.

"Don't you know people overdose on cocaine, too, silly?" Suga replied, shaking her head in disbelief of what she was hearing.

"Suga, you have to do an awful lot of coke to overdose. I just want to try a little bit, damn lighten up. It's my birthday. You act like it's the end of the world!" Monee was getting annoyed with Suga being so protective of her. Just then, she saw Geno step behind the bar, and Janet darted for the ladies' room.

"So, you really gonna try that shit, huh?" Suga took a big swallow of her Hennessy. Monee didn't say anything; she just took another sip of her vodka and cranberry.

"Well, one thing I have learned about you, Nikki, is that when your mind is made up about something, there is no changing it!" Just then, Janet walked back behind that bar.

"You got that right, sweetie pie!" Monee jumped up from her chair, blew Suga a kiss, and headed for the ladies' room. When she got inside the bathroom, she saw a lottery ticket folded on top of the toilet cover.

"What the hell?" Monee thought as she slowly unfolded the lottery ticket. It was a

white powder inside the ticket. Monee had seen the movie *Scarface* enough times, so she took her pinky finger and scooped up a little of the powder and snorted hard. She didn't feel anything, so she scooped up some more. Then snorted up the other nostril even harder. This time, she felt a rush like she had just got a jolt of energy. She quickly folded the ticket back up, checked her nose, and walked out of the bathroom.

Monee walked back to her seat. Suga was now on-stage dancing. Janet came over to Monee and leaned over the bar. Monee went to hand Janet the lottery ticket.

"Keep it, happy birthday, Nikki!" Janet slid her a drink and said, "This is from the gentleman over there." Janet pointed to an older Caucasian guy with curly black hair sitting by the stage. Monee looked over at the guy, and he raised his drink and smiled.

Monee felt like she was on cloud nine. Every sensation in her body was enhanced. Nothing bothered her the rest of the night. She had drink after drink and never once did she begin to feel like she was getting nauseous or tired. She felt like an Energizer bunny. When she hit the stage, she was a shining star. Monee was in full character, and Darling Nikki was her name. Moving her body so seductively and fluid, Nikki was smooth with her body and sealed the deal with her smile. She had men going to the ATM to give her more money. Monee didn't realize she was playing a dangerous game. A game that she would find hard to stop playing.

○ ○ ○

"Honestly, Ms. Isis," Monee said, deciding to be honest, "it was my twenty-first birthday, and I was in an environment where I had access to it. I just decided that I wanted to try it to see how it would make me feel. I was young, and it was something inside of me that made me feel that it was the right thing to do at the time."

"The devil is cunning," Ms. Isis said, nodding. "He will make you believe that something that will destroy you is good for you. If you had a bag when you got pulled over that landed you in here, then it is safe to assume that your twenty-first birthday was the first but not your last time?" Ms. Isis was like a priest trying to exorcise a demon out of Monee. Monee was beginning to feel a bit uncomfortable.

Monee grimaced. *"Who the hell she thinks she is interrogating me? She locked up in here just like me."* she thought. But she continued with the conversation to see where Ms. Isis was going with all these questions.

"You are right," Monee replied. Her lip quivered as she added, "I had a cousin that was killed by his friend who accidentally shot him when they were playing with a gun. I started using more frequently after I went home for the funeral."

"I am sorry to hear that. Were you close to your cousin? You were grieving—that's what made you want to get high?" Ms. Isis asked sympathetically.

"No, it wasn't that. At that time, I was living in Columbus, Ohio, and I was an exotic dancer. My mom had called me to tell me my cousin had been killed, and I needed to come home to Cleveland for the funeral. I had told her previously that I was no longer in college and had started stripping. I made her promise not to tell anyone. Not my family, not my siblings, no one. I wasn't proud of what I was doing and didn't want anyone in my hometown to know."

Sighing, she added, "Well, I went home for the funeral, and the repast was at the house I grew up in in Cleveland. During the repast, I was in the basement with some of my family members, and we were playing cards and drinking. Well, my mom came down in the basement, and you know the song by Marvin Gaye, 'Sexual Healing'?"

"Of course, who doesn't know that song? It's a classic!" blurted out Precious.

"Exactly!" Monee said, agreeing with Precious. "Well, that song began to play, and a few of my relatives started dancing. My mom blurts out, 'Monee can show yawl some of her dance moves. She's a stripper! Yeah, she been stripping in a strip club in Columbus'!"

Monee lowered her head and slumped her shoulders. "When she announced that," she said, "I could feel my heart drop to the floor. I was so ashamed, and I had felt betrayed by the person I trusted the most. My brother jumped up out of his seat, yelling, 'She doing what!?' and my aunt told me to climb up on a pole and show them how it is done. My uncle told me to give him a lap dance." Monee paused for a moment, shook her head and fought back the tears swelling in her eyes.

Ms. Isis and Precious were stunned by what they were hearing. Monee could tell by the looks on the two women's faces that they could feel her pain, but she kept going.

"I was devastated. The entire time, everyone was ridiculing me and joking about me being a stripper. No one came to me and asked me why I was stripping. That was no one's concern. It was like my mother had stuck a dagger in my back that pierced through to my heart, and they pushed it in deeper." A tear fell from Monee's left eye, but she quickly wiped it away.

"Monee, God placed a powerful strength in you," Ms. Isis said.

"Damn now that's fucked up!" Precious said in a slow, disbelieving tone.

"Well, I wasn't too strong, Ms. Isis," Monee said. "That bothered me deeply, and when I went back to Columbus a few days later, I started using cocaine more often."

"You started to self-medicate," Ms. Isis said sadly.

"Yes. It helped me take my mind off all the bullshit I was carrying inside of me. Like a friend of mine said, it helped chase away the demons haunting me."

Monee was beginning to understand that not only was it the bad things that happened to her that was destroying her. It was also the way she was dealing with the bad things in her life. *"Maybe if I would have gotten therapy when I was raped, I would have empowered myself with the knowledge to help deal with the self-destructive thoughts and low self-esteem. Maybe there are people in this world that could have helped me see things from a more positive prospective?"* Monee contemplated then fell silent and began reflecting on what happened after she left her family and went back to Columbus.

○ ○ ○

After attending her cousin's funeral in Cleveland, Monee returned to Columbus and continued to work at Club Illusions. She was happy to get back to Columbus; going home had its ups and downs, and after her mother had betrayed her and revealed Monee's secret, Monee wasn't too motivated to go back home anytime soon. Monee and Red were back together, and he moved in with Monee in Columbus.

Brown Suga had invited Monee to make some extra money working at these events called Female Reviews. During a Female Review, several strippers, oftentimes from other cities, put on a show at a club or a private venue where men paid an entry fee or purchased a ticket to see some new girls, or their favorite strippers put on an exotic show. This was where many dance tricks and other novelties happened that usually would not happen at a regular strip club. The last time Brown Suga asked Monee to go with her, she made close to eight hundred dollars in one night. But that was when they had drove to Memphis and worked at a female review and then a private party afterwards.

The money was great for one night of work, but Monee was exhausted afterwards.

The adult entertainment industry wasn't all it was cracked up to be. Guys always asked Monee to take pictures with them, and she always declined. She knew this was a temporary hustle and that she didn't want pictures of her stripping to surface when she became successful. Monee was often propositioned to do sexual favors for customers, and they even offered to pay her for sex. When Monee first started stripping, she was appalled by such offers and would explain night after night that she was an exotic dancer, and this was a job to make money and that she was a professional not a prostitute. But after a few more months working at Club Illusions and doing private shows, Monee quickly realized that men were going to always try to get over and unfortunately getting propositioned, declining and cussing men out was all part of the job.

On Sunday, Monee and Brown Suga went to Club Emerald to participate in a female review. That night, Monee had a weird feeling about going, but since she had just got back from Cleveland and hadn't worked for a few days, she could use the money. When they arrived, the club was already packed with men and women.

"Suga, I didn't know women were allowed to be here for the female review." Monee was a bit nervous; she had danced for a few women that had come into Club Illusions but never at a regular club where the women were allowed to remain in the club.

"What, you scared to dance in a regular club? Nikki, it's no big deal. Some women tip better than men!" Suga was surprised that Nikki was acting a bit intimidated. "Besides, most women leave anyway once the show starts."

"Well, I am going to get a drink before we have to dance." Monee was feeling a bit uneasy. Club Emerald was a big club, and Monee wasn't expecting the crowd to be so large on a Sunday night. Suga and Monee had already changed into their dance outfits, so that made Monee even more uncomfortable walking around the club in lingerie, but guys could ask for table dances, so Monee had to be ready to make that money.

"Come on, girl, I want one, too." Monee and Suga headed over to the bar to order drinks.

Monee bombarded her way close to the bartender and accidently bumped into a lady. "Oh, excuse me, I didn't mean to bump you!" Monee and the lady turned and looked at each other simultaneously.

THE DEVIL'S BEDROOM | 111

"Oh, hey, Samantha, how are you!" Monee was surprised to see someone she knew at the club. It was her old hair stylist from Cleveland.

"Hey, girl! How have you been? Long time no see!" Samantha said, waving her drink and then taking a sip.

"I am doing good, girl, just out here making this money," Monee said.

"Girl, I don't blame you. Hell, if I wasn't so fat, I would be doing the same thing. Girl, we all got bills to pay, and you know my ex-husband ain't paying his alimony or child support! I tell ya niggas ain't shit!" Samantha said, while sipping on her drink again.

"I feel ya, I haven't even got a pack of diapers out of my son's father. Girl, we got to choose better!" Monee said, laughing.

"Monee, so you dance at a strip club, too?

"Yeah, girl, it's been almost a year now," Monee said.

"Girl, you need to move to Atlanta! You haven't heard that the Olympics is going on there this summer! Girl, I got girlfriends down there making a killing dancing. If you want to make a lot of money that is when you need to be!" Samantha took another sip of her drink.

"Nikki, come on! The DJ is calling all of the girls to the dance booth!" Brown Suga nudged Monee's arm.

"Gotta go, girl, take care!" Monee and Suga made their way to the DJ booth. When they got there, twelve other girls already there. The girls received the order in which they were going to do their featured dance on the stage. Monee and Brown Suga always did their featured routine together. While the other girls were on stage, the rest of the dancers circulated the club and gave table dances for the men. Monee had found a small stage in a corner to dance on.

She was getting plenty of attention and tips, which caused her to forget all about being uncomfortable in front of such a huge crowd. She was leaning down in front of a guy so that he could put the tip in her garter belt when she heard someone say, "Monee?"

It was a guy's voice, and he sounded like he was in disbelief. Monee had quickly turned to the opposite side of the stage to see who it was.

"Oh, hey, Dabir!" Monee said, trying to play it cool. "Monee! What the hell are you doing?" Dabir was in shock. Monee and Dabir hadn't seen each other since Dabir had left college to do an abroad internship in Africa. Their friendship had stopped once Monee and Red started their relationship. Plus, Monee never got closure from the whole episode with him lying to her and the whole Leah drama. Monee's heart was beating fast, but she wasn't about to give him any satisfaction that she still cared for him. Not after the way her treated her.

"So, you are back from Africa, huh?" Monee asked as she kept winding to R. Kelly's "Bump and Grind" and giving the other guys attention.

"Yeah, I got back last week. I was asking Bruce about you. What the hell are you doing up there, Monee! Can you get down for a sec and let me talk to you?" Dabir was livid. Monee could tell in his tone that he was angry and a bit jealous. However, she was over it and wasn't about to let Dabir pull her back on an emotional roller coaster again.

"Sorry, I am working right now, Dabir. Maybe some other time." She bent over and shook her breasts in Dabir's face.

"You are tripping, Monee! Have you lost your mind? Come on, get down from there and let me talk to you!" Dabir was yelling now and could no longer keep cool.

"You want a table dance, baby? My time is money, and I ain't got no time for games!" Monee was enjoying every minute of seeing him upset, but her heart was still hurting and wasn't in agreement with her mind.

"Oh, ok is that what you want, money now? Here!" Dabir pulled out a $20 and tossed it on the stage.

Monee picked up the twenty dollars along with the rest of her tips and got down from that stage and stood in front of Dabir silently. She was curious what he possibly could have to say to her.

"Look, Monee, I know I have been gone a while, but I need to talk to you. I know that I left things in a mess, and I didn't get a chance to clean things up between us before I left for Africa… but I still—"

"Look, Dabir, don't worry about it. We are cool. I have moved on. I am with Red now. Glad you back, but I gotta go. See you around." Monee walked away and headed to the ladies' room for a break. Dabir was left there looking clueless.

○ ○ ○

Precious' and Ms. Isis's loud laughter interrupted Monee from her flashback.

"Monee, are you with us?" Precious asked. "We been sittin' here talking, and you ain't said a word in a minute. I was telling Ms. Isis about the time I got caught smoking cigarettes butts in my mom's room. Did you hear what I was saying?"

Before Monee could answer, that loud intruding click of their cell door opened, ending their conversation for the time being. It was time for lunch and phone calls.

Monee hadn't spoken to Nefarius or her children since she had been locked up, so she darted to the phones once their jail cell door slid open. She was praying that Nefarius would accept her collect call.

Monee could hear Nathan say hello, but the operator protruded, asking would he accept that charges. "Yes, ma'am," Nathan said politely.

"Hey, baby! How is my big boy doing?" Monee was trying to sound happy even though the guilt she was feeling by letting her children down was weighing heavy on her.

"Hey, Ma! I'm ok. Ma, Dad had took us over Granma's house today, and she told us you were on drugs! Grandma said that is why you got arrested. Why you using drugs, Ma?" Nathan began crying.

Monee was speechless. *"Why the hell would my mother tell my children that shit?"* she thought. *"Damn, she doesn't hesitate to take every opportunity she gets to humiliate and embarrass me to the ones I love the most! Damn her!"* Monee could feel that same dagger in her back that she felt in the basement back at home when her mother told everyone she was a stripper. Her heart was aching, but she couldn't focus on her pain because her son was hurting now from her actions.

"Well, son, it's a long story, but basically, I got pulled over while I was drinking alcohol. I do use drugs sometimes, but I am not a drug addict. Sometimes, adults use drugs and alcohol to take the pain away that they are feeling. It's not good to do that, and I would never want you to use drugs. I will explain everything when I get home. I am soooo sorry that Mommy didn't come home that night. I feel terrible." Tears ran down Monee's face.

"It's ok, Ma. I am glad that you are ok, and I forgive you." Nathan had always been a laid-back kid. Even as a baby, he rarely gave Monee any problems. "I love you, Nathan. Thank you for forgiving me!"

"I love you, too, Ma. When are you coming home?" Nathan sadly asked.

"I am not sure yet, but hopefully it will be very soon." Monee's tears burned her cheeks. She had been through a lot, but this was one of the hardest moments in her life. Not being able to be there for her children, having no control of the situation, and she couldn't blame anyone but herself. It was breaking her down.

"Baby, I don't have much time to talk where is your father and your brother and sister?"

"Dad is upstairs, and Gideon and Eternity are sitting right here."

"Let me speak to Gideon, please."

"Hey, Mama! When are you coming home? I miss you!" Gideon started crying.

"Gideon, please don't cry. I will be home soon, but I am going to need you to be strong, ok?"

"Ok, Mama." Gideon gave the phone to his little sister.

"Hi, Mommy!"

"Hey, babe, how is my princess doing?"

"I am ok. Nathan keeps eating all the cookies! Mommy, can you tell him to share?"

"Yes, baby, tell Nathan I said to share the cookies!" That was the first time Monee had smiled all day. She knew that if her baby girl was fussing about cookies, then they were just fine. "Eternity, I need to talk to you father. Tell him to get the phone."

"Ok, Mommy. I love you!"

"I love you, too, Princess!"

There was a brief pause, but Monee could hear her daughter's feet walking up the stairs and knock on the bedroom door. "Daddy, Mommy is on the phone." Monee could hear the silence then the phone being shuffled.

"Hey," Nefarius said as if he was half sleep.

"Hey, how are you?" Monee asked, trying to feel Nefarius out.

"I'm all right. Just trying to figure out what the hell is wrong with you?" Nefarius said in a matter-of-fact way.

"What's wrong with me... what do you mean?" Monee was confused. "You are the one who was threatening me! All because I am trying to keep us afloat and not drown! I got bills to pay and children to feed, Nefarius. I don't know where the hell your mind is at sometimes, like you don't have any kind of hustle in you! Like you just don't give a damn about nothing or no one but yourself!" Monee's blood was boiling.

"You just don't get it, do you," Nefarius said, searching for words. "You think I need you to be in some bar all night. All up in niggas' faces selling alcohol to pay some fucking bills? I don't need no wife like that! I need a wife that is going to understand that her place is at home taking care of my children and our home. I told you that shit when you was strippin! I pulled you out the strip club but you still act like a damn stripper!" Nefarius' tone was nasty and cold.

"Well, if you want me home, that means you would have to pay some damn bills and not sit on your ass! You've been waiting on some big deal that doesn't look like it's going to happen! What happen to your ambition?" Monee was trying to stay focused, but her mind drifted to when she first met Nefarius.

○ ○ ○

It was early June of 1996 and Monee was walking into Club Illusions to work her last night shift there before leaving to move to Atlanta. Monee had decided to take Red up on his offer for her to leave Columbus and move to Atlanta right before the Olympics was going to be held there. Monee had several people tell her that she should move to Atlanta and dance there as a stripper during the Olympics because the potential to make a lot of money was exceedingly greater than it would ever be working at a club in Columbus. Two weeks after seeing her beautician from Cleveland at Club Emerald, Red's college buddy Omar showed up in Columbus stating that he was going to head to Savannah, Georgia for a week and then hang out in Atlanta to visit with some friends.

Omar wanted Red to come, enticing him with the opportunity to make a tremendous amount money during the Olympics selling marijuana. Red told Monee and Monee knew this was her opportunity to relocate to the "city where dreams come true" and make a lot of money in the Adult Entertainment Industry. Everything seemed to fall in place, she called her sister Lisa back in Cleveland and she agreed to take care of Nathan while she went to Atlanta. Monee's plan was to get a job and a place to live in Atlanta, then get Nathan from Lisa. It worked out because Lisa had a daughter close in age with Nathan.

Monee and Red packed up all of Monee's furniture and belongings and moved everything into a storage unit in Columbus not too far from the college campus where they were living. Two weeks later Monee and Red drove Nathan to Cleveland with Lisa. The couple jumped back on the road immediately and drove back to

Columbus. They were fueled with excitement about starting a new life together in Atlanta. The next day was Monee's last day to work at Club Illusions. She had told Brown Suga and the entire staff that she was moving to Atlanta two weeks prior. Brown Suga took the announcement hard and was not happy to hear that she was about to lose the only other stripper in club that she considered a good friend. Monee and Brown Sugar had grown very close and spent as much time together out of the club as they did when they were working.

Monee remembered how hot it was her last day working at Club Illusions. She couldn't wait to get out of the hot car and into the air-conditioned club. Red liked to ride with the windows down and he dropped Monee off at the club. He used her car to run a few errands and say his goodbyes to a few of his friends while Monee worked her final shift. Monee didn't mind Red using her car even though his license was suspended because her driver's license was also suspended. Monee had got a speeding ticket a few months ago driving back home to Cleveland. Once she realized that she had forgotten to pay the ticket and missed her court date to appear in Cleveland's traffic court her license was already suspended. Monee's birthday was in May; she wasn't able to renew her registration nor get auto insurance but was still irresponsibly driving her car.

Although Monee was making decent money dancing at the club, she spent her money haphazardly. Monee had intelligence, street smarts, and a good heart but lacked discipline. Monee would make four hundred dollars in one night but would not save the money. Instead, she would tell herself that she can make it back the next night. She never thought to create a budgeting system that would help her manage her finances effectively. She had the same problem a drug dealer has; when you make money fast often you spend it fast too. It is the minority who can manage to live a street lifestyle and successfully use it as an exit strategy to live a legitimate life. Most who play the hustle game never win the game but find themselves in a self-destructive cycle of splurging and never master the science of being discipline and saving. Usually, the drugs, sex and alcohol have them too distracted to even think clearly and/or they are making a lot of money and still have a poverty mind set and the money never amasses into wealth.

Red and Omar pulls up at Club Illusions at three am and see Monee, Brown Suga and Nick, the security guard walking out of the club saying their goodbyes. It was

Omar's idea for them to come with him to Savannah for a few days to his grand-mother's house and then later drive back to Atlanta and reside there, however, Omar didn't have a car. Monee was the only one that had transportation to make the trip happen. Even though they would be driving with expired registration tags, no auto insurance and none of them had valid driver's license. They were ignorance on fire, and nothing was going to stop them from taking that leap of faith.

Brown Suga was crying as she hugged Monee for the last time. Monee was in tears too and it was bittersweet to lose a good friend for the hopes of gaining a better life. Monee promised Brown Suga that she would keep in touch, and Monee waved goodbye until Brown Suga were no longer in sight. Red was driving Monee's car as they left the club and headed for interstate 71 south towards Cincinnati. Monee wasn't in a position to drive; she had been drinking and dancing all night. In fact Monee didn't drive the entire way to Savanah, Georgia. When Red got tired his friend Omar drove. Monee was nervous and praying the entire time Omar was driv-ing because he recklessly drove at least twenty miles over the legal speed limit even though he was aware that none of them had a valid driver's license.

They arrived in Savannah later that afternoon and stayed more days than Monee had expected. Monee didn't make much money her last night working. After giving Lisa money to take care of Nathan's needs, gas money, storage fees and food and she didn't have much money left. Monee was down to her last fifty dollars and after four days in Savannah on Jekyll Island the heavy cigarette smoking and change in atmosphere had Monee struggling to breathe. She had no choice but to go to the emergency room to get medical attention. The doctor told her if she didn't quit smoking cigarettes her bronchitis was going to progress into emphysema and gave her a prescription to get some medication. Monee left the hospital and lit up a cigarette and spent her last fifty dollars at the pharmacy to buy the medication and they headed to Atlanta.

They arrived in Austell, Georgia later that evening at Omar's friend's townhouse. There were four guys living in the townhouse. Monee and Red crashed on the sofa in the living room and Omar slept somewhere upstairs. The first few days in Austell were fun and exciting for Monee. Her bronchitis had healed, and she was back to drinking and smoking every day. Actually, she never stopped. She was partying, lis-tening to the southern hip hop music and learning the bank head bounce and many of the other southern dances from the guys that were their new roommates. The four guys were very hospitable to Monee and Red. They were often barbecuing outside on the patio and were very generous with the meals. That helped ease Monee's worries about not having any money temporarily. However, after a few days Monee was ready to start making some money and decided to go visit some strip clubs.

Monee went to the Blue Flame Gentleman's club that wasn't too far from the townhouse community that she was living at. She spoke with the owner of the club who told her that she needed a dancing permit to strip in Atlanta. Monee also discovered during that interview that the Adult Entertainment Industry in Columbus was like learning how to ride a bike with training wheels compared to riding a motorcycle in Atlanta. Stripping in Columbus wasn't really "stripping," and Monee now understood why it was called "exotic dancing." Monee was an exotic dancer not a stripper. Monee danced in costumes and G-strings, the clubs she worked at were not topless. She was never required to take off her bikini bra and g-strings, and it was illegal to dance nude in Ohio.

Monee performed mostly on stage and the no touching was strongly enforced at Club Illusions. The customers were required to buy the dancers drinks in exchange for their conversation. Which was easy for Monee because she was very versatile and articulate. The establishment paid the dancers the total amount of the drinks purchased on their behalf, and they kept all the tips they were given. However the adult entertainment industry in Atlanta was a totally different level of entertainment and Monee had no instructions and was a rookie to the game she was getting ready to play.

Monee was devastated, not only did she have to go downtown and register for a dance permit, but she didn't have a valid driver's license. To make matters worse, she didn't have the money to pay for the permit and she learned from the manager at Blue Flame that she would be required to dance completely. This was more than Monee had planned for but what could she do now? There was no turning back.

Monee left the Blue Flame feeling defeated and returned to the townhouse full of men. *"How did I get myself in shit twelve feet deep!"* Monee thought to herself as she looked at her gas tank and realized the gas needle was almost on empty. *"Damn, I got to get Red to put some gas in this car."* She was beginning to feel anxiety trying to invade her mind. Then she remembered what Susie, the owner of Club Illusions had said to her when she told her that she was moving to Atlanta, "You can go anywhere in the world but the sad part about is you can't run from you." Susie said as she rolled her eyes. Monee didn't understand what she meant exactly when she said those words to her, but now she was feeling like lady luck was no longer with her and that she brought struggle to Atlanta.

That night Monee and Red sat in her car talking and discussed their plans. Monee shared with Red the information and the obstacles that she had to overcome for her to start stripping. Red shared with her that his older brother that lived in New York offered him a position with his marketing firm. His brother even offered to send Red some money and purchase his flight to get him to New York.

"That's great Red! I am so happy for you! When do you leave for New York?" Monee asked with a big smile on her face. *"At least one of them had good news."* she thought.

"Well I didn't say I was leaving Monee." Red said a little agitated.

"What do you mean you aren't leaving? This sounds like a great opportunity for you to advance your career and make some good money!" Monee was confused.

"Yeah, it sound good, but I don't want to leave you. I want to stay here in Atlanta with you. Is it something wrong with that Monee? Oh I get it you got down here to Hotlanta and now you wide open! I see how that nigga Ray been looking at you since we got here. Trying to teach you how to bank head bounce and shit! What, you like that nigga now?" Red was angry and was jumping to conclusions.

"No! This doesn't have anything to do with me wanting to be with another guy. You know I love you Red, and that is why I am thinking of what is best for you. Going to New York and taking the job with your brother is good for us! I don't know how my situation is going to turn out. But at least you have a solid opportunity. That's why I think you should go. What are you going to do if you stay here?" Monee turned in her seat and looked intensely at Red.

"Good question. Omar got a connect where he can get pounds of premium weed for four hundred dollars. I told him to plug me in and I can start moving that while you strip and then we good Monee!"

"Something doesn't sound right. So Omar is going to give you some pounds of weed for free and let you pay him back after you sell them?" Monee was in disbelief.

"No, he ain't going to do that, come on now you know Omar is a criminal. He ain't got no generous heart like that! I was thinking you could loan it to me, and I would give it back to you after I sell my first pound."

"Me? How am I going to loan you four hundred dollars? I don't even have thirty dollars to get a work permit!" Monee snatched her pack of cigarettes from the dashboard of the car.

"Come on Monee you know you a go getter. You gonna find a way and you will be working real soon in one of the hottest strip clubs in Atlanta! Making plenty of money! It won't be nothing for you to loan me four hundred dollars." Red grabbed one of Monee's cigarettes from her pack and lit it.

"So you betting on me coming up with the money to get my permit, start stripping and hopefully make enough money to loan you four hundred dollars and we don't even have a place to live yet? I see you got a lot of faith in my body and my hustle huh? Nah, I ain't loaning you shit! I ain't got shit to loan you and you need to take your sorry ass to New York cause I am through with you!" Monee jumped out the car and ran into the townhouse. The guys were having a barbeque so there were more people there than usual. Monee went and sat down on the couch sulking when Ray came and sat down next to her.

"Where's that pretty smile that you usually have on your face?" Ray asked.

"Atlanta is too much than I had bargained for, I think it is time for me to go back home." Monee said as her eyes watered.

"Nah you don't have to go anywhere, what happened did that nigga do something to you? You can talk to me, tell me what's wrong Monee?" Ray was able to make Monee feel comfortable. Some of what Red said was true. Ray made it obvious that he was strongly attracted to Monee when they first arrived. But Monee never reciprocated the flirtatious looks or vibes that he was sending her. Ray was attractive, tall, slim and muscles everywhere. He had piercing hazel eyes with a butterscotch complexion. However, Monee's focus was on changing her life not complicating it by flirting with another guy. But now Red had pissed her off. Hearing him say that he was going to wait until she is in a position to loan him some money to sell weed and wasn't going to take a legitimate job opportunity for growth and stable pay was a reality check for Monee. Monee had lost a tremendous amount of respect for Red and was hurt at the thought of him trying to use her.

"Well I'm dealing with a lot. I have had a very rough day." Monee said sadly.

"You want a drink? Come on let's go get a drink and we can go to my room to talk." Ray stood up and grabbed Monee's hand and helped her up from the couch. They both went into the kitchen where there were people dancing and some sitting at the kitchen table playing cards. It made Monee smile, kinda reminded her of back home. Ray poured to vodka and cranberry juice into two glasses. He turned around and handed her one of the glasses and said,

"Taste it, I want to make sure it is straight before we go upstairs. Is it ok?"

Monee took a sip of the drink and nodded yes.

"Thank you, it's cool." And she took another sip.

He grabbed her empty hand and lead her through the kitchen and up the stairs into his bedroom.

"I thought this was just a three-bedroom townhouse. Naw its four, the other two just share a bathroom. Now what is wrong with you beautiful?"

Monee told Ray how she went to the Blue Flame and found out that she needed a permit and how she didn't expect to have to dance nude. She also shared with him the conversation that she had with Red.

"Damn that's not good for that nigga to be relying on his woman to win. That brother aint right!" Ray said shaking his head.

"Yeah tell me about it." Monee took another sip of her drink.

"Well I am headed to medical school in Florida in the morning. That's why my room so empty and they guys is having this little gathering for me. I will let the guys know that you will be sleeping in my room until you either find a place to stay or the lease ends here. At least that will give you a little more privacy until you figure things out and you don't have to be exposed to that asshole if you don't want to."

"You don't have to give me your room Ray! Plus I can't contribute to the rent right now either."

"No you don't have too. I still must pay the rent until the lease end in September, so you good at least for two months. Come on I will be happy to know that a beautiful fine thing like yourself is sleeping in my bed." They both began laughing. Then they heard a knock at the door.

"Come on in." Ray said loudly. It was Red,

"Monee, I need to speak with you for a minute." Red said as he stood in the doorway.

"I am already having a conversation Red what's up?" Monee rolled her eyes and took another sip of her vodka.

"Can you come here for a minute please?" Red looked like he had lost his best friend, which he did.

"No I don't want to talk to you right now Red."

"Monee I am serious we need to talk, how you up here in his room with the door closed? So this how you gonna act?"

"Aye man I know you Omar's boy and all but it ain't no disrespect! We just talking. But if Monee say she don't want to talk right now I think you should respect her wishes ma man." Ray said in a firm tone.

Red looked at the both of then shook his head and closed the door. Monee knew he was regretting his decision to ask her to borrow four hundred dollars. Monee didn't care about his feelings anymore. She was hurt and angry and fed up with Red's lack of ambition. She felt that it was a win-win for Red to live with her in Columbus because he was good with Nathan and it helped her to focus on work knowing that her son was safe. However, it did bother her at times that a sitter and sex was all she could expect from him. Monee knew that she deserved so much more but she loved him. But now she realized that Red had become too dependent on her ambitions and not enough on his own. It was time for them to separate. Monee turned to Ray,

"I apologize for our drama Ray."

"No need to apologize. I don't blame him for being upset that you up here in my room with me. Hell, I am asking myself why I haven't made a move right now. Monee you sexy as hell but quite honestly, I know that is not what you want and damn show ain't what you need right now. I just want to help you in any way I can. So take my room and know that everything will work out, ok?" Ray chugged down half of his drink.

"Ok and thank you so much Ray. I really appreciate you!" Monee smiled and gave him a big hug. Monee stood up off the bed and turned towards the door.

"I'm gonna go downstairs and get something to eat, you coming?"

"You go ahead I got to take a piss first" Ray laughed and went into the bathroom.

The rest of that night Monee tried to take her mind off everything and enjoy the party, however the tension was high between her and Red. He tried a few times to approach her again, but she knew she needed to distance herself from him so that he would make the right decision and go to New York.

The next Morning Ray left for Florida to go to medical school and Monee moved into his bedroom. Monee was very grateful to have some privacy and solitude. She was amazed at how this guy who just met her was so nice to her and just had a willingness in his heart to help her. Later that morning Monee was in her new room contemplating on what to do about her situation. She was trying to decide if she should drive back to Cleveland, which really wasn't an option because she didn't have enough money and the chance of going to jail.

Monee knew when she made the decision to drive to Atlanta under those risky circumstances, that if they made it without getting pulled over and going to jail for driving with suspended license that there was no turning back until she could get legit. So Monee felt that by making it this far, there was only one way out of the mess and that was to keep moving forward with her plan.

"Monee, can I come in?" It was Red's voice on the other side of the door.

"Yeah, come on." Monee said as she sighed.

Monee was lying on her back on the bed staring at the ceiling and she didn't bother to move when Red walked in.

"Listen, I know that I hurt you and I want to make things right between us before I leave." Red said as he sat down on the bed next to her.

"Leave? Where are you going?" Monee asked brimming with curiosity.

"I decided to accept my brother's offer and go to New York. It is a paid internship that will last until the end of October. I figured that it would be the best decision especially since you don't want me to stay here with you. Omar is leaving tomorrow to go to New Orleans to meet his connect, so that really isn't an option for me right now with no money. I want to apologize for the way I made you feel yesterday. What I was trying to express just came out wrong. I am not trying to use you. We make a good team and I love you Monee. I am in love with you! You know that!"

Monee could feel Red's sincerity and his sadness. She knew he was hurting too. Monee believed that he wanted to do more for her but unfortunately, he just didn't know how. Monee loved Red, but she questioned if she was in love with him. She knew Red just wasn't the kind of man that was strong enough to handle Monee's strong will and ambition. They were at the fork in the road and their destinies was taking them in two different directions.

"I love you too Red! I know I hurt your feelings as well. I know sometimes when I get angry, I can say harsh and disrespectful words without thinking. I am proud of you for making the right decision! So when do you leave?" Monee sat up on the bed.

"Tomorrow. My brother already booked my flight this morning when I spoke with him. He also is going to wire me some money tomorrow as well so that I won't be broke traveling. I can give you the thirty dollars you need to get your dancing permit. I just want to know that you will still be mine when I come back in October? I still want us to work Monee. You were right, when I get to New York I will be making consistent money and will be in a better position to help you more. I just need to know are you going to stay down with me and not let all these ballers out here blow your head up and having you thinking you too good for me?" Red grabbed Monee's hands.

"Red, you know I love you but honestly, I don't know what the future holds for us. I don't know where my path is taking me but yes, I am open to us being together, however, I think we should wait until we both get ourselves together. I need to focus on getting a job so that I can get a place to live so I can go and get Nathan. We have been in Georgia for three weeks and I haven't made any progress and I am out of money."

"Ok Monee I hear you. You want to keep your options open huh?" Red snatched his hands out of Monee's hands.

"No, that is not what I am saying Red. I am saying we need to get ourselves together first then discuss our relationship." Monee wasn't sure who she was convincing herself or Red.

"Ok." Red said with a blank stare on his face.

"So will you still give me the money to get my permit?" Monee knew Red was upset and didn't like her response, but Monee loved him too much to lie to him. She had to be honest so that he could focus on himself and not allow their relationship to be a distraction.

"Yeah I got you." Red said as he stood up and walked out of the room.

Monee's mind went to work. Red agreeing to give her the money for the permit was the spark that lit her fire back up. She knew that if she tried to go to Fulton country to apply for a permit that they would run a background check. She wasn't sure if the warrant for her arrest due to failure to appear in court for the speeding ticket would appear on the background check. Monee couldn't take that risk. She heard of people getting expedited from one state to another to report to court to answer a warrant.

Monee called her sister Lisa and asked Lisa to mail her driver's license to Monee. She would use her sister's license and birth certificate to get her permit. That way Monee would pass the background check and then she would just mail the documents back to Lisa once she got her permit. Monee's license wasn't expired it was just suspended so she would still be able to use it for identification to prove her age.

Monee had her answer to the problem that was plaguing her most. Red would give her the money tomorrow and then all she had to do is wait for the license and birth certificate to come in the mail to the townhouse. Monee exhaled but for some reason she couldn't relax. Monee went to the subdivision pool to go for a swim. That night Monee didn't sleep well she had this reoccurring dream about children being trapped in the attic of this house. Although the children were trapped, they appeared to be ghost or spirits that for some reason were bound to the attic. The house would sometimes be different, but the dream was always the same Monee trying to free the trapped children but was never successful.

The next day Monee woke up early due to not really sleeping at all. She went downstairs and saw Red putting his bags inside Greg's SUV. Greg was one of the roommates that lived in the townhouse. Ironically, Chase another one of the roommates was leaving to visit his parents in Mississippi for a few weeks and was going to the airport that morning to catch a flight too. So Greg agreed to take Red to the check cashing store so that Red could get the money that his brother was wiring him, before dropping them both off at the airport.

"Hey Monee, you riding with us? Greg asked her.

"Sure I will ride." Monee responded wondering why Red didn't tell her they were getting ready to leave.

She looked at Red as he pretended to be focused on loading the SUV with his bags and didn't respond when Monee when she said good morning to him. They all got into the SUV and Chase was in the front with Greg. Monee and Red were in the backseat. Monee asked Red was he ok and he replied,

"Yeah" very firm and dry.

Monee knew he was lying and was still angry with her. They pulled up to the check cashing store and Red hopped out and went inside. Ten minutes later he got back into the SUV and didn't say a word to Monee. He told Greg that he was good to go and head to the airport. Monee's heart was beating frantically. She now knew why she had an uneasy feeling last night. After she told Red that she didn't want to be in a relationship right now, he didn't want to help her get the permit. Greg pulled up to the airport and Monee looked over at Red. "Ugh, so you not going to say anything to me?" Monee asked as her voice cracked.

"What do you want me to say Monee? You made things very clear to me yesterday. Take care. Peace!" Red slammed the door and walked to the back of the SUV grabbed his bags. He gave Greg a handshake and hug and walked into the airport. Chase opened Monee's door gave her a hug and told her it was nice meeting her and that he wished her the best.

"Thank you, Chase, same to you." Monee managed to crack a smile.

Greg got back inside the SUV and told Monee to get in the front passenger seat. Monee was in a daze, she got in the front seat and put on the seatbelt. Greg looked over at her and said,

"What you think I'm your chauffeur?" and he began to laugh, but all Monee could do is cry. She had been fighting back her tears since they had left the check cashing store because her intuition had confirmed that Red had no intention of giving her the thirty dollars to get her permit. She was devastated. Greg abruptly stopped laughing.

"Damn, Monee I was just joking! You don't have to cry."

"I know. I am not crying because of your corny joke. I will be ok." Monee said sadly.

"Oh you sad because your man is leaving you to go to New York?" Greg asked.

"No, he's not my man anymore, we broke up and not that's not why I am crying. I am crying because he lied to me and told me he was going to give me the money so that I can get my dancing permit and he didn't. That selfish bastard is mad at me, but it's ok God will make a way somehow."

After speaking those words Monee felt determination rise from within her. This wasn't the first time she felt the thrust of the deep dagger of betrayal into her back. Monee wiped her tears from her eyes and let the hurt fuel her desire to survive. She got quiet and searched her mind for someone she could call to ask for the money.

"No one." Monee and her mother weren't speaking, and Lisa was taking care of

Nathan so she wouldn't dare ask Lisa for money. She would be getting the license in the mail within the next day or so. Monee had isolated herself from her other siblings and family after her mother announce that she was stripper. Monee felt like no one understood her and that she was alone on her journey, and she had accepted that. So calling Cleveland for help wasn't an option.

"Monee there is a strip club off Stewart Avenue, that is always looking for pretty girls with bad bodies to work there. You should go there tonight and see if they will let you work. I understand that you think you need a dance permit but hell this is the Atl, and every club aren't enforcing that shit. Especially a chick bad as you are walking up in there do you really think they are going to turn you away?" Greg had just given Monee a new perspective that she hadn't considered before.

"Are you serious Greg? You really think they might let me dance without a permit?" Monee was getting excited.

"Hell yeah. Me and the fellas go in there sometimes and not half of them strippers got a body like yours!" Greg said as he glanced over at Monee.

"Ok well if I am going to go tonight I got to do something to my hair. Can you loan me five dollars so I can go get some gel from the beauty supply store please? Monee humbly asked.

"Sure I got you." Greg replied as he pulled into the beauty supply store down the street from the townhouse on Six Flags Drive.

Greg reached into his pocket and gave Monee a five-dollar bill and Monee hopped out and went into the store. When they got back to the house Monee washed her hair and used the gel to pull her hair up into a ponytail. It was her signature look when money was tight, and time did not allow for her to sew-in a weave. After Monee finished her hair and got dressed, she was ready to go and make something happen. She was fueled with a burning passion to win and confidence that could kill. This was a do or die moment in her life and she would be damned if she was going to allow Red to get the last laugh.

"He thought he was hurting me humph! I will show his ass, joke is on you jack!" Monee thought to herself as she headed down the stairs to find Greg. She could hear voices coming from the living room. Monee walked in and saw Greg and Rick sitting on the couching watching sports on television and drinking beers. Rick and Greg were the last two remaining roommates in the townhouse. It was crazy how within a few

weeks everything had changed. Monee didn't expect to be roommates with two guys and have her own room, but she was happy that it worked out that way.

"Damn girl! We need to be going to the club with you! I would give you all my money if I had some to give! Greg said and gave Rick a fist pound.

"Yea Monee you gonna take all them niggas money! Greg told me you were going to The Basement tonight." Ricked laughed.

"Yes, I am getting ready to leave now. Greg, tell me how to get there again?"

Monee listened intently to the directions, grabbed her dance bag, and then got in her car and left. Monee couldn't believe that she still managed to have gas in her car. But she was grateful that she did. She was on a quarter of a tank and was hoping Greg was right and the club wasn't very far. She followed Greg's directions and arrived at the strip club just to discover that it was closed. The building didn't have a soul insight.

"Awe shit! Now what!" Monee yelled out loud as she sat in her car beating the steering wheel. Then she heard that still small voice say "Drive." Monee obeyed she pulled out the Basement Lounge parking lot and turned left. Then she went through a green light, and she heard "Right!" Then she turned right and saw a big marquis sign in front of a club that said, "Club Nikki's dancers wanted inquire within." Monee couldn't believe it!

She pulled into the parking lot and checked her face in her rear-view mirror and hopped out the car, grabbed her dance bag from the back seat and walked into the club. Monee had decided to wear her black denim mini skirt with a white halter top and her white stiletto heels. She felt confident and sexy. She was ready to make some money.

Monee walked into the club and there was a big dark-skinned security guard standing there looking at her.

"You here to work?" the guard asked in a deep voice.

"Yes, but I haven't been hired yet. I wanted to speak with the hiring manager, I saw the sign that y'all need some dancers?" Monee said confidently.

"Yeah, you got to speak with M.C. hold up a minute." The security guard disappeared, and Monee scanned the club.

The club was huge and upscale. There were a lot of girls working even though it was early evening, and the sun was still shining. There were a lot of men spending money inside the club too.

"Wow, it's this busy at almost seven in the evening, I can imagine the crowd at night!" Monee cheerful thought to herself.

Monee also notice that most of the strippers were naked. Some had on very skimpy lingerie but most of the women on and off the stages were naked. Monee couldn't believe it. Dancers were giving the men lap dances naked! Monee got nervous and uncomfortable.

"I don't know if I can do this." She whispered.

"Hey sexy I am M.C.! You wanna work here tonight beautiful?" Monee turned around and saw this brown-skinned,short slim guy with very nice waves in his hair. He was dressed in an all-white suit and had gold rings on most of his fingers and three gold chains, all different lengths around his neck. He also was holding a large cigar but it hadn't been lit yet. Monee thought he was attractive, and he looked like money!

"Yes, I would like to start now if possible?" Monee asked

"You got your permit? How old are you? You look like a sweet young tender!" He said as his eyes examined her from head to toe.

"I am twenty-one. I just arrived her from Ohio and I haven't gotten my permit yet. I was hoping I could work tonight and get my permit in the morning?" Monee was reaching.

"Nah I am sorry Shawty but the law be watching my place heavily. You know how haters be when they want what you got, but don't have a clue as to how to get it? But I tell you what, when you get your permit tomorrow you come back here, and you definitely can work. You're beautiful shawty, what you say yo name is? M.C. hadn't taken his eyes off of Monee.

"Nickee, my name is Nickee." Monee said and then shot him a sexy smile.

"Alright then Nickee you make sure you come back once you get your papers ok?" M.C. smiled took one last look and turned and walked away. Monee stood there for a moment frozen. *"Damn that didn't go as I had planned."* She was thinking.

"Why didn't I tell him I didn't have any money to get the permit? Monee asked herself as she turned and walked out of the club. Deep down Monee knew that even if she would have shared her story with M.C. the outcome would have been the same. He wouldn't have helped her. One thing Monee knew was how to read people and

working in a strip club Monee had perfected that gift. Nine times out of ten Monee was right about the vibes she felt from people.

Monee got in the car and that still small voice told her to turn right out of the parking lot. Monee obeyed and a mile down the road Monee notice another strip club on the left-hand side of the street. It was Club Body. Monee pulled into the parking lot and parked. She walked in and asked security guard at the door to speak with the manager. The security guard who was sitting on a stool by the door didn't move. He just pointed to a guy who was standing next to the DJ booth.

"That's him over there."

"Thanks." Monee replied and walked toward a young handsome caramel-complexion muscular guy that was about six feet. He had on a metallic blue adidas jogging suit and white adidas shell toe sneakers with navy strips. He had on one gold chain and a nice diamond and gold bracelet on his right wrist and a diamond gold watch on the left wrist. Monee was caught off guard because she didn't expect for the manager to be so young. He looked to be only a few years older than Monee. He seemed to be very mature, and Monee could tell that he was a no-nonsense kind of guy.

"What can I do for you sweetie?" The guy said as he approached Monee.

"Yes, hi, I was wanting to speak with your hiring manager..." Monee said nervously.

"I'm Darren, the owner, I make all the decisions what's up?" Darren didn't crack a smile, nor did he really even look at Monee.

Something clicked inside of Monee when she heard him say that he was the owner and he make all the decisions. Monee opened her heart and briefly told him her situation.

"I'm Nickee and I just moved here from Ohio. I was an exotic dancer in Columbus and came here to work during the Olympics. What I didn't know is that the county makes dancers pay to get a permit to dance here in Atlanta. I have been here for three weeks, and I have run out of money. Darren, I have no money to get my permit, but I promise you if you let me work tonight so that I can make enough money to get my permit I will be able to repay you tomorrow. Please help me, I have nowhere else to go." Monee pleaded almost in tears.

Darren looked at her intently.

"Ok. I will let you dance this one time without a permit. Get dressed, the dressing room is over there to the back." Darren said as he pointed to the back of the club.

"Thank you so much!" Monee said to Darren and darted towards the dressing room. That was the first time that Monee took all her clothes off and danced completely naked in the club. Although, Monee made a lot of money that night, she felt worthless dancing naked in front of strangers

The next day Lisa's driver's license and birth certificate came in the mail and Monee went downtown and got her permit. Although Darren had a heart to allow Monee to work there without her permit, she knew she had the potential to make the most money at Club Niki's. Club Niki's was one of Atlanta's most popular upscale strip clubs and she knew that club would be where many tourists would frequent.

After her first week working at Club Niki's, Monee got a hotel room on Fulton Industrial, not too far from the townhouse where she was staying. Monee decided to stay Austell, she had become very familiar with the area and the rates were reasonable. Monee thought that she would be happy once she started working, but that was far from the truth.

Working at Club Nikki's was hard for Monee. She started drinking heavily again because she couldn't bring herself to be in that environment sober. She did become good friends with a guy who owned a hand car wash in the club parking lot. He would clean the customers' cars for them while they were inside the club partying. It was a very lucrative business. Monee would often sit out there with him and talk before going inside to dance. He would always give her encouraging words and tell her that everything was going to work out for her. Marsalis was the only light in a dark environment.

Monee had been there for over three weeks but hadn't made friends with any of the other girls that worked at the club. She wasn't interested in getting to know anyone, and plus she had witnessed a lot of fights between the strippers, and she wanted to stay as far away from drama as she could. Monee did, however, meet a guy named Bull, who was a regular at Club Nikki's. He had paid for her to give him several lap dances the first night she worked there. Every time he was there, Bull would find Monee and buy dances while he begged for her number. Monee got to know him, and they did begin to talk on the phone when Monee wasn't working. Bull was twenty-five and lived a street lifestyle. He wouldn't tell Monee many details about what he did to make money, but she knew it wasn't legal. He had a new Mercedes convertible and always wore the latest new tennis shoes and jogging suits and starter hat to match. He told Monee he wanted her to be his girlfriend; however, Monee was hesitant about getting involved with him because he seemed to be very controlling.

Monee had also spoken to Red, and he apologized to her about leaving and not giving her the money for her permit. Monee forgave him, and he sent her some money to get an apartment for the both of them. Red was coming back to Atlanta in two weeks. The next day Monee was leaving the hotel she was staying at, and she was walking past the front desk when Bill the morning shift front desk manager stopped her.

"Ms. Green! I was getting ready to call your hotel room phone. Do you have a minute?" Bill said as he waved to stop her from walking out of the door.

"Sure, Bill, what's up?" Monee asked as she turned and walked toward the front desk.

"Well, Ms. Green, it seems that this will be the last day that you can remain in your hotel room," Bill said in a timid tone.

"What do you mean last day? I already paid for the entire week. Today is only Thursday. I am good until Monday." Monee was flustered.

"I know, and we are going to have to refund your money. Unfortunately, the room you are staying in was reserved three months ago by a customer that is coming to Atlanta for the Olympics. The customer just confirmed their reservation and will be arriving to check in tomorrow. I do apologize it was clearly an oversight made when the front desk clerk took your weekly payment without checking the existing reservations for the entire week. I do apologize," Bill said regretfully.

"No problem. Just switch me to another room, Bill," Monee responded, thinking her suggestion would easily resolve the problem.

"I thought the same thing, too, until I checked our reservations, and our entire hotel is completely sold out until next weekend. The Olympics has been very good for business, and we just don't have any more rooms." Bill looked at Monee and then looked at his computer screen as if he was searching for a room to miraculously appear available.

Monee was infuriated!

"What the hell. How could y'all allow this to happen without giving me prior notification? You tell me this and expect me to checkout my room today! This is insanity! How unprofessional! This is unbelievable!" Monee shouted.

But she knew that there was nothing she could do but try to go and find another hotel before she had to be at work at seven that evening.

"Ok, I will be back to check out later. Thanks, Bill." Monee turned and stormed out of the hotel. She was leaving with the intention of going to look at some apartments, but she didn't have enough time to look at apartments and find somewhere to sleep that night before having to go to work. Monee knew that even if she found an apartment today, she wouldn't be able to sleep the with no furniture. So, she headed down Fulton Industrial to find another hotel to stay.

Monee went to three other main hotels that were on the same street, and they all were sold out. Monee was driving back toward her hotel when she noticed a hotel on the left side of the street that was behind another building, which made it difficult to see from the street. Monee turned on the side street that led to the hotel parking lot. Monee parked and went inside. The hotel was undergoing some major renovations, and the lobby was in disarray, but Monee didn't have time to drive all over Atlanta to find a room, and the odds were very slim to find a hotel that wasn't sold out. So, she walked up to the front desk and asked the lady behind the desk did the hotel have any rooms available. She said yes, and Monee paid for a room and got her hotel room key.

Then she left and went back to the current hotel she was staying at to pack up her belongs. Monee managed to pack up all her bags and luggage. She realized she had managed to accumulate a substantial number of personal items such as a salon style hair dryer and two additional suitcases. One suitcase was full of nothing but new lingerie and costumes for work, and the other was new clothes she had to buy to accommodate the hotter temperatures during the summer in Atlanta. Monee had everything packed into her car and drove to the front of the hotel so that she could check out and get her refund.

Monee walked up to the front desk and Bill looked up at her smiled.

"Ms. Green! So good to see you! Did you get my message that I left you on your room phone?"

"No, I did not. I was out looking for another room," Monee said with a bit of irritation in her tone.

"I had called you to notify you that I had two customers cancel their reservations shortly after I had spoken to you. You can remain in your room, and I can put the customer that reserved your room into the second room that came available. Isn't that great?" Bill said as if he was proud of himself.

"Bill, that would be great if it wasn't for the fact that I already paid for a room down the street and have my car loaded up with all of my stuff! I will just take my refund for the weekend, and I will be on my way. Thanks."

Monee couldn't believe what she had just heard. She was once again infuriated that she went through all of this effort to find another room just to be told that she didn't have to go anywhere. Although the hotel she was currently at was a much better-quality hotel, the rate at the hotel down the street was much cheaper. Plus, she would just commit to finding her and Red a place to stay after the weekend.

Monee pulled up to her new hotel and immediately became more irritated when she saw nine men standing in front of the hotel outside. Most of them were dressed in sweatsuits with matching shoes and had platinum chains around their necks.

"Ugh! Lord, you know that I don't want to be bothered today. I am not in the mood to be dealing with some thirsty ass dudes trying to get my number!" Monee yelled aloud. Monee was out of sorts. When she woke up that morning, she was expecting the day to be just as routine as any other day. She had no idea that her life would forever be changed.

Monee got out of her small little Ford Escort and began to dig through her luggage and bags to determine how she could carry it all inside the hotel at once.

"You need some help with that?" Monee heard one of the men yell to her.

She didn't even look up.

"Nah I'm good!" she shouted back, and then whispered, "Now leave me the hell alone!"

Monee began to assess her load, and she realized that there was no way she would be able to carry all of her belongings in one trip. And she knew she didn't have much time before she had to get ready to go to work.

"Ugh, it looks like I do need some help!" Monee called out to the men still all standing by the building watching her. Two men jogged toward her, so she began to pull her suitcases out of the car. One guy was short with a light-colored complexion.

The other guy was much taller and very slim with a round head. The tall guy began grabbing bags and suitcases.

"How you are doing today, ma'am? I'm Nefarius but folks just call me Nef." Monee looked at the man and noticed he was smiling at her.

"I am fine. Thank you for helping me with my bags," Monee said with her arms full of luggage as she headed toward the hotel entrance.

"I know you're fine but what's ya name?" Nefarius slammed Monee's trunk and hurried to catch up to her. The three of them were able to carry all of Monee's belongings on one trip and was at the elevator door when the tall guy began jumping around shouting,

"God is so good to me! What's ya name Shawty?"

Monee looked at the man, wondering what he was so happy about.

"Monee." Shaking her head with a slight grin. She pushed number seven as they stepped into the elevator.

"You know that this hotel is going to get shut down in a few hours?" Nefarius said the elevator door opened to the seventh floor.

"No it's not stop playing!" Monee laughed.

"Yes it is. My partna told me the fire Marshall will be here in a few hours. I've been waiting on him to meet me here because we got some business to handle. His ass always late. Yeah, Shawty you got somewhere else to go?"

"I'm good. Thank you both for helping me. I appreciate it!" Monee opened the hotel room door. "Y'all can leave my stuff right here, I got it. Thanks!"

"Alright Shawty, you take care now." Nefarius and his friend headed towards the elevator and Monee took her bags into her room and began to get ready to go to work. She had just got out of the shower when she heard a know at her hotel room door. Monee grabbed her robe as she heard a second knock at the door.

"Fire Marshall!" Monee peeped through the peek hole and saw that it was indeed a fire man standing on the other side of the door. Monee cracked opened the door,

"Hi Ma'am, I am the Fire Marshall for Fulton County here to notify all patrons that this building is unsuitable for occupancy and must be vacated immediately."

"Are you serious? I just checked in this room earlier today!" Monee couldn't believe that Nefarius was right.

"I understand Ma'am. You need to get your money back. The owners of this hotel are fully aware of the unsafe conditions of this hotel. You shouldn't have any problems getting your money back. But you do need to vacate this hotel immediately." The Fire Marshall said firmly.

"Alright, I have to finished getting dressed and then I will check out. Thank you, Sir." Monee closed the door and flopped down on the bed. She stared at the mirror in front of her. Looking at her reflection, as if looking at a total stranger. She was in shock, but she had no time to get stressed out. Monee knew that she had to stay focused and moved all her stuff back downstairs and get to work at the club in a couple of hours. Monee finished getting dressed and packed her things. Luckily, she found a old luggage cart in the hall to take her things to the lobby.

The hotel clerk refunded Monee her money without any hesitation. While Monee was standing waiting for the clerk to give her refund, a guy walks up beside her.

"You got something to put in that babe?" The guy asked as he undressed Monee with his eyes and then pointed to the blunt package on the counter. Monee dumped a bunch of items on the counter when the clerk had asked for her driver's license to issue her refund. Her papers to roll her blunt was on the counter along with her keys and a tube of lipstick.

"Something to put in what?" Monee snapped. She was about to go off on the guy but before she could open her mouth she heard, "I got something to put in that!" from behind her.

Monee turned around; it was Nefarius.

"Fat Back get out this beautiful woman's face beggin! Thirsty ass!" Nefarius walked on the other side of Monee as Fat Back walked away.

"Oh that's ya boy? Huh?" Monee asked annoyed.

"Yeah, Fat Back good folks. He just doesn't know how to act around beautiful women. Can you blame him? Look at yo fine ass! I see you got your luggage down on this raggedy ass cart. Come on, I got it. I will take it to your car." Nefarius grabs the cart and heads out the hotel door to the parking lot.

"Ok. Thank you." Monee says as the clerk hands her the money for the room. Monee quickly grabs her things off the counter and puts them back into her purse and walks out the door. Nefarius was waiting by her trunk.

"I told you they were shutting this place down. You didn't think I knew what I was talking about did you? Nefarius said boastfully as he put Monee's luggage in the trunk.

"Nope, I didn't believe you. I thought you were crazy, but you were right." Monee said as she opened the driver's door of her car. "Come on get in, you said you got some weed, right?" Monee smiled. Nefarius closed her trunk and got into the passenger seat.

He handed Monee a bag of weed and she began to roll the blunt.

"So where you gonna go? I know you out here all alone from Ohio. Now you ain't got nowhere to stay and the hotels are booked! Shit the Olympics got Atlanta on fire right now!" Nefarius was proud.

"I'm not all alone. I got folks here. I'm good. I'm bout to go to work and then…"

"Oh you gotta go to work? Where you work at?" Nefarius interrupted.

"I work at Nikki's strip club." Monee lit the bunt.

"Oh you bartend, waitress.." Nefarius stuttered.

"I dance!" Monee exploded into laughter.

"Oh, ok well I understand. You out here doing what you think you got to do. That's good you got hustle in you, and I can tell you got heart. But look here, sometimes it ok to need some help. I'm a God-fearing man. I live alone and I ain't gonna do nothing shady to a lady. So, here is my number and if you need somewhere to go tonight when you get off work call me. I'm serious. I ain't gonna let nothing happen to you on my watch. That's real Shawty." Nefarius looked deeply into Monee's eyes as he gave her his business card. "This your dance bag right here?" Nefarius pointed to the bookbag on Monee's back seat.

"Yes." Monee giggled as she handed him the blunt. Nefarius grabbed the blunt and put it in between his lips, then reached in the back and put another one of his cards in Monee's bookbag.

"Now, just in case you lose that one you got my card in your bag. Matter of fact, here." Nefarius reached in his pocket and puts another card in Monee's glove compartment. Monee began laughing hysterically. She was impressed by his persistence and sincerity.

"Alright, alright! I got somewhere to go but I appreciate your offer. I got to head to work but it was nice meeting you Nefarius." Monee said blushing.

"Alright Monee, nice meeting you too! Don't forget what I said. Be safe!" Nefarius said as he got out of the car and walked back toward the hotel lobby.

That night at work Monee felt as if she was at a crossroads. She didn't have her own safe place to go and she knew making the wrong decision could be dangerous. Her friend Bull was at the club that night begging her to leave with him. Monee liked Bull but deep down she felt like that would have been the wrong decision. So at 3 am, Monee went into the dressing room and called Nefarius. He answered on the first ring. Monee went to his home and never left. Monee quit dancing and they became inseparable. After the Olympics was over Monee started to miss home. So they decided to move to Cleveland.

Monee was brought out of her flashback when she heard an inmate next to her on the phone screaming frantically then slammed the phone on the receiver and walked away. Monee took a deep breath.

"Look I didn't call you to argue. I need you to get me out of here, Nefarius. My bond has been set. Can you get the money to get me out?"

Monee was calm again. She really wanted them to be able to work through their issues for the sake of their children. Nefarius and Monee had been at odds often over the years. Things hadn't been the same between them since Nefarius initially left her in November of 2000, three days before thanksgiving. The strange thing was it was for the very reason that he was upset with Monee now... for getting a job.

"I don't have any money to get you out! I'm taking care of our children that you left home alone to go get high!" Nefarius was throwing punches with his words.

"Nefarius, that is a low blow! Especially considering the fact that you are the major contributing factor to my stress! You never take responsibility for your actions! It's always my fault! You never do anything wrong!" Monee began crying again. She was hoping that for once Nefarius would show some compassion and help her get out of jail.

"Where are all the niggas at that you be out in the streets getting high with? Have them get your ass out of jail! They keep calling your cell phone since you been in there, so call them to help you!" Nefarius now had the gloves off and was street fighting. "Better yet, you say you love God so much, why don't you ask him to get you out?" Nefarius began laughing. If he had any empathy for Monee, it was six feet deep in the same casket that his love for her was buried in.

Monee was devastated. Her sister Lisa had come to the jail yesterday and picked up all of Monee's belongings that she had in the car when she was arrested. Monee had instructed Lisa to give Nefarius everything but her cell phone. She told Lisa to keep her cell phone until she gets out of jail. Now, she knew that Lisa had given Nefarius the cell phone, too. Although Monee had several male friends that she was communicating with, she was not involved with any of them. However, she knew Nefarius would never believe that, so she didn't try to explain. It wouldn't have mattered anyway because Nefarius didn't want Monee having any platonic male friends at all.

"Are you really going to do this to me again, Nefarius?" Monee asked helplessly, hating that her life seemed to cycle bad situations—and she never seemed to learn from them. Her mind drifted back to that dreadful night that she had hit rock bottom.

○ ○ ○

"Monee! Hello, Monee! Answer me, what is wrong with you? I haven't heard from you all day." Monee's sister Lisa was on the other end of the phone, and Monee was just holding the phone to her ear sobbing silently. "I am here, Lisa. I just am done. I can't do this anymore," Monee said lifelessly.

"You can't do what anymore? What is wrong with you, Monee? What is going on?" Lisa was frantic. She felt helpless because she was in Ohio, and Monee was twelve hours away in Atlanta, but she wanted to be there for her sister. She knew Monee was going through a rough time with Nefarius since they reunited after a bad break up. Nefarius had started physically abusing Monee when they were living in Cleveland and Monee was pregnant with Eternity. Monee had had enough when Nefarius had spit on her after coming home from having dinner and drinks with a few friends. She was ready to leave him then. But it didn't last. After about six months, Monee was back in Nefarius' arms again, believing all the false promises that he would never hurt her again.

It wasn't until Nefarius had made some bad business decisions and a large shipment of cocaine that he was supposed to sell was confiscated by the police in Mexico. Nefarius was depending on the shipment to sell to another dealer. The deal was going to offset the amount of money he had lost in some other investments and make him three hundred thousand in profit. When the deal fell through, Nefarius was in serious debt. Monee volunteered to get a job to help with the bills. But Nefarius wasn't having it. The day Monee accepted a position with a non-profit organization, Nefarius left Monee and their children three days before Thanksgiving and moved back to Atlanta. Monee was devastated. She had no money, little food, and no transportation. Nefarius had taken both vehicles to make sure that Monee would surely suffer in his absence. After a couple of years passed Monee left Cleveland moved to Atlanta to reconcile with Nefarius.

"I can't take this anymore! All the pain and hurting… why am I living?" Monee had cried to her sister. "This is not a life, this is hell, and I want out! I tried so badly to stay with him so that my children could have their father raise them. But I am dying! His family is tormenting us. I have no one, Lisa! No one! I am here all alone, and he doesn't give a damn about no one but himself! I have no job, no money, and no home… I am done." Monee continued to sob, struggling to see through her tears as she swerved on the highway into another lane.

"Monee, what did you do?" Lisa and Monee were always spiritually in tuned with each other ever since they were little girls. Monee would finish Lisa's sentences, and they could look at each other at times and know what the other was thinking. Lisa could feel her sister's pain all the way in Ohio and knew that Monee was in a grave situation.

"I took a whole bunch of pain pills… I'm just going to drive until I blackout," Monee exclaimed hopelessly.

"Monee! Why did you do that? You are not going to die! Those pills aren't going to kill you. They are going to just damage your kidneys and liver! You are going to mess up your organs!"

Monee was in shock from what she was hearing from her sister. She had a vision of herself in a wheelchair and the fear of living the rest of her life on dialysis. She snapped out of her drug-induced daze while noticing the exit sign on the side of the highway that read "Union City next exit in half a mile." In a state of panic and fear, Monee quickly put her right signal on and got into the exit lane on the highway.

"Are you for real or are you just telling me this to scare me?" Monee slowly asked Lisa.

"I am very serious! You not going to die, Monee!" Lisa was still shouting, trying desperately to reach her sister before it was too late.

"Ok, I am getting off the highway now. There is a gas station right off the exit, and I will go there and make myself throw up. I will call you back." Monee quickly pushed the end call button on her cell phone before Lisa was able to say anything else.

Fighting to see clearly through her tears to prevent from hitting the car in front of her, Monee was still feeling the effects of all the drugs and alcohol that she had been putting in her body earlier that day. It was now nighttime, and that made it even more difficult for her to see clearly.

Earlier that morning, Monee was at Nefarius' mother's house when she and Nefarius had gotten into a fist fight after Monee tried to take her keys to the storage space that had contained all of her and her children's belongings from their home back in Cleveland. Monee was fed up with waiting for Nefarius to find them a home and had decided to make a change and leave Nefarius once again.

After Nefarius left her and their children in Cleveland, Monee was working for the non-profit organization, her mother helped her get a new car, and was living in a nice three-bedroom home. She even started dating Louis who she had met at a night club hanging out with her sister Lisa. However, Nefarius had his hold on her son Gideon, who had become very rebellious and was always angry and demanding to be with his father.

Monee was trying to move on with her life, but she still loved Nefarius and seeing her children, especially Gideon, hurting from their separation from their father caused guilt to haunt her daily. Monee fell in love with Louis, but they, too, had relationship issues that caused her to question the longevity of their relationship. Depression was riding Monee's back heavily, and the pressure of it all caused Monee to quit her job, end her relationship with Louis, pack up all of her and the kids' belongings and furniture, and moved back to Atlanta with Nefarius. Monee made this rash decision in one day.

Two weeks after deciding to sacrifice everything that she worked to establish in Cleveland, she was homeless in Atlanta with vindictive Nefarius. Louis was devastated to say the least. Monee was hurting all the while, but she thought sacrificing her new relationship and job security for the sake of keeping her family together was the right thing to do, and eventually, she would find happiness again with Nefarius.

Nefarius had promised her that he had a home for his family to move into in Atlanta and that everything would be fine. Once they arrived in Atlanta, the first stop was to unload all of Monee's belongings into a storage unit not far from where Nefarius lived in College Park, GA. However, it didn't take long for Monee to realize that the promises Nefarius was telling her to convince her to move back to Atlanta with him were all lies. The home that Nefarius said he had for his family turned out to be two condos that his mother and younger sister lived in Decatur. Monee and her three children were now homeless and living between two condos in chaos!

Nefarius was cold and aloof toward Monee. He would leave early that morning and wouldn't return until late that evening. Monee had intentions on going back to college when she got to Atlanta, but that was quickly eliminated as an option when she tried to register and discovered that the registration deadline for receiving student financial aid had passed. She would have to wait until the following semester to register for school.

Monee had applied for housing assistance, but her application was low on the priority list due to all the refugees that migrated to Atlanta at the same time after Hurricane Katrina. Monee was broke, and homeless with three children and in a city where the only people she knew was Nefarius and his family. Nefarius' mother never liked Monee, and she made that very clear by the way she treated her and her children while they were living between the two condos. When Monee decided that she couldn't continue to live in such a chaotic environment, she went to the storage facility to get a copy of the keys.

Nefarius had refused to give her the keys to her storage in hopes of keeping control of her. He thought that if she didn't have access to her property then she would have to consult him with every decision she made concerning leaving him or the condos. He knew Monee was strong minded, and he wanted security that she would not try to leave him again.

Earlier that day, Monee discovered that Nefarius did not register the storage unit in both of their names. Nefarius was not only deceitful but conniving enough to put his best friend's name on the paperwork as an alternate user and not Monee's name. Monee was too trusting and naive and believed the devil had a heart and would finally do right by her. So, she had decided to call her mother and ask for help. Monee wanted money to move into an extended stay until she could find permanent housing for her and her kids. But Virginia wasn't going for it. Once Monee explained the situation to Virginia about how Nefarius was refusing to give Monee the keys to her storage, Virginia still refused to help Monee. Virginia told Monee she was afraid of what Nefarius would do to Monee if she tried to leave him. Monee was devastated; who else could she turn to for help?

Monee wouldn't dare ask Louis who was begging her to move back to Cleveland and be with him. As much as she loved Louis, something deep inside of her knew that moving back to Cleveland wasn't the answer. She was afraid of looking like a fool to all her family and friends. Plus, she didn't want to go back to that dreary city, which was where her pain lived, and she wanted a new beginning where she could put her past behind her. Monee didn't realize that she wasn't running from her pain nor her past, but she wasn't loving herself.

Once her mother had deserted her, Monee had lost all hope. She had decided to find her storage key, and when the kids returned from the park with their aunt, she would grab them and leave. She didn't know where she was going to go, but she was willing to go to a homeless shelter if she had to. However, her plan had been diverted when Nefarius had returned to the condo late that morning and found her rummaging through his drawers.

"What the hell are you doing?" Nefarius was pissed. "Why is this room a mess, Monee! What the hell are you looking for?" Nefarius approached her with fury on his face.

"I am looking for my damn key!" Monee said in a frustrated and angry tone. "I can't take this bullshit anymore! You ain't shit! You lied to me! You brought me back to Atlanta to get revenge for me falling in love with Louis! You never had any intention on forgiving me, did you?" Monee's heart was pounding through her chest.

She always knew how to use her words to cut through a man's heart like a sharp machete, and she was ready for war. She knew every time she pulled her machete out Nefarius would not be able to win with his words, so he resulted to using his fists. An all-too-common occurrence with all the previous abusive men in her past. Monee loved hard, but when the man she loved betrayed her, that betrayal ripped the un-healed wound wide open. Once that wound began to bleed out, Monee would say every vicious combination of curse words and book words she could spit out to rip her betrayer to bloody shreds of flesh.

"You just didn't want me to be happy, did you? Well, muthafuker, I am going to be happy 'cause I am leaving your triflin' ass! Now give me my damn key!"

Nefarius' eyes bulged out of his head like an over boiled egg busting threw its shell. "Bitch, I ain't giving you shit, and you ain't going nowhere!"

Nefarius had his hands around her neck and began to push her back up against the wall behind her. He began to squeeze both hands until they touched, and Monee began gaging. She knew she had to do something to get him to release his hold before she passed out, so she quickly kneed him in his scrotum. Once he bent down to grab himself, Monee grabbed her purse and car keys then ran out of the condo. She managed to get into her car and sped off as she watched him from her rearview mirror running out of the condo and screaming for her to come back.

Monee was still fighting to get air back into her lungs as she made her way down the street. She decided to go to Creel Park in College Park to pull herself together. Her breathing was regulated by the time she had pulled into parking lot of the park. Her adrenaline was still pumping through her veins, and she was too angry to shed a tear. As she drove through the parking lot, she noticed three guys standing close to one of the parked cars, smoking a blunt. She could hear Tupac's "Me Against the World" playing from inside the car. Monee scanned the park to see if she wanted to stay. She noticed a few kids playing on the playground and a few other parked cars closer to the back. But they were all empty. She assumed they belonged to the lady walking the dog and the couple playing tennis toward the back of the park.

"Long as they don't bother me, I won't fuck with them!" Monee said about the three guys smoking. They appeared to be average guys around Monee's age. They didn't look like gang bangers or thugs, just some guys that might be hanging out on their day off of work. So, Monee parked closer toward the empty cars by the tennis courts. She turned the car off and pulled out her pack of cigarettes; she was looking through her purse for her lighter when she noticed that one of the guys that was standing by the car smoking the blunt was walking toward her car with a cup in his hand. Her windows were already down since it was about eighty degrees outside, and with all the surrounding trees, there was a gratifying breeze flowing through the park.

"What's up?" Monee decided not to wait for the guy to get too close to her car before finding out what his intentions were.

"Hey, boo, you all right? You having car trouble or something? I am just checking to see if you need any help." The guy cracked a half smile, and that's when Monee realized that the guy was quite attractive.

"Yeah, I'm good. No car trouble over here. Thanks for checking." Monee didn't smile back but instead looked to see if the other two guys were making their way over to her car as well. But they were both back inside of the car talking and still listening to Tupac.

"I'm Dillion. what's your name, beautiful?" The guy was now close to the passenger side of Monee's car. He was talking through the open window, but he was so tall that he was standing a few feet away in order to be able to see Monee inside the car.

"Look, I ain't in the mood for no conversation, so I would appreciate it if you would just leave me alone," Monee said in a slow, low voice.

"Oh, ma, my fault no disrespect intended. You do seem a bit stressed. What's wrong with you? Tell Dillion who he need to go fuck up!"

Monee looked at Dillion, and they both laughed, then Dillion took a sip from his cup.

"What are you drinking in that red cup of yours?" Monee asked.

"Some vodka and cranberry. Why, you wanna a drink?" Dillion asked, feeling hopeful that she would say yes. He was drawn to Monee; she seemed intriguing, and he noticed her beauty from the time she had first entered the parking lot. He couldn't resist her sitting several feet from him alone in the car and miss the opportunity to find out who this mysterious beauty was.

"Yeah, I need a drink!" Monee exhaled.

"I got you, Shawty, hold up," Dillion said then quickly jogged back over to the car with the two other guys. He returned with a brown paper bag and another empty cup.

"You mind if I get in your car?" Dillion asked as he placed his hand on the car door handle and paused. Monee smiled and hit the unlock button, and Dillion got in. Whether it was being under age in nightclubs or dating drug dealers and gang-bangers, ever since Monee was a teenager, she always was in the streets. She realized early on that she had to pay close attention to the people she trusted and allowed to get close to her. She had been betrayed enough to pick up on bad vibes. Nefarius was where she would lose all sense of good judgment and make decisions based off her emotions and what she wanted to force to happen. With Dillion, however, Monee could sense that he was a good dude with no intentions of harming her. She could see admiration and wonder all in his eyes when he looked at her.

"Here, I will let you pour your own drink so you don't think I am trying anything." Dillion chuckled as he handed her the brown bag with the bottle of Vodka and cranberry juice inside. "So, beautiful, you gonna tell me your name now or am I just gonna have to call you Beautiful?" Dillion smiled at her.

"Beautiful is fine." Monee gently laughed. "Monee, my name is Monee."

"You mean like Money?" Dillion asked her.

"Kinda but not spelled the same and pronounced slightly different, more feminine. Monee!" Monee said her name again, accentuating the vowels.

"That's different, never met anyone with that name before, but I sure do love me some money!" They both looked at each other and laughed. Dillion held up his cup toward Monee and said, "Here's to more Monee! More Monee! More Monee!"

Monee raised her cup with a smile on her face and tapped Dillion's red cup. They both take a sip from their cups.

"So, what else do you indulge in? You smoke, Molly, X, white gurl?" Dillion asked as he reached in his pocket and pulled out a plastic bag.

"Hmmm, I smoke, and I mess with coke from time to time. Why, you got some?" Monee asked, slightly amazed how she always managed to meet the right people that always had her drug of choice. Dillion passed Monee his bag of coke, and they talked for another twenty-minutes.

"Damn, girl, you cool! I gotta go. We gotta go bend a few corners, but let me get your number?" Dillion asked as he began bagging up his liquor. "You want some more of this before I put it up?"

Monee grabbed the bottle of Vodka and poured some more into her cup. Then she grabbed Dillion's phone and put her number into his contacts.

"Thanks, Dillion, you're cool, too! You are a little sunshine on my rainy day." Monee smiled and reached over and gave him a hug. Dillion blushed and got out of the car. "All right, girl, call me later, let's link back up." Dillion turned and walked away.

Monee sighed and sat there silent, realizing that for a brief moment Dillion had distracted her from thinking about Nefarius and her dreadful situation. She didn't share with Dillion what she was going through, which made it easier for her to take her mind off the hurt and despair she was feeling. The drugs and the alcohol were like putting a dirty bandage on a bloody wound. It would stop the bleeding, but it would never help heal the wound and maybe even infect the wound and prevent it from healing.

"Now what?" Monee whispered. She could feel the effects of the alcohol and coke, and it wasn't making her feel better. The more and more she sat in the car smoking cigarettes and thinking about her situation, the darker and more depressed she became. She felt so alone and was searching her mind to find a positive thought to focus on. She saw her three beautiful children laughing and playing in her mind's eye. Monee's heart became warm, and she took a long, deep breath. She started the car and knew it was time to go back to what meant the most to her in this world, her children. As she drove out of Creel Park, she was surprised that the sun was now going down, and it was getting dark.

O O O

When Monee got back to the condo, she could see the children playing on the community playground in the subdivision. She took comfort in knowing that her children could still be children and play. Even though they had been exposed to so much dysfunctionality, they were resilient and positive. Monee was pulling into a parking spot in front of the condo when she saw Nefarius bust out of the door and charge the car.

"Where the fuck you been?" he yelled as he grabbed the car door handle to open the car door.

"Why are you asking? I know you aren't worried about me?" Monee snapped in a sarcastic tone.

"You don't give a fuck about nobody but yourself, do you?" A few neighbors that were outside were now beginning to look over at the two of them. Monee looked around, and she could see her children running toward them leaving from the playground.

"Look, I don't want to argue with you right now. Let's go inside and talk, try to sort this out," Monee said, lowering her voice.

"Oh, so now you want to talk, huh? You smell like liquor. You always begging for money, but you sure do manage to get your vices, don't you?" Nefarius wasn't letting up.

Monee could never understand how he was ever the man that she fell in love with several years ago. Monee's cell phone rang in her back pocket. Nefarius stood directly in front of her, pinning her in between him and her car. Monee tried to reach in her back pocket for the phone, but Nefarius grabbed her arm and twisted her around to grab the phone out of her pocket first.

"Why are trying to hide the phone? What you trying to hide, huh?" Nefarius answered the phone. By this time, Monee's children were walking up to the car.

"Hey, Ma," Gideon said, out of breath from running there.

"We were playing flag football and got thirsty," Nathan said excitedly. The children had no idea that their parents were at war.

"Ok, honey, y'all go into the house and ask your grandma to give y'all some water," Monee said, trying to remove the distress from her voice.

"OK!" Nathan said as the three of them ran into the condo.

"Yeah, what you say your name is, bruh? Dillion, don't call my wife again, or it's going to be a mutherfucking problem!" Nefarius hung up the phone, threw it down, and slapped Monee across the face. Monee fell to the ground and was able to pick up the cell phone. She knew if she had gotten back up, he would hit her again.

Nefarius stood there lecturing her on how disrespectful she was and how she was trying to embarrass him the same way she did when they were in Cleveland when she started dating Louis. Monee had zoned out. Her heart began hurting as it was pounding inside her chest. She couldn't believe that she had given up everything she worked so hard to rebuild after Nefarius had walked out on her and the kids in Cleveland. Just so he could get her back to Atlanta and take advantage of the fact that she had nothing or no one to turn to. She felt the fire of devastation burning her soul and the smoke of despair suffocating the life out of her body. This was too much. Monee couldn't take anymore.

She jumped up, pushed Nefarius away from her car door, jumped inside the car, and locked the door. He stumbled back to the car, but it was too late. Monee had already started the car and was backing out of the parking lot. She was speeding out of the subdivision because she knew he would follow behind her if he felt he could catch up to her. Monee was hysterical. Tears ran down her face, and her mind raced. She was trying so hard to be strong for her children, but in this moment, the darkness that she had been eluding had completely consumed her. All hope was lost, and even her children's smiles and laughter were no longer enough for her to continue to fight. Monee had been fighting all her life, and she was tired.

She pulled into the Kroger parking lot with no money. She was afraid of getting caught for stealing so she went to the "Cough and Cold" section by the pharmacy and quickly grabbed a bottle of extra strength Tylenol, then headed for the women's bathroom.

Tears streaming down her face, she cracked open the bottle and turned on the cold water. She began frantically shoving large, big blue pills down her throat then flushing as much water as she could down her throat, to force the pills down. She continued this until she began to feel like she was about to vomit. She looked into the mirror and saw that her eyes were swollen and blood shot red. She had blue dye from the pills around her mouth. The devil was winning, and death was waiting.

"I think I swallowed about 10 to 15 pills." Monee's mind was slowing down, but she wasn't sure if she had taken enough, so she poured half of the remaining bottle in her jean's pocket, threw the bottle and box into the trash, cleaned her mouth, and walked out of the store.

When she got to her car, she saw Nefarius jumping out of his truck, which was directly parked in the parking space in front of her. Monee was walking slow and was feeling satisfied that she knew it was only a matter of time before her body would catch up to her mind and give up so she would no longer have to suffer in this cruel, wicked world.

"Look at y'all mama! She high as a kite! You should be ashamed of your damn self! You are pathetic!" Nefarius was yelling, pointing to Monee as she was getting closer to her car. Monee heard what he was saying, and when she looked inside Nefarius' truck and saw her three babies sitting in the back seat, it was like he had just lit the match and tossed it on her gasoline saturated body. Everything she once believed in about her life and love was going up in flames.

The man that she had entrusted her mind, body, and heart to, the man that once saved her and built her up now did everything in his power to tear her down. Monee always had taken pride in protecting her children from all her pain and darkness, but that was no longer the case. The reality was their father was using them as pawns to hurt Monee because he knew how much they loved and respected their mother. Nefarius wanted to transfer the guilt he was carrying from leaving his children to their mother. He wanted them to see her flaws so they would know that he wasn't the only one with flaws and that Monee wasn't the perfect mother. It didn't matter to him that by destroying their mother's image he was destroying his own family.

Monee had no fight left in her. She just hung her head, got into her car, and pulled off. The dark cloud of hopelessness that was over her had sunken down upon her as a heavy fog of misery. She knew that would be the last time she would ever see her children again. She was numb, she couldn't feel anything anymore. It was as if something snapped inside her brain that turned off the "I care" button. Nefarius had managed to push her to the point of no return.

"Well, God, I guess this is it. I'm done." Monee had decided that she would just drive until she passed out on the highway. Monee's cell phone rang; it was her sister Lisa.

After Lisa told her that she wasn't going to die. Monee had gone to the nearest gas station bathroom and forced herself to vomit as much as she could. Walking from the bathroom back to her car, she couldn't even feel the ground. It was surreal, like she was floating. She couldn't believe that this was happening to her. All the pain and suffering she had experience in her life had taken its toll on her. Monee stumbled to her car and fell into the driver's seat. Her phone was ringing. It was her mother crying asking her why she tried to kill herself. Virginia told Monee that she was going to get on the next plane to Atlanta. Monee told her not to do that and that she would call her back. Monee hung up on her mother and called Nefarius.

"What do you want, Monee?" Nefarius sounded irritated and tired.

"I am at the gas station on Flat Shoals. I took a bunch of pills... come get me. I can't drive." Monee couldn't say anything else. Her head felt as if it was spinning, and before she could push the end call button on her cell phone, she had passed out.

Monee woke up to Nefarius pushing her over into the passenger seat. "Girl, what is wrong with you?" Nefarius asked Monee with disappointment in his voice.

"Mommy, are you ok?" It was Monee's daughter. Monee managed to lift her head up and see her three children sitting in the back seat of her car. *"I can't believe this bastard! He just won't let up! Why would he bring the children to see me like this?"*

Those were her words, but she was so out of it that she couldn't speak to them. Just thoughts in her head. Nefarius left his truck at the gas station and drove Monee's car back to the condos.

"Ma'am, what did you take? Ma'am, can you hear me?"

Monee was once again brought out of her unconsciousness—this time by a flashlight in her eyes and a man's voice demanding to know what she had taken. She opened her eyes and saw that she was inside her car, but now there was an EMS truck parked next to her car, and she could see a crowd of people all looking at her. The man yelling at her was a paramedic examining the pupils of her eyes. Monee managed to tell him and a female paramedic that she had taken about fifteen pain pills and that she had made herself vomit. The paramedic told Nefarius that they were going to transport her to the hospital and did he want to go with her. He refused and said that he would remain home with the children. Even though his mother and sister were there to take care of the kids. He just didn't have any compassion in his heart for Monee. No desire to be there for her at the time when she needed support and encouragement the most. Nefarius was darkness residing in a tomb called flesh.

Monee woke up in the hospital and then was transported to Dekalb Medical for a 5150 Psychiatric Hold. Monee didn't know that anyone who attempted suicide in the state of Georgia automatically was put on an involuntary psychiatric hold for 72 hours for observation and treatment. Monee was transported to the psychiatric ward in the medical center. She had to participate in group therapy sessions and was in private counseling sessions with a psychiatrist. Monee was in shock. She wasn't crazy, she was just very depressed. She spoke to her mother and her sister Lisa and discovered that Nefarius was telling them lies to have them believe that she was a drug addict and was smoking crack.

He told them that he was going to take Monee to court and gain custody of their children. But Monee knew better. She knew that Nefarius didn't want the kids; he was again trying to destroy her and kill her character. Monee realized that she was making it easy for him to destroy her character by her own self-destructive behavior; it was the fuel he used to ignite the fire of persecution.

On the first night that she was in the psychiatric ward, Monee woke up in a pool of blood. She was terrified. She thought she was hemorrhaging, but she had started her menstrual cycle. The stress and toxins that were still in her body were causing her flow to be very heavy. Her panties were soaked in blood, and the nurse suggested that Monee call her husband to bring her some more clothes. Monee was reluctant because she wasn't ready to speak to Nefarius yet, but she had no choice. She only had the clothes that she was wearing when she was taken to the hospital. She called Nefarius, and he refused to bring her anything. Monee cried and cried in the bed all that night. She was alone and heartbroken. This devil had her deceived that he was a God-fearing man, but to her demise, he was a wicked serpent filled with life-destroying venom.

But when Monee spoke to her sister Lisa the next morning, that victim button was shut off, and her warrior inside took control.

"Hey, Monee, how are you feeling today?" Lisa asked her sister in a gentle tone.

"I'm ok, I am just praying to God to show me why am I going through all this drama." Monee sighed deeply.

"Well, Nefarius said that you need help, so maybe this would be a good opportunity to take some time for you and let him take the kids for a while?" Lisa was still speaking in her gentle voice as if she was speaking to a child. She was very concerned about her sister, and Nefarius had done a great job of convincing her that Monee was strung out on drugs.

"What? Lisa, why are you talking to me like this?" Monee was agitated that Lisa was really believing that she was a drug addict. "Lisa, I am not addicted to drugs, and you know I would never smoke crack!" Monee yelled. "Yes, I snort coke sometimes, and it was stupid of me to allow myself to get that depressed to want to take my life, but I am not a drug addict! This man is trying to destroy me! I love my kids and will never allow him to corrupt them into hating me! I got to get the hell out of here and get my kids back!" A fire was lit inside of Monee that had been snuffed out years ago from all the hardship and battles she was fighting. But the realization that she was being spiritually attacked by the man whom she loved and married, the father of her children was enough to wake her up out of her misery. She was no longer the victim; she was the wounded warrior and was ready for war. Monee regained her inner strength and will to live.

"Look, Lisa, I am gonna be ok. The devastation that this man lied to me and pretended to want to reconcile our marriage—I gave up everything for him! I gave up my job, my home, my life to come to Atlanta! And for what? To find out that not only did he lie about having a home for us, but he used my personal belongs and furniture as ransom to control me! His family turned on me and my children. Living with his mother and sister to be reminded every day that we were not welcome!

"My own mother abandoned me when I needed her help the most! Here I am homeless with no money and no one to turn to! It was just too much! Way too much for me to keep it together, but you know what? I get it now! I gotta love myself even if no one else loves me. I know God loves me and he had you call me in Divine time to save my life, and I thank you both for that! I didn't die, and I am still here for a reason! Now, I am going to get the hell out of here and get my children back and restore my life. I love you, Lisa, and I will talk with you soon."

Monee was breathing heavily; her heart was beating fast, and her adrenaline was pumping. She was ready to fight for her children and her life.

"I love you, too, Monee, and I am sorry for believing his lies. I am with you, and I wish I could help you more. I will be praying for you and my nephews and niece!"

"Thanks, sis, talk to you later." Monee hung up the phone and went to go find her psychiatrist.

Monee went to the psychiatrist's office and found her doctor on the phone. She motioned for Monee to come into her office. Monee sat down in the chair across from the doctor's desk.

"Hi, Monee, how are you feeling today?" the doctor asked with a smile.

"I am better. I have a clear mind. Listen, Doc, I got to get out of here and get my children from their father. My husband is trying to destroy my character and take custody of my children, and I can't let that happen." Monee was looking at the doctor directly in her eyes and was speaking with a firm and calm tone.

"I understand. Monee, you did come to us as an attempted suicide patient and with a substantial amount of alcohol and drugs in your system. You don't think drug treatment would help you with your drug abuse?"

"Doctor, my problem isn't drugs. My problem is me allowing my husband to abuse me mentally and physically. My problem is not loving myself enough to recognize that I do not deserve this kind of abuse from anyone even if he is the father of my children and my husband."

"Yes, I understand that Monee, but you are also abusing yourself by using drugs."

"Yes, I have suffered a lot of abuse in my life, and I began to abuse myself because I didn't value myself. I learned at an early age that the way to deal with my stress and problems is to get high and drink alcohol. I now understand what self-medicating is, and all I wanted to do is numb the pain. Get high so that I didn't have to deal with my emotions and feel the hurt from my traumas. But I am by no means an addict. I consciously made a decision to use coke and alcohol the day I decided to take my life. I was hurting and was in my own pool of self-pity. I now realize that I am here in the world for a reason, and I do love myself, and I love my children, and they need me!"

Tears swelled up in Monee's eyes.

"Ok, I really do believe you, Monee. However, I am not sure that it is safe for me to discharge you, and you have nowhere else to go but back to your husband, and he is abusing you." The doctor sounded very concerned for Monee's safety.

"I understand. I am going to leave him when I get out of here. I am going to get my kids, and I will go to a shelter if I have to. Please, doctor, my children need me!"

"I have tried to call your husband several times, and he has not returned my phone calls. I would like to at least speak with him before discharging you so that maybe he will agree for the two of you to seek family counseling when you are discharged. I tell you what I will do. I will call him today and see if he will come here tomorrow for a meeting with the two of us. Tomorrow is your third day here anyway, so technically, you must remain here for 72 hours. Just complete your group sessions today, and we will speak again tomorrow."

"Ok, but I really don't think he is going to return your call. What if he doesn't agree to meet with us?"

"Well let's cross that bridge when we get to it, ok?" the doctor replied.

"Ok thank you, Doctor." Monee sighed and left the office.

During group therapy, Monee heard some very heart-wrenching testimonies from several patients in the psychiatric ward. Monee heard a prostitute share how she was forced into prostitution by her ex-boyfriend, and she eventually contracted HIV. From her anger and hatred of men, she kept prostituting and spreading the virus to her johns. She heard a homosexual man share how he was raped by his stepfather when he was younger and how it still haunts him today. Monee was in tears listening to these real-life horror stories. She realized that she had so much to be grateful for and that even though she had to struggle, things could be a lot worst.

"God, thank you for my blessings! Thank you that I did not die! But damn, God, why is it so much pain in this world?" Monee thought while sitting there listening to the other patients share.

That night, Monee wrote a prayer to God.

HEAVENLY FATHER, CREATOR OF ALL LIVING THINGS,

FATHER, I COME TO YOU TODAY WITH A BROKEN HEART AND CONTRITE SPIRIT. SOMETIMES, IT IS VERY DIFFICULT FOR ME TO HAVE HOPE IN A WORLD FILLED WITH SO MUCH PAIN AND DESPAIR. I KNOW I HIT ROCK BOTTOM AND FELT ALL HOPE WAS LOST; HOWEVER, YOU SPARED MY LIFE AND DIDN'T ALLOW ME TO COME HOME. I KNOW THAT AS LONG AS I AM BREATHING, I STILL HAVE A REASON TO BE HERE. YOU ARE SO MERCIFUL TO ME! THANK YOU FOR DIVINELY PROTECTING ME WHEN I REFUSED TO PROTECT MYSELF. THANK YOU FOR LOVING ME UNCONDITIONALLY EVEN THOUGH I HAVE NO CLUE HOW TO LOVE MYSELF. BUT WITH YOUR DIVINE WILL AND MY DESIRE TO HEAL AND SUCCEED AT THIS THING CALLED LIFE, I KNOW YOU WILL TEACH ME HOW TO LOVE MYSELF. GOD, YOU ARE THE WAY MAKER, YOU ARE THE MIRACLE WORKER, AND I NOW AM TRUSTING YOU TO DELIVER ME FROM THIS PIT OF DARKNESS AND REMOVE THESE RAVENOUS WOLVES IN SHEEP'S CLOTHING PRETENDING TO LOVE ME BUT THE ENTIRE TIME DESPISE MY LIGHT. THEY ARE INTIMIDATED BY MY STRENGTH AND AMAZED AT HOW I AM STILL BREATHING. NO WEAPONS FORMED AGAINST ME SHALL PROSPER, AND WITH YOU, FATHER I KNOW ANYTHING IS POSSIBLE! THANK YOU FOR SPARING MY LIFE SO THAT I CAN BE HERE FOR MY CHILDREN. THANK YOU FOR FORGIVING ME AS I WORK ON FORGIVING MYSELF!

I WILL ALWAYS PRAISE AND GLORIFY YOUR DIVINE NAME AND YOUR SON'S NAME,

SELAH

The next morning, Monee attended the required group therapy session. It was difficult for her to be present because all she kept thinking about was getting back to her children and starting a new life. She knew she didn't want to go back to Cleveland. Although Cleveland was home, she intuitively knew that if she went back, she was going back to her past, and she wanted a fresh start. It was time for her to start a new life, and Monee felt Atlanta would be the perfect city to do just that.

When the session was over, Monee headed straight to the doctor's office and was relieved to find the doctor in her office.

"Hi, Monee, come in. I was expecting you. How are you feeling this morning?" the doctor asked her in a clinical and professional tone.

"I am great! I am ready to start a new beginning. Did you speak with my husband?" Monee asked all in one breath.

"No, I didn't. He has not returned my calls. I am concerned for your safety, Monee. I can tell that your husband is not supportive of you and has not shown any interest in your recovery. However, I can tell that you made a bad decision and that you really do love yourself and your children. It is very difficult to be in an abusive relationship, and oftentimes, women don't see a logical way out. I will sign off on your discharge today on one condition…" The psychiatrist took a deep breath and was staring at Monee intensely. Monee was staring back at the doctor and hanging onto her every word. Monee wasn't breathing; she didn't want to miss not one word that the doctor was getting ready to speak. "Monee, here is my card. I want you to call me when you leave and let me know that you and your children are safe. Can you promise me that you will do that?" The doctor handed Monee her card.

"Oh, absolutely, Doc! I promise you I will call you, and I thank you so much for understanding what I have been going through and not judging me for making a terrible decision!" Monee exhaled and put the doctor's card into her hospital pants pocket. She had been wearing scrubs for the past two days since she had soiled her clothes in blood the first night there.

"Ok good. I will send your discharge papers to the nurse, and you should be ready to leave in a few hours or less. Once your paperwork has been completed, the nurse will come get you from your room. Do you have someone to come get you?"

"Yes, I will make arrangements when I get back to my room. Thank you again, doctor!" Monee said with a big smile on her face as she got up to leave the doctor's office.

Monee got back to her room and flopped on the hospital bed, staring at the phone on the table next to the bed. She knew that she had to call Nefarius to come get her because he had her car.

"Please, Lord, let this man do right and come get me from this hospital," Monee said before taking a deep breath and picking up the phone.

"Hello?" Nefarius asked, not recognizing the phone number.

"Hi, it's me. I am getting discharged now. Can you come get me from the hospital, please?" Monee knew this was not the time to show any animosity or anger toward her husband. She knew if she wanted to get her kids and leave him, it would have to be done in a way that he didn't see it coming. She had to pretend that she wanted to work things out long enough to figure out an exit strategy.

Monee was sitting by the window in the emergency room waiting area, watching every car that rode by anticipating seeing her car pull up to get her. About an hour has passed when she saw her car pull into the roundabout drop off section in front of the ER. Monee opened the car door and saw that it wasn't Nefarius driving her car. It was his best friend Que. Monee's blood began to boil. She was pissed.

"How the hell this devil gonna send Que to come get me in my car and this nigga ain't even got license to drive!" Monee thought, but she knew not to show any anger because Que would report every word to Nefarius once they returned. She took a deep breath and exhaled.

"Hey, Que," she said as she got into the passenger side of her car. "Why Nefarius didn't come?" Monee asked, not showing any emotion.

"Oh, he at home. He is cooking for you and the kids. So, he asked me could I come get you," Que said, pulling out of the parking lot.

"Oh, thanks for coming to get me, Que," Monee said sincerely. She always called Que Nefarius's crony. He did anything Nefarius would tell him and never stood up for himself. Monee hated the way Nefarius would talk about Que like he wasn't good for anything then would have him selling drugs and would take most of the profits.

"I am glad that you are all right, Monee. I know it's been rough for you since you been back in Atlanta. But I know you and Nef love each other, and y'all can work things out," Que said as he glanced over a Monee.

"Thanks, Que." Monee smirked and looked out of the car window. She wasn't in the mood to have a conversation; she was contemplating her plan to leave. Monee was consumed in her thoughts and didn't even realize that they were pulling up in front of the condo when Que said, "Welcome back!"

Monee got out of the car, and soon as she got to the door, her children ran up to her, grabbing her and hugging her. Monee was so happy to be reunited with her children, but it was bittersweet to have to interact with Nefarius and his family after all the chaos and drama they had been through. At first, Monee felt humiliation and embarrassment having to still live with Nefarius' mother and sister after attempting to take her own life. But then, she had a conversation with Nefarius' sister, and his sister apologized for how she had been isolating Monee and never took into consideration what Monee was going through dealing with her cold-hearted brother. At least his sister was able to be honest and show compassion for what Monee was going through. Monee felt relieved to know that at least someone acknowledged the madness that was going on, and even though it didn't make it right, it did for Monee make it real and that the spousal abuse was obvious to many who saw how Nefarius was mistreating her.

Monee was back at the condo for three days, and things seemed to become routine. Summer was coming to an end, so Monee knew she had to make some decisions quickly to get the children registered for school. Early one morning, there was a knock at the door of Nefarius' mother's condo. It was still dark outside, and everyone in the condo was still sleeping. Nefarius came out of his bedroom and asked Monee did she hear a knock at the door. Monee who had been sleeping with the kids on a pullout couch bed in the living room sat up on the bed and told him that she did hear a loud knock at the door.

Nefarius went to the door and opened the door with his gun in his back pants. It was a large man dressed in mechanic clothes with a clipboard standing at the door.

"Ugh good morning, sir, I'm John with Ford Motor Financial, and I am looking for Mrs. Monee Green," the man said in a firm but respectful voice. Monee could see that there was flashing red and yellow lights that was reflecting from the man's vehicle onto the front door. Monee stood up, and her heart fell to her feet. *"I know this can't be the police coming to arrest me for attempted suicide!"* Monee thought. She could barely breathe as she walked to the front door.

"John, what is this concerning?" Nefarius asked as he noticed that Monee was heading toward the door.

"Hi, are you Monee Green?" John asked as Monee stepped into the doorway next to Nefarius.

"Yes, I am," Monee said, slowly fighting to quiet her heartbeat so that she could hear what the man was going to say next.

"Ma'am, I am with Ford Motor Financial, and I have been instructed to come and take back your Ford Escape. I understand that $1,516.57 is past due on your finance loan for your vehicle, and unfortunately, we need the car back. Can you please sign right here and then retrieve all your belongings out of the Ford Escape please?" The man handed her the clipboard and pen. Monee took the clipboard out of John's hand.

"So, you are here to repossess my car?" Monee asked in denial but also was grateful that it wasn't the police. She took a long deep breath and then exhaled. She was searching her mind to say something to try to reverse the situation, but she knew the cold hard truth was she didn't have the money, and Nefarius was not helping her financially at all. She exhaled again.

"Yes, ma'am, unfortunately that is the case." He handed her the ink pen.

"How did you find me?" Monee asked as she took the pen from John.

"You made a phone call from a telephone number two months ago stating that you had intentions on paying your car payment, you just needed a few more weeks to get the money. The number was traced to this address." John looked at Monee as she stared blankly back at him. She could tell that he was beginning to feel uncomfortable with both Monee and Nefarius staring at him, and he began to slowly back out of the doorway onto the porch. Monee, however, had no intentions on being confrontational with this man. She understood that he was just doing his job, and she was grateful that he did give her an opportunity to get her belongings out of the car.

Monee's car had been her only place of refuge since she had been there. Her car was like her private bedroom. It was where she would go to talk on her phone to her family and friends back in Cleveland, smoke her cigarettes, cry, and pray without having to do so in the condo. Now, her place of refuge was gone. Monee stood out on the porch and watched John with Ford Motor Financial load her Ford Escape up onto the tow truck as tears rolled down her face.

"What next, Lord… what next?" Monee exclaimed.

Nefarius turned and went into the house and didn't say one word. He knew he was wrong, but his ego was too huge to allow him to acknowledge that he had failed his wife as a supporter and provider. Monee could hear Nefarius' mother asking her son what the hell was going on and Nefarius snapping at her telling her to go back to sleep. Monee stood on the porch until the tow truck was no longer in sight, and she heard a still small voice in her left ear say, "It's time for you to go, too." Monee went inside and laid back down with her children and cried until she fell asleep.

The next morning, Monee took the kids to the playground that was inside the condominium community. The playground was now Monee's new place of refuge. Monee watched her children play, and she decided it was time to make a move. Monee always had a hard time asking for help, but she knew that she was not going to get out of this mess alone. Monee reached out to her ex-co-worker Will, who had become a very good friend of hers back in Cleveland. He worked with her at the Department of Justice before she left Cleveland and moved back to Atlanta. Will was a great guy who loved Monee, but he was married. They became friends by him always putting fruit and flowers on her desk anonymously. This went on for at least three weeks until Monee got to work early, and he was the only one there. She asked him was he responsible for the mysterious gifts, and he confessed that he had a crush on her and wanted to become her friend. After that, they would often go to lunch together and meet for drinks during happy hour.

Monee called him and told him how things had gone seriously downhill with her and Nefarius' reconciliation. She shared with Will how she had lost all hope and tried to take her life. Will was Monee's confidante and was furious with her for not calling him to get the money for her to pay the first month's rent that she needed to move into the house or even to help her with her car payment before it got to the repossessed. Monee found out that the landlord rented the house out to someone else, so now, Monee had to find another place for her and the kids to go. Will suggested that he mail her his credit card, and they get a room at an extended stay until she could find a permeant home. Monee was so grateful, and for the first time in a long time she was beginning to see some light at the end of the long dark tunnel she was traveling down.

Monee stayed at the condo for a few more days, until she received the credit card in the mail. She kept her interaction with Nefarius to a bare minimum, which was easy to do because he had moved out of his mother's condo and went to live at his brother's house in East Point. Monee didn't mind because she didn't want to have anything to do with him. The day after Monee received the credit card in the mail, she packed up all of her and the kids' things, and Nefarius' sister dropped them off at the extended stay. His sister promised that she was not going to tell anyone where they were so that Nefarius would not find them. Monee was forced to come back to the present moment.

"*Crazy bitch*!" Nefarius shouted, into the jail phone.

O O O

"Do what to you again? You are a selfish, crazy bitch, I hope you know that, Monee!" Nefarius was furious.

"I'm a crazy bitch? Yeah, you know what, you are right! I got to be a crazy bitch to let you back into my life again after all of the hell you have put me through! And for me to think I was helping you! I let you back into my heart, my house, and my life again! You are right, I am a crazy bitch, but guess what, I bet you this is the last time I fall for your dumb shit!" Monee yelled and then slammed the phone down on the receiver. The other inmate who was on the phone next to her was annoyed.

"Damn, I am glad you got off the phone with that nigga. I couldn't even hear my boo! Yo ass talking so damn loud!" The inmate rolled her eyes and began talking on the phone again. Monee was pissed, and this was an opportunity to take it out on someone else.

"What the hell did you just say to me?" Monee snapped at the inmate that was on the phone next to her.

"You heard what I said—"

The corrections officer that was in the glass booth in the center of the jail belted out over the intercom, "Monee Green! Monee Green, report to the red line. You have a visit!"

Lost or Losing

God don't put no more on you than you can bare.
Well, then, why do my tears flow,
and my heart still has a huge tear?
All my life I try to do what's right,
but my life is dark as night.
I keep trying to hold on and fight,
but all the lies, deception, misconceptions,
and stress is taking away my bite.

What does it mean to live a righteous life?
A man can leave his kids and wife.
A woman can tolerate pain during childbirth
and continue to live in pain all of
her days on Earth.

Searching for answers,
looking in all directions,
desperately trying to make connections
to rectify the missed directions.
The sun is shining brightly,
but my mind is running crazy,
and all this bullshit is fazing me!
Things getting better, I try to see,
but I am so ready to give up
that I feel death calling me!
This is pushing me closer and closer to the ledge!
Between you and me is a huge wedge.

I am angry because of all the
false promises.

It's not up to me…
it's up to you,
so, what are you going to do?
You say call on you…
maybe I am not hearing You?
Maybe I am so lost
that peace I can't find?
Maybe that's what's causing me
to go out of my mind?

Reflections

Hitting Rock Bottom

Our environment in which we grew up has a direct impact on our perception of the world, how we interact in our relationships, and how we feel about ourselves. A "perfect" family and/or "perfect" childhood is nonexistent because there are no "perfect" human beings. We all make mistakes and have suffered pain in some way. Many of us have suffered through a traumatic event, even if we aren't aware that the experience was traumatic. Trauma is the response to a very disturbing event that severely hinders an individual's ability to function with a healthy state of mind and minimizes their sense of self and their ability to properly feel a full range of emotions and experiences. Trauma is subjective to the individual experiencing the event. Two people can experience the same trauma and process the experience differently. Abuse of power, sexual abuse, physical abuse, psychological abuse, neglect, betrayal, and loss of a loved one are all examples of circumstances that can cause trauma.

Traumatic events can cause an individual to experience a feeling of helplessness. Especially if that individual has experienced multiple traumatic experiences. Monee was raped at the age of five and molested a few years later. She witnessed domestic violence, first watching her mother being physically beaten and then experiencing physical abuse in her relationships with men as well. Never getting therapy or counseling to assist with healing and processing all the abuse, she learned to cope in her own dysfunctional way.

Self-medicating with drugs and alcohol are usually the most common methods that individuals try to numb or eliminate the pain they are experiencing from the emotions that are triggered by memories of the events. It was the verbal and physical abuse and betrayal that Monee experienced when she moved back to Atlanta to reconcile with Nefarius that sent her into a deep feeling of helplessness. When she realized she had nowhere to go and no support system, she lost the little hope she was holding onto and hit rock bottom. She thought taking her own life was her only way to free herself from all the pain she was feeling. Fortunately, she was not successful and found the strength and courage to get up from the bottom and take a stand and fight for her life. Monee realized that her life was just as important as her children's lives, and if she didn't nurture and take care of Monee first, she was not able to love and take care of anyone else.

Contemplate on the traumatic events that you have experienced in your life.

Do you feel you have healed? Why or Why not?

_____

_____

_____

_____

_____

_____

_____

_____

_____

_____

_____

_____

_____

_____

_____

_____

If your response was no, you do not feel that you have been healed? Write down the ways in which you feel those events are affecting you.

_____

_____

_____

_____

_____

_____

_____

_____

_____

_____

_____

_____

_____

_____

_____

_____

_____

_____

_____

_____

_____

_____

When we can look at ourselves and be honest enough to face our darkness within, then and only then are we able to begin the healing process. If we stay in denial and refuse to admit that we need to do our healing work, we prolong our healing and growth. If we wait too long, the Universe and/or God has a way of forcing us out of our comfort zones to see the light and begin to do the work. It is Monee's faith in a higher power inside and outside of herself that she connected with no matter what she was experiencing in her life. Her faith is what helped her rise from the pit of hopelessness and stand in her truth of empowerment to change her life.

Can you reflect and see how God/Source was using trials and traumatic events in your life to cause you to grow and learn more about yourself? What are some key lessons that you have learned by experiencing trauma?

_____

_____

_____

_____

_____

_____

_____

_____

_____

_____

_____

_____

_____

_____

_____

When Monee reflected on the traumatic events that she suffered in childhood, she began to question the Universal Law that she heard repeated so often, "Everything happens for a reason."

Do you see any events that you triumphed over and can offer assistance to help someone else that has experienced that same trauma? If so, how can you help someone?

_____

_____

_____

_____

_____

_____

_____

_____

_____

_____

_____

_____

_____

_____

_____

_____

_____

_____

_____

_____

_____

_____

_____

Affirmations for Healing from Trauma

I am healed.

My wellbeing and health are my top priority, and I am making right choices in all aspects of my life.

I am now listening to my body, loving my body, and giving it what it needs to heal.

I love my mind, I love my soul, and I love my body.

I am pure life force in a human body, and I am strong.

I am healing deeply and letting go of all thoughts, actions, and people who are not in alignment with my highest good.

I am allowing the intelligence of my body to heal naturally and completely.

I am thankful to be alive right now!

I declare healing over my body, mind, organs, cells, and spirit right now!

I am filling my mind with empowering thoughts.

I am in control of my thoughts and emotions, and I am safe. I am free, and I am love.

Scriptures to Read to Overcome Trauma, Trials, and Tribulations

The entire Book of Psalm is great to read.

Psalm 34 – Seek the Lord It is very encouraging; I recommend reading the entire Psalm. Here is an excerpt:
v 15. "The eyes of the Lord are on the righteous,
and His ears are open to their cry.
16. The face of the Lord is against those who do evil, to cut off the remembrance of them from the earth.
17. The righteous cry out and the Lord hears and delivers them out of all their troubles.
18. The Lord is near to those that have a broken heart and saves such as have a contrite spirit.
19. Many are the afflictions of the righteous, But the Lord delivers them out of them all.

Psalm 27 – Trust in the Lord and Be Not Afraid
v. 13 "I would have lost heart, unless I had believed that I would see the goodness of the Lord, In the land of the living.
v.14 Wait on the LORD; be of good courage, and HE shall strengthen your heart; Wait, I say, on the LORD!"

Psalm 147 – God Heals the Brokenhearted
v.3 "He heals the brokenhearted and binds up their wounds.
v. 4 He counts the number of the stars; He calls them all by name.
v.5 Great is our Lord, and mighty in power; His understanding is infinite.
v 6 The LORD lifts up the humble; He casts the wicked down to the ground"

Two Sides of the Same Coin

From the darkness of the womb came forth the light of the Earth!
From the deception of the mind to the truth of rebirth.
The flesh may conceal the sickness of the heart,
but with Faith, one's spirit can truly heal and have a new start.
Close your eyes so that they can become open.
Shut your mouth so that you can gain focus.
The Holy Spirit is real, this ain't no hocus pocus,
or some fake magic trick,
you must respect and repent,
and know that miracles are Heaven sent.
Don't be confused, Satan has abused all of God's children.
But with Trust and Faith in God,
Satan will never win!
Don't give up the fight
because from darkness emerges Light!

Chapter 5

God is Real

Monee completely forgot about arguing with the other female inmate and immediately went to the red line in front of the glass door. She was wondering who her visitor was as she waited impatiently for the large thick glass door to unlock and slide open. Monee stood there contemplating who knew she was in jail to even come to visit her. *"Maybe it's my mom and she changed her mind and is ready to bond me out?"* Monee was hopeful. While she was lost in her thoughts, she was startled by the loud click of the glass door unlocking. She walked through the door and went up the stairs to the visitation section of the jail. "Monee Green report to visitation booth number 3" the correction officer blurted loudly over the intercom.

Monee walked pasted the other inmates that were in booth one and two and took the seat in booth three. She was surprised to see that her visitor was Steven. Steven was Monee's manager and photographer when she was modeling. Monee was living in the townhouse for a few months and one day there was a knock at Monee's door, and it was Steven. He introduced himself as that guy that lived in the townhouse before Monee, and he wanted to know if Monee had been receiving his mail. He told her that he had to leave to go back to New York and didn't have time to submit a change of address to the post office before he moved.

Monee had in fact been saving the mail and had intentions on taking the mail to the post office but never got around to doing so. When she gave him the mail, he had asked her did she ever consider modeling and that was the beginning of their friendship and modeling venture. However, Monee fired Steven as her manager when she discovered that every time, he took her to industry parties and events he did not want her to network and promote herself to anyone. He wanted full control of Monee and her career.

"Steven! What are you doing here? How did you find out I was locked up?" Monee said with wonder and curiosity.

"That is what I should be asking you! Monee, girl what are you doing in jail? I went to your house after I had called you a few times and your husband was answering your phone. When I got to your house he and your kids was there. He told me you were in jail. I couldn't believe it! I asked him did the kids need anything and he got offended. Telling me to mind my own business and that everybody is fine. I said "What about Monee? Is she fine too? When is she getting out? How much is her bail?" Steven barely stopped to take a breath.

"Wow, yeah it's a long story but basically I got a possession charge and DUI. When did you go to my house? I just talked to Nefarius, and he didn't mention you to me. Maybe that is why he was so angry." Monee said.

"I went over there two days ago. Monee this guy doesn't seem to be doing anything to get you out of here. He seems content just taking care of the kids and living in your house. I see he is driving your car too. He pulled up as I was leaving because no one was there when I first arrived at your house. Where is your mother? Why hasn't she gotten you out?" Steven was genuinely concerned Monee could see it all over his face and in his questioning.

"She told me she was going to leave me in here. She thinks I was trying to kill myself." Monee said and then sighed.

"What is her number? This can't be happening; you need to be home taking care of your kids Monee! They need you. I am going to call your mother and talk to her. We are going to get you out of here, ok?" Steven said in a firm and determined tone.

"Thank you, Steven, I do need to be home with my kids! Please help me!" Monee gave Steven her mother's cell number, and the visitation time was up. Monee felt relieved that Steven came to see her and said he was going to help get her out of jail. However, she was also devastated to get the confirmation that Nefarius was really doing the same thing he did when she was at Dekalb Medical, showing that he really is a narcissist and loves only himself.

Monee returned to her cell to find Precious sleep under her cover and Ms. Isis was still out in common population waiting to use the phone. Monee climbed to her bunk and laid there staring at the ceiling. She was furious and panting. She couldn't believe that she settled once again. Sacrificed her principles and went against all logic and thought intuitively that it was her job to help Nefarius get back on his feet. *"How could I have been so stupid! I really thought God's was telling me to help him."*

Monee was distraught. *"I have been making major life changing decisions trying to force my life to be the way I think it should be. But even during those times that I thought I had things all figured out, ultimately it was a power greater than myself that was looking out for my highest good. God, you know me better than I know myself and I thank you for not allowing me to self-destruct!"* Hot tears began to run down her face.

She began to think about how everything fell into place after she left the hospital after her attempting suicide. Monee laid there and reflected on the synchronicities that helped her meet the right people to help her start her new life in Atlanta. *"Damn, it's very ironic that most of the devils that hurt me in my life were men. However, most of the angels that helped me were men too! Life is crazy!"* Monee thought to herself as she could hear Mr. Moses saying, "That's so sad Monee, so sad." in her head as she remembered how he helped her when she was homeless and staying in the extended stay.

○ ○ ○

After Monee had left the condo in Decatur, her and her children stayed at an extended stay for a couple of weeks. Monee had met a realtor who put her in touch with the owner of a vacant townhouse in College Park.

Monee spoke to the owner who lived in New York and told him her story. She poured her heart out to this stranger on the other side of the phone. All he kept saying was "That is so sad…that is so sad." The owner of the townhouse agreed to allow Monee to move in after she promised that she would clean it herself and use her own appliances which she had in storage. He agreed to give her a month to pay the first month rent. Monee was elated! She and her children were no longer homeless! God was showing up and showing out in Monee's life!

Monee had another angel help her at the storage center. The same employee who rented Nefarius that U-Haul truck that he used to move Monee to Atlanta. Told Monee that the only way she could get access to her storage unit if she had Nefarius call the storage facility and tell the employee that it was ok to add Monee to the account. The employee winked at Monee as she was telling her this. So, Monee was able to discern that the girl was giving her away to get her belongings. Monee had Will call and say he was Nefarius and to add Monee to the paperwork and that it was ok for her to get her things out of storage.

Monee was so relieved to finally have a place of peace, somewhere that they could call home. She was so thankful for the angels that God had strategically place in her life to help her on her journey. Within one month of Monee attempting to give up on herself and her creator, she was no longer homeless and was working a full-time job. Monee hadn't spoken to Nefarius since she left the condo. She was still communicating with his sister Carla who took her to the extended stay. Carla would give her the update on Nefarius and how he had got an apartment in College Park with his friend Que. Although Monee stilled loved Nefarius her feelings were numb towards him. She was focused on her and her children and starting a new life for them.

Monee was working as a bartender at a local club on Old National not too far from where she lived. After two months of working late nights and having to bum a ride home or take a taxi, Monee decided it was time to buy a car. One of the regulars that came to the club she was working at, gave her a business card of a car dealer that sold used cars to customers with bad credit and repossessions on their credit report. Monee decided to go to the dealership on her day off and hopefully get a car. When Monee got to the dealership everything seemed to go smoothly.

The car salesman told Monee that since she was working, she could get financing and walked her outside to show her some of the cars that were for sale and in Monee's price range. Monee saw an ice blue Honda Civic that grabbed her attention. The car salesman was showing her the features of the car when another salesman from the building shouted that he had an urgent call and needed to come quickly. The car salesman ran inside, and Monee continued to look at the Honda. While she was inspecting the tires, she noticed a utility vehicle pull into the car lot and park not too far from her. A man gets out of the vehicle and beings to inspect a convertible corvette parked three cars down from the Honda. He looked over and noticed Monee looking at the tire and shouted, "You not going to buy that car are you?" The man asked as he walked towards Monee.

"Why you want to buy it?" Monee asked turning towards the guard.

"No, I see you looking at the tires, do you know how many miles is on it?" The stranger asked Monee but didn't wait for her response. She opened the car door, turned the ignition key, and inspected the dashboard. "Un huh one-hundred and fifty thousand miles not bad for a Honda. But this ain't your car Miss." he said as he closed the car door and smiled at Monee.

"This ain't my car? Yes, it is, the car salesman just told me that this is a good running car and is in my price range, so if I wanted it, it's mine! It's not my car right now but it will be in an hour or so once we finish the paperwork." Monee said confidently.

"Yes, I understand what you are saying however, I am telling you this isn't your car. Mark my words, this maybe your car temporarily, but I feel like something better is coming your way. By the way, my name is Reggie. I own my own transportation company, here is my card in case you need anything please don't hesitate to call me." Reggie smiled at Monee as he handed her his business card. Monee was perplexed. *"Who is this guy and why is he telling me this isn't my car? He doesn't even know me. Who the hell do he think he is?"* Monee thought to herself as she took his card and began to examine it.

"My name is Monee, what kind of transportation services do you provide?" Monee said feeling very skeptical of this man's intentions but she's getting a "good old country boy" vibe from him. She noticed he had a wedding band on his finger, but she knew all too well that for most men being married didn't deter them from pursuing what they want.

"Monee, that's a pretty name for a beautiful lady! Where are you from, I know you aren't from around these parts." Reggie belts out a big deep hearty chuckle.

"I'm from Cleveland, I moved back here a few months ago. Where are you from?"

"I'm practically from Atlanta as long as I have been living here over 25 years, but I am originally from Mississippi..." Reggie was about to say more when the car salesman ran up to them and spoke to Reggie. Then told Monee that he needed to get going with the paperwork inside for the Honda because he had a family emergency and would need to leave soon.

"Well Monee it was a pleasure meeting you and you got my card, don't forget to call me if you need anything, seriously." Reggie turned and got into his vehicle and was gone as quickly as he had appeared. Monee and the car salesman went inside and took care of all the paperwork and within an hour Monee was driving off the lot in a 1996 Honda Civic! She was ecstatic, she was shouting and praising God all the way home. "Miracles do still happen!" she shouted.

Three days passed and Monee got a call from the car salesman who sold her the Honda, telling her that he was unsuccessful with getting a finance company to finance her loan with the recent repossession and her only being on her job for less than three months. The car salesman told Monee that she had to bring the car back within the next 24 hours.

Monee was devastated. She couldn't believe what she was hearing. "Damn why am I so unlucky? Why me God? Why am I going through this? All I want to do is take care of my kids and succeed in life! When am I going to win? When?" Monee shouted as she was driving to pick the kids up from school with tears running down her face. Monee pulled into the school parking lot and pulled over to wipe her tears and get herself together. She was a firm believer that she was the mother and that she would carry her burdens and not project them on her kids. They had suffered enough with dealing with Monee and Nefarius' separation. Then uprooting them and bringing them to Atlanta just to witness their parents fighting and their mother being suicidal and homeless. Her children were resilient through it all and they didn't need to carry her burdens now or forever more.

Monee picked up the kids from school and told them that they had to take the car back, but everything was going to be ok. She told them that it wasn't a good car and that they would just have to wait a little while longer until she could get a better car for them. Monee decided to stop at the grocery store and then drop the kids off at their townhouse before taking the car back to the dealership. The car salesman already told her that he would drive her back home, so she didn't have to worry about getting a ride home.

Monee and her children went to the grocery store and when they got to the car to put the groceries inside the trunk, she couldn't find the car keys in her purse. She looked inside the car and discovered that she had locked the car doors and had left the key in the ignition. "Oh no! Oh my God how could I have done something so stupid!" Monee exclaimed while staring at the keys. "What's wrong Mommy?" asked Eternity. "I locked the keys in the car!" Monee was in a panic. She could feel anxiety trying to invade her mind. Monee closed her eyes and took a long deep breath a technique she learned from the psychiatrist when she was at Dekalb Medical. Monee exhaled slowly, then she heard that still small voice in her left ear say, "Call Reggie." Monee thought to herself "Who is Reggie?" Then she remembered "The transportation guy!" she shouted out loud. Monee frantically searched through her purse and pulled out his business card. Next Monee pulled her cell phone out of her purse.

"It's gonna be ok y'all I am going to call this nice guy I met he should be able to unlock the car door. You all go and sit on the bench over there by the store for a minute. The children obeyed and darted off towards the bench that was in front of the store.

Monee dialed the phone number on the card. "Lord please let him answer." She said quietly to herself.

"Top Notch Transportation!" a man said with a deep and cheerful voice.

"Ugh yes, I am trying to reach Mr. Reggie…" Monee said.

"This is Reggie, how may I help you?"

"Hi Reggie, this is Monee. I met you a few days ago…"

"Yes hey Monee! I remember you! I gave you my card at the dealership on Jonesboro rd. How are things going girl?" Monee was relieved and she could tell he was happy to hear from her.

"Hi Reggie things aren't going too well right now. I am at the grocery store with my kids, and I locked the car key in the car. Do you happen to have that tool to un-lock car doors?" Monee asked prayerfully.

"Oh, so you did get the Honda Civic huh?"

"Yes and no. Seems as if your prediction came true. I got to return the car today. The car salesman said that he couldn't get me any financing." Monee said sadly.

"Oh wow, yeah, my spirit told me that that situation wasn't going to work out for you. Where are you at now?"

Monee told Reggie her location and he said that he wasn't too far from where she was. Reggie got there and was able to unlock the car door. He offered to take her home from the dealership, after some convincing on Reggie's part, Monee agreed to let him take her. Her intuition was telling her that he was a God-fearing man and that he was here to help. Monee told Reggie that she would call him when she was head-ed to the car lot, and he would meet her there.

That was the beginning of their friendship. Monee returned the Honda Civic and Reggie took her home. They sat out in his limousine and talked for hours. Reggie told her how his transportation business was very successful, but he was unhappily mar-ried. Monee shared how she had been through hell and back dealing with her husband

and how she had to fight to get her name on her storage unit but wasn't able to afford to pay to get a U-Haul and get her furniture from the storage unit yet.

Reggie was an angel in disguise. He told Monee that God told him to help her when he saw her at the car dealership. He didn't know how and when but that was why he gave her his business card. Now it was making sense to him. Reggie paid two guys and the U-Haul storage fee and took Monee to get her things out of storage that weekend.

Monee was in awe! She knew God was real but to witness and be a recipient of so many miracles was humbling for her. She was feeling so blessed and grateful that after so many people that she allowed into her life that betrayed her, she was hesitant to allow anyone to get close to her again. However, Reggie made it easy for her to trust him and his friendship was difficult to resist. He had a heart of gold and a genuine interest in Monee. He showed her compassion and a willingness to help that made her heart melt.

A month later Reggie had called Monee and told her that he was driving down Old National and saw a car for sale for $1000 and wanted to take her to look at it. Monee told Reggie that she didn't have that much saved yet and he insisted that they go and look at the car. Monee finally agreed since the car was around the corner on Old National. Two hours later they were at the seller's house looking at the car. It was a white Nissan sedan.

"Do you like it Monee? It's in good condition and doesn't have an excessive number of miles on it. I think it will be a good temporary car for you and the kids until you can afford something better." Reggie said.

"Yes, I do like it however Reggie I told you that I don't have a thousand dollars right now." Monee sighed.

"I didn't ask you for any money, did I?" Reggie stated in a firm tone and then smiled. He turned to the woman who was selling the car and handed her a wad of cash.

"Ma'am that is one thousand dollars cash, all we need it the title and we will take this car off of your hands." Reggie said then turned and looked at Monee who was smiling from ear to ear. The woman turned to go inside her house to get the title. Monee ran to Reggie and gave him a huge hug and said, "Thank you, thank you, thank you!"

"I can pay you back, how about I pay you fifty dollars a week until I pay it off? Will that work for you?" Monee asked sincerely.

"You just don't get it do you? Monee, I didn't ask you for any money. When God places it on someone's heart to bless you receive it. Otherwise, you are telling God that you are not worthy of His blessings! Do you not feel worthy?" Reggie said then sighed.

Monee stared at Reggie as she processed the words of wisdom, he had just shared with her. Tears swelled in her eyes and began to fall. She realized that what Reggie said was truth. She had learned about the law of attraction when she was in college and was in network marketing with Dabir, but she threw a lot of that out the window when her marriage became so dysfunctional. Sometimes in life, our greatest problems are attached to those we love, so that we can learn our greatest lessons.

Monee took a long deep breath. "I am worthy, and I am grateful to you and to God for sending you to be my friend. Thank you, Reggie!"

o O o

Monee was interrupted from her memory "Hey girl, I didn't hear you come back in here, where's Ms. Isis?" Precious asked as she raised up from under her sheet like the dead being resurrected from the grave.

"She still waiting to get her phone call. I came back to calm down after arguing with my husband." Monee sighed.

"Again! Damn y'all argue every time y'all talk. What was the argument about this time?" Precious asked feeling concerned and irritated.

"Girl, he ain't going to do a damn thing to get me out of here. He's laying up in my house, driving my car and taking care of our kids so he good. He don't need me to come back anytime soon. I guess he going to just ride this wave until it takes him to the shore. You know Precious as I was laying here contemplating about my life. I now realize that for every devil that tried to destroy me, God sent one of his angels to help build me back up!" Monee said with a sense of gratitude in her voice and in her heart. Before Precious could respond the loud clicking sound that the steel jail cell door made every time it unlocked to slide open; interrupted the inmates conversation. As the door slide open Ms. Isis waddled in breathing hard and sweating.

"Ms. Isis are you ok you don't look too well." Monee asked as she sat up on her bunk bed.

"Chile, I don't know why these folks can't get my meds right! It just doesn't make any sense. I had a bottle of my high blood pressure pills in my purse when they arrested me, but they want to prescribe me a new prescription instead of giving me my meds my doctor prescribed me! Now these pills have my heart racing and my body temperature all out of whack. I will be alright I just need to sit down and rest for a little while." Ms. Isis plopped down on the bottom bunk beneath Monee and slid her back up against the wall to give her support as she sat on the bed.

"Ms. Isis are you ok? I can hear you breathing way up here!" Monee was concerned she had never heard Ms. Isis panting so hard. There was a total of thirteen steps from the lower level of the jail where the common eating area, showers and phones were to get to the second level where their jail cells are located. It shouldn't cause anyone to breathe that heavily to climb those steps.

"Chile, I don't know, I am feeling a bit light headed. I should be ok in a few minutes once I rest. It just doesn't make any sense why all the inmates in this pod have to use the phone at the same time. It took forever for me to get a chance to call my son! But the Lawd is so merciful! I was able to speak to my son and tell him how much I love him before he left to go to work." Ms. Isis says with a mild chuckle and then she begins to choke.

"Monee something not right with her! She looks very pale in the face!" Precious stated in a panic. Ms. Isis begins to grasp for air. Monee jumps down from her top bunk to look at Ms. Isis.

"Yeah, she is very pale! Ms. Isis can you hear me? Isis!" Monee is now in a panic too. Ms. Isis eyes are now closed, and her body slowly slides from her upright position, and she collapses on the bunk bed. Monee bends over her to listen to see if she is still breathing and realizes the Ms. Isis's breathing is very shallow.

"Precious get help!!!" Monee yells. Precious jumps up from her mat on the floor and runs to the big steel locked door and begins banging hysterically on the door. Monee grabs he wash cloth and runs the cold water from the sink on it, quickly squeezes it and places it across Ms. Isis' sweating forehead.

"Ms. Isis can you hear me? Say something please!" Monee pleaded.

"Monee, God told me to tell you that You are a star, and you need to let your light shine...don't dim your light even if you are in a room full of dark souls. You shine Monee. Shine!" Ms. Isis said in a very weak voice as she grabbed Monee's hand and squeezed her hand so tight Monee thought she was trying to hurt her. Ms. Isis words triggered a memory that Monee has never been able to forget.

○ ○ ○

Monee was twelve years old, and it was Easter Sunday. Monee, her mother, and her Aunt Veronica was attending Easter Sunday service at a local church not too far from where Monee lived. Pastor Ann Jackson was a wise older woman that loved Jesus Christ and was known throughout the congregation to have the gift of prophesy. Pastor Jackson was the residing Pastor of this non-denominational Christian church. Monee and her mother were invited to attend by Virginia's sister Veronica. None of Monee's siblings wanted to come and remained home.

After Virginia almost died from the abusive hands of her third husband and she divorced him; she began to seek out a greater meaning for life. Virginia was hungry to discover her true purpose in life and began her quest for inner peace by visiting different churches, temples and spiritual classes. As a young girl Monee found religion interesting and her father would often read the Watch Tower magazines to her when she went to visit him. Her father was Jehovah Witness. Monee and her dad would discuss religion and his beliefs often. Monee always found religion and the mysteries of a higher power interesting.

So, when her mother would go visit the different religion services Monee always would go with her. Monee found Pastor Jackson to be intriguing. This was the first time that she attended a church service that was led by a female pastor. Pastor Jackson was very beautiful to Monee as well. She was tall and very thin with caramel smooth skin with small wrinkles in her face. Her eyes were hazel and were very mystical and she had short sandy brown, curly hair. Monee estimated that the beautiful God-fearing woman was at least in her early sixties. Pastor Jackson emanated a power and strength that Monee admired.

Monee listened casually to the sermon, but towards the end of the sermon she heard Pastor Ann state that she was going to invoke the power of Jesus Christ to fill and anoint the entire church. That captured Monee's attention. After Pastor Ann belted out a long prayer and invocation to Jesus. She instructed the entire congregation to close their eyes and visualize themselves in a circle of divine white protective light. Monee obeyed and did exactly as the Pastor said. Then Pastor Ann instructed the congregation to include their loved ones within the circle of divine white all around them as well. Then she told them to include Jesus and God, hovering over them and the congregation all within the divine white healing light.

Next Pastor Ann told the entire congregation to join hands. So, Monee who was sitting in between her aunt and her mother grabbed both of their hands. Pastor Ann began to walk in the middle of the aisle starting with the row of member that were closest to the alter and she would grab the hands of both of the people that were sitting in the first chair that was closest to the aisle. All the while Pastor Ann was shouting for the holy presence of Christ to fill the church and make his presence known to the congregation.

Monee could hear a few people began to scream and cry as Pastor Ann grabbed the hands of the two people in each row. Monee was sitting in about the seventh row from the alter and she kept her eyes closed even though she could tell Pastor Ann voice was getting closer as she continued to shout, praise, and worship to Jesus and invoke him to make his powerful presence known.

Monee could feel that Pastor Ann was now holding her mother's hand because she was sitting in the chair closest to the aisle. She heard Pastor Ann speaking in tongues and shouting praises to Jesus when Monee felt an energetic force enter her body from the center of the top of her head and quickly travel down through the center of her body until the force was at her navel and then she felt a circular swirl of the energy before quickly exiting her body through her feet.

Monee opened her eyes, turned to her mother, and asked her mother did she feel the same energetic force and her mother asked her what she was talking about. Monee told her mother what she had just felt and then turned to her Aunt Veronica and asked her did she fell the same energy, her Aunt told her no. Monee was amazed! She couldn't understand why she was the only one between the three of them that felt what she experienced.

Once service was over Aunt Veronica took Monee and her mother to meet Pastor Ann. Pastor Ann looked at Monee and cupped Monee's chin with her right hand, smiled and said, "Shine bright star, shine your light." the tall thin Pastor smiled and gave Monee a tight hug. Monee wanted to tell the Pastor about what she had experienced during her invocation, but she was too shy to speak and kept quiet. However, Monee left that church that day knowing that there was a higher power and God is real.

"Monee! Monee what is happening? Is she breathing?" Monee could hear Precious' voice coming from a faint background noise to a loud persistent yell in Monee's ears. Monee looked down at Ms. Isis and her eyes were fluttering.

"I think she is having a heart attack Precious!" Monee runs to the door and start banging on the door too. both inmates are yelling from the top of their lungs for help. It seemed like they were banging on the door for at least fifteen minutes before they could hear the loud click of the door unlocking and Officer Tate is standing at the door as it slowly slides open.

"What the hell is going on in here, are you too fighting? Get back both of you! Get back into your cell now!" Officer Tate yelled.

"Please Officer it is Ms. Isis! I think she is having a heart attack! Help her please!" Monee yelled. Officer Tate spoke into her walkie talkie to call for back up.

"Move Monee you two get up against that wall! Move now!"

Monee and Precious backed up against the wall opposite the bunk beds and watched Officer Tate called out to Ms. Isis and examined her. Officer Tate spoke into her walkie talkie and stated that the inmate is nonresponsive and medical assistance is requested. Officer Tate began to perform CPR on Ms. Isis immediately. Precious began crying hysterically and Monee told her to stay calm. Monee was in shock, but she knew Ms. Isis was going to be ok. Monee began praying.

"God please heal Ms. Isis and let her be ok." Monee said as tears began to run down her face as well. Three more officers rushed into the jail cell. One of the officers commanded Monee and Precious to step outside of the cell and face the wall. The girls obeyed and they could hear the officers working on Ms. Isis. A feeling of dread consumed Monee and she looked towards the cell to see several officers run up the steps with a gurney. Moments later the officers were leaving back out the room with Ms. Isis on the gurney and a sheet over her body.

"No! No! No! She's not dead! She just needed the right medication! Y'all killed her!!!" Monee yelled as she collapsed to the floor crying and screaming. Precious was screaming and cussing too. "Y'all devils is going to pay for this! Murders! Y'all all got blood on your hands!" Precious yelled at the officers. Two of the remaining officers that did not help take Ms. Isis out of the room came over to Monee and Precious and instructed them to go back into their cell.

"You mean to tell me that we got to go back in that cell after Ms. Isis just died in there?" Precious was hysterical.

"Yes, you do! You think you at the Marriott or something? Get your ass back into your cell!" The officer grabbed Precious and shoved her into the cell as Monee obediently followed them back into the cell and said nothing. Monee was in shock. She couldn't believe what was happening.

Reflections

Intuition & Synchronies

When we leave the spirit realm to enter this physical dimension, we are equipped with an inner guidance system also known as intuition. Intuition is an inner knowing or feeling about something without having to get conscious confirmation before making a decision or taking certain action. It is commonly known as our "sixth sense," or "gut feeling," and "something told me…" It wasn't until Monee moved to Atlanta that she begin to listen to her intuition more. Challenges and obstacles in our lives can cause a person to use dormant gifts that they didn't even realize they had.

Adversity has a way of causing a person to stretch and grow spiritually and mentally. Imagine being lost in a dense forest without a map and compass. You know that you must find a road before it gets dark, and the temperature drops to below freezing and it is possible you won't survive until the morning. What would you do? You would use everything you have to survive. Whatever items you have in your pack, your knowledge about the forest and your instincts to help you find the road before dark.

Can you think of a time in your life where you listened to your intuition? If so, write down how that benefited you during that time.

_____

_____

_____

_____

_____

_____

_____

_____

_____

_____

_____

_____

_____

Meditation, chanting mantras and breathing techniques are a few tools that are used to strengthen the ability to use this "sixth sense," without having to experience a challenge to tap into this gift.

Would you like to use or strengthen your gift of intuition? If so, write down a few techniques that you would be interested in learning more about:

_____

_____

_____

_____

_____

_____

_____

_____

_____

_____

_____

Monee had a supernatural experience in church where she felt the spirit of God. After that event, her life was forever changed because that experience caused her to no longer question if there was a power greater than herself. She knew that it was. Therefore, the experience increased her faith and caused her to pray and talk to God throughout her entire life. Even though she wasn't completely conscious of how God was working in and through her life she knew there was a God.

Do you believe in a power greater than yourself? If so, have you had any supernatural experiences or witnessed any miracles in your life that has increased your faith or encouraged you in some way? Write down how these events affected you:

_____

_____

_____

_____

_____

_____

_____

_____

_____

_____

_____

_____

_____

_____

_____

_____

_____

_____

The Universal Law of Oneness and the Power of Synchronicities

Everything and everyone is connected on an energetic level, this is the Universal Law of Divine Oneness. Synchronicities occur because our thoughts, feelings and actions are all energy. Energy is transmitted through the universe through waves and vibration, thus depending on the vibrational frequency of our thoughts, feelings and actions will determine the result. If an individual is thinking negative thoughts that vibration is lower than an individual that is thinking thoughts of abundance.

Monee wanted a desire for a better life when she was living in Ohio. Her thoughts were an inquiry of how she can obtain a better life for her and her son. She began to receive messages from people that suggested that she should move to Atlanta. She was open to the idea and an opportunity presented itself for her to move to Atlanta. Although, Monee faced challenges in Atlanta; it was those challenges that caused her to grow and expand her consciousness.

Some people choose to ignore synchronistic messages and justify it as nothing but coincidence. However, that can result in missed opportunities and life cycles repeating. Synchronicities can occur when overcoming obstacles in life, creative inspiration, to receive answers, confirmation when in doubt what to do, confirmation to act on an idea or hunch. Every situation is different; however, it is our job to be aware and conscious that we are in communication with the Universe and God daily. Therefore, be aware of the messages we send out and receiving.

Can you identify a synchronistic event that happened in your life? Write down how that synchronistic assisted you in some way:

_____

_____

_____

_____

_____

_____

_____

_____

_____

_____

_____

_____

_____

_____

_____

_____

_____

_____

_____

_____

_____

_____

_____

Affirmations for Increasing Your Intuition

I am allowing my life to unfold. Everything is how it should be, and I am safe.

I am grateful to have a gift of intuition and I am connected to my higher self now.

I am trusting the intuitive guidance that I receive.

I am trusting my inner voice.

I am opening up to receive wisdom and guidance that is for my highest good.

I am a spiritual warrior of light, and I am always connected to Source Energy.

I am all that is, and all is within me.

I am the light and the more I listen to my inner guidance; the more life gets easier to navigate.

I am controlling my thoughts, emotions, and actions to work to manifest all things that are in alignment with my highest good.

Scriptures to Read to Gain Inner Wisdom

Psalm 119 v.18 "Open my eyes, that I may see wonderous things from Your law."

John Chapter 14 v. 26 "But the Helper, the Holy Spirit, whom the Father will send in My name, He will teach you all things, and bring to your remembrance all things that I said to you."

John Chapter 15 v. 26 "But when the Helper comes, whom I shall send to you from the Father, the Spirit of truth who proceeds from the Father, He will testify of Me."

Genesis Chapter 1 v 27 "So God created man in His own image; in the image of God He created him; male and female He created them.

1 Corinthians Chapter 2 – Read the entire chapter to get the full understanding of Heavenly Wisdom. Here are a few verses:
v. 12 "Now we have received, not the spirit of the world, but the Spirit who is from God, that we might know the things that have been freely given to us by God.

v. 13 These things we also speak, not in words which man's wisdom teaches but which the Holy Spirit teaches, comparing spiritual things with spiritual.
v. 14 But the natural man does not receive the things of the Spirit of God, for they are foolishness to him; nor can he know them because they are spiritually discerned.

v. 15 But he who is spiritual judges all things, yet he himself is rightly judged by no one."

I Forgive

Through all the days that we live our lives
there are times we hurt and experience things
that cause us tears.
Some of those days are filled with
wails and cries.

Some of the hurt is caused by
life's trials and tribulations,
but often there are people
who inflict the most dreadful pain.

A child's life should be
filled with joy and happiness…
some of God's children grow up with
a deep inner sadness.

They became the prey of raging vicious wolves,
trying to eat away at their flesh.
Pain caused by all
the unbearable madness.

Through all the days of
our lives…
Some of those days are filled with
wails and cries.

Pain is often inflicted by people
whose souls have been constricted.
Their energy is misdirected
because from their creator
they are disconnected.
Forced to interact
God's righteous children the wicked affect.
The scars of all the dreadful pain are re-opened when
the devil attacks us once again.
Greater is the one who can forgive
than the one who holds hate
in their heart refusing to forgive.
Live and let Live!

Chapter 6

The Devil is a Liar

Monee and Precious was left alone in their cell to process Ms. Isis' death on their own. It was surreal. Monee was sitting on the top bunk in a daze and Precious on her mat hugging her knees rocking back and forth as if in a trance.

"I have lost a lot of loved ones in my life, but I never actually witness someone dying." Monee said feeling broken.

"I lost my mother when I was seven. She was beautiful and miserable. I came home one day from school and found her on her bedroom floor in a pool of blood. I turned her over and she was bleeding from her neck. My stepfather had cut her throat earlier that morning." Precious began to cry harder. "I still can smell her blood!"

Monee jumped down from her bunk and sat next to her cellmate and grabbed her.

"That is awful Precious! My God, I am so sorry to hear that! Why did he do that do her?" Monee couldn't believe what she was hearing.

"He thought that she was having an affair, but she wasn't. He was the real jealous, possessive type that had an inferiority complex. My mother couldn't go anywhere without him questioning her or accusing her of being with another man. It was all in his head. He was crazy! He took my mother away from me!"

Precious began sobbing in Monee's arms. "That's why I will never give myself to a crazy, perverted twisted ass man! They are all devils! He would come into my room at night when my mother was sleep and rape me! He told me not to say anything or he would kill my mother. For six years I let him do that to me and he killed her anyway!" Precious yelled hysterically.

"That is horrible, I am so sorry that happened to you! I witnessed my mother go through a very abusive marriage too. This was her third marriage to an ex-convict, and he was evil too. She went through four years of getting black eyes, broken bones and being called every curse word that exists. Every night I would lay in my bed and cringe when I would hear his fists hitting her and my mother wailing in agony. For those four years every day I wanted to kill myself." Monee said sadly.

"Why did you want to kill yourself Monee?" Precious asked as she got up to get the roll of hard toilet paper from the steel sink to blow her nose.

"Because I could have prevented the marriage." Monee began to cry.

"My mother moved him in our home before they were even engaged and one afternoon during nap time, he got in the bed with me and made me touch and squeeze his penis. This grown ass, dirty man grabs my hand and makes me jack him off! And I never told my mother! I never said anything. I was so stupid; how could I have let her suffer for that long? I could have saved her from all that pain and misery!" Monee broke down.

She had never shared that story with anyone and to actually speak those words brought it all to the surface and it was devasting. However, hearing Precious' testimony Monee realized that her suffering in silence was nothing compared to finding your mother dead in a pool of blood. No matter what we are going through there is someone else going through something ten times worst!

"I usually write my prayers, but I feel like praying for Ms. Isis and for the both of us right now. Precious would you pray with me?" Monee asked staring at Precious intensely. Monee slid in front of Precious on her mat and grabbed Precious' hands into hers as they both were sitting with their legs crossed. Both closed their eyes and Monee took a long deep sigh.

"Dear Heavenly Father, Creator of all things. Father, I first want to thank you for granting us life! Thank you for Your Divine Mercy, Grace and Lovingkindness. Thank you for Your miracles for I know you are a miracle worker! Father, I know that you make ways out of no way! Father, we just witnessed the passing of Ms. Isis and we both know that she is now with you. May you bless her soul. Father, I ask that You heal your children on this Earth! We have suffered so much pain and misery, but I know that it all is for naught. I know it will be for Your Glory Father! Hallelujah! Father, I ask that You heal Precious, comfort her, and remove the demons that are still haunting her and myself as well. Send Your Divine Healing Light to surround us now even as we sit here in this jail cell not knowing what the future holds for the both of us. We trust you and know that You are in control. As it is spoken so let it be done. Selah" Monee took another deep sigh.

"That was beautiful Monee and I actually feel better!" Precious said and then gave Monee a tight hug. Monee climbed back up to her bed.

"You know Precious, I have been through a lot in my life. I was raped when I was five years old and it seemed that once that happened to me the Devil just kept coming in many forms in my life, but mainly through men. Since I have been locked up, I have been experiencing flashbacks of parts of my life and I am realizing that the Devil only have as much power that we, God's children; give him in our lives. What is the Devil exactly? Is he really some demon with horns and a long tail traveling through the earth to get God's children to sell their soul? I think not. I have been studying the bible for years now and from my research, I believe that yes, Lucifer was a fallen angel and was cast down here on earth along with one-third of the other angels. However, to me the devil is a spirit. It is the spirit of evil, ego, hatred, selfishness, any negative thoughts, and behaviors that contaminate our mind, body and soul." Monee took a brief pause to contemplate her own words.

"Wow Monee, I have never heard it put that way. That is something to think about. My mother use to take me to church, but I started to hate going to church because the more she went it seemed the more depressed she got. She always thought of herself as a sinner and that she was being punished for her sins. She told me that being born in this world as a sinner comes with the consequence of suffering and the blessings of accepting Christ as our Lord and Savior. I used to ask her, "Mommy if there are blessings accepting Christ and you accepted Christ as your Lord and Savior years ago then why are we not being blessed? And you know what Monee? She could never answer my question! She would always tell me to go play or would get angry with me and start yelling at me!" Precious said shaking her head.

"Yes, I feel religion is like a riddle that the believer must solve to find the true passageway to enlightenment. Christ, Buddha, Gandhi, Mohammad, all ascended masters are beacons of light to be examples of the divine power that is within us all. The power just remains dormant inside of us because we don't believe that we can achieve higher spiritual consciousness. We are trained to think of God as being an external deity in heaven and not a God force that dwell within us that we have access to all the time." Monee paused and looked down at Precious. Precious was lying on her mat, snuggled up with her sheet as if it was a teddy bear listening intensively to Monee.

"But you know what Precious? I don't understand how a loving and merciful God would allow so many bad things to happen to children! I can't understand how God would allow a child to get abused and hurt, hell good people have been suffering at the hands of evil doers since the beginning of mankind, so I don't know girl, I just am babbling." Monee sighed.

"Monee do you think Ms. Isis died because they gave her the wrong medication, or do you think it was her time to go?" Precious asked in a slow monotone voice as if to be pondering the answer at the same time she was asking the question.

"I think it was both. I think the prison system is not designed to provide adequate care for the prisoners. It is all a business and at the end of the day, each inmate is only worth free labor and revenue. It is institutionalized slavery and when Ms. Isis kept telling them that she was having adverse effects from the medication the jail doctor prescribed her, he should have prescribed her the medication that she was taking when she came in here! So yes, I believe the doctor must take some responsibility for her death, but I also think she was ready to go because she didn't resist. Precious, it just seemed like one minute she was here and the next minute she was gone! And you know the look in her eyes when she was talking to me was like she had seen God, if that makes any sense? What she said to me struck my soul because I was told that before. It was eerie girl!" Monee looked down at Precious to see that she had fallen asleep.

Monee wasn't surprised because in jail that is one of the main things inmates do to pass time is read, sleep and exercise. Monee was tired too; she had experienced so many emotions within a few hours, and she hadn't had a chance to process any of it. Especially seeing Steven and what he confirmed about Nefarius not caring nor wanting to do anything to get her out of jail.

"All of this because I went through a stupid roadblock! Damn!" Monee mumbled to herself as she rolled over and fell asleep.

"Monee! Monee! Wake up! Wake up girl are you ok?" Precious was standing on the bottom bunk leaning over Monee shaking her to wake her. Monee sits up startled.

"Yeah, girl what's wrong? Why are you shaking me?" Monee asked confused and a bit irritated with Precious.

"You were making loud moaning sounds in your sleep and your body was jerking periodically like you were being shaken or tossed around! Look at your shirt you are soaking wet! You are sweating like you have been working out!" Precious was looking at Monee like she was crazy as she stood in front of the bed staring at Monee.

"That's crazy! I was dreaming that I was on a large ship in a storm. The sky was like a dark indigo blue and was filled with thick storm clouds. It was thundering and lightening loud, and the waves of the ocean was forcing the ship to violently rock back and forth like it was almost about to capsize! I was so scared, I felt like I was about to die! Suddenly, the storm stopped, and the sun came out. The sky was a beautiful azure blue and the ship stopped rocking and that's when you woke me up." Monee said as she examined her shirt realizing how sweaty she was.

"Azure blue! What the hell is that? Damn they got me locked up with a street nerd!" Precious began laughing hysterically, Monee joined in. Their laughter was abruptly interrupted, and their bodies jolted by the loud click of the jail cell door unlocking and slowly slid open.

"What is going on now? We already had dinner." Precious blurted out while throwing her hands on her hips.

"Girl, I don't know." Monee smacked her lips and hopped down from her bunk and quickly grabbed another green shirt with "INMATE" written across the back of it from underneath her mattress. She managed to change shirts right before hearing Officer Tate over the intercom, commanding all inmates to step out of their cells and stand against the wall.

Monee and Precious stepped out of their cell and stood with their backs up against the wall and quietly watched the other female inmates emerge from their cells and do the same. The main entrance door unlocked and in walks the County Sheriff Napoleon Hill with four other officers following him. Sheriff Hill was the head of the county jail and he made sure the entire city, his staff and inmates knew he was in charge. He often usurped his power unjustly and was rumored to be involved in some city corruption. He was known for making routine appearances in each jail, male and female to keep the inmates in submission to his authority.

"Today, I was informed that an inmate in this pod passed away from natural causes. In unfortunate times like these, we know how disheartening and difficult it can be for some to handle. Myself and my staff are aware that Ms. Isis, although she had not been here for a long time, made a positive impact on many of you in this pod. So, this evening, I have decided to allow Chaplin Bryant to hold an hour prayer circle and memorial service in honor of Ms. Isis' life. This service is starting now for any inmate who would like to attend and for those who do not want to attend, can return to their cells now." Sheriff Hill said in a firm but solemn voice. Then he left the pod. The four officers remained to keep order and to watch as some of the inmates began to head to the jail sanctuary and others returned to their cells.

"Come on Precious ain't you gonna go?" Monee asked her cellmate as Precious turned to walk back inside their jail cell. "Nah, I don't have much to say to God right now. I'm good. I already said my goodbye to Ms. Isis…she's in a better place now…hopefully. You go. I'm going back to sleep." Precious said indifferently.

"Yes, I get it. I have issues with the Lord too, but I know He is real, and we can never stop seeking His mercy and grace!" Monee said loudly hoping her cellmate would change her mind. But she didn't, after Precious walked into the cell that intimidating loud click sounded and all the jail cell doors simultaneously slid closed. The sound of Ms. Isis struggling to breathe haunted Monee as she walked down the stairs and head to the sanctuary.

Monee walked inside the sanctuary and was quite impressed with the décor. It looked like a mini church and felt like one too. For a second, Monee forgot that she was inside of a jail. The alter was elevated on a small stage and there were violet drapes that covered the wall behind the alter. There were real flowers sitting in tall vases on both ends of the stage and there were five rows of real church benches on both sides of the room with a violet carpet that flowed down the center of the aisle for the inmates to walk on as they entered the sanctuary. Monee walked down the middle aisle to find a seat. She was surprised that it was about twenty women sitting randomly on the church benches on both sides of the room.

"Wow Ms. Isis, so I see I wasn't the only one that you shared your wisdom with. May God bless your sweet soul!" Monee whispered as she sat down in the first row on the right side of the sanctuary, next to another inmate who was reading one of the bibles that were placed in pockets attached to the benches.

The chaplain came out of an office that she used for private counsel for the inmates. She walked up to the alter with bible in hand. She gracefully laid the bible on the pulpit and slowly opened it.

"Good evening everyone, I am Chaplin Bryant, most of you know me by Chaplin Debra. I have been Chaplin here for over twenty years and I have watched many inmates come and go and sometimes return. I spoke with Ms. Isis briefly the other day before the Lord called her home. She was a kind-hearted woman with a mighty spirit! Let's bow our heads in prayer."

Chaplin Bryant was a short and stout woman with long brown hair. She wore huge glasses that constantly kept sliding down on her nose. Monee found it a bit distracting to watch her continuously push them up while she was speaking. However, the Chaplin has a very strong and comforting voice that resonated peace. She had a very nurturing air about her. As Chaplin Bryant said prayer Monee could feel what she sometimes felt in the past when she visited a few churches, the presence of God. She knew when the Holy spirit dwelled with in a church because she would experience chills and a strong feeling of unconditional love and peace throughout her body. Monee often felt that having the ability to sense the holy spirit was related to the supernatural experience she had on Easter Sunday when she was twelve.

Chaplin Bryant finished her prayer and played three gospel hymns over the speakers where she and several other inmates sung along. Monee knew one of the songs from when she was a member of her high school gospel choir. It made her feel encouraged as she belted out the words "He Is Worthy!" Monee clapped and rocked from side to side and her mind drifted off to when she was a senior in high school, and she was on stage singing her solo gospel song

"Oh Happy Day!" Monee knew she wasn't the best singer in the choir, she wasn't even a good singer but something inside of her wanted to praise her creator in front of the entire school. She remembered when she told the gospel choir instructor that she wanted to do a solo and Mr. Fisher just smiled and said,

"Alright Monee we just need to find the perfect song for your voice." He never discouraged her, and he smiled and encouraged her the entire time she sang that song on stage. Sometimes it is so easy to get so consumed with darkness that we forget to illuminate the light. Monee never realized how being a member of her high school gospel choir gave her an outlet to temporarily escape from all the confusion and chaos that was happening around her. It instilled in her, the spirit of tenacity and encouragement. Monee didn't realize that singing gospel songs, writing her prayers and poems during the rough times were the tools that was divinely placed in her life to help her persevere. That memory made Monee smile as she continued to clap and rock until the song ended.

"Yes, let's give Jesus and loud praise amen!" Chaplin Debra shouted as she pushed her glasses up on her face.

"Amen! Amen! At this time, I would like to extend the invitation to anyone who would like to say a few kind words about Ms. Isis or a testimony. Even if something is troubling you, please stand up and get it out. This is a time where believers need to come together and encourage one another and although you ladies are incarcerated at this time Jesus loves you and His love is unconditional. God knows the hearts of man and he watches over the good and the evil, but He is merciful and bestows forgiveness and lovingkindness to us sinners that repent. Amen!" Chaplin Debra shouted.

Everyone began to clap and there were several "amens" that echoed through the sanctuary. Then a woman sitting in the last row on the left side of the sanctuary stood up.

"I have been here for six months now awaiting my trial. I have been charged with shooting my husband. Although, I have been married to him for eleven years and he had been beating me for ten years of our marriage. There are several police reports that show that I had made calls for the police to come to our home for domestic violence. Even though there was evidence of spouse abuse, I was still charged for attempted murder and manslaughter! But I know that my God knows it was self-defense! I serve a mighty God and what the devil does to destroy us, God uses it to build us up! Hallelujah!" the woman yelled.

"I thank Jesus for every day that I am breathing, and I know it gets greater later amen!" The woman began to jump and shout, and other women began to wail and scream, "Hallelujah thank you Jesus!"

Monee could tell the woman had been through hell because her top lip was crooked with a visible scar as if it had been severed, and she walked with a slight limp. Monee felt overwhelmed with compassion and shouted, "Glory to God!" She was amazed at this woman's testimony and that the woman wasn't bitter but grateful for still being alive.

Chaplin Bryant chimed in and said "Yes Lawd, God bless you sister! God is telling me to tell you to stay faithful because all charges will be dropped against you, and you will soon be free! Just keep praising Him and He will get the glory!" Again, all the women began clapping and shouting praises. Then the praises began to quiet, and the Chaplin asked was there anyone else who had something to say.

Another woman stood up.

"I just wanted to share that I have been using drugs since I was fifteen years old and witnessed my older brother being stabbed to death by a neighborhood thug who was trying to rob us walking home from the corner store. I have tried all my life to beat this drug addiction, but it wasn't until I met Ms. Isis who helped me realize the reason why I haven't be able to stop using. I didn't even have to share much of my story with her before she told me that I was feeling guilty and responsible for my brother's murder. It was my nagging about wanting to go to the store was the reason why we were there in the first place. She was right! I never realized that, but I have been re-living that horrible day for fifteen years now. Ms. Isis encouraged me and told me that I was not responsible and that every soul has a divine time when they will be called home and it was my brother's time to pass on..." The woman started crying hysterically and couldn't finish her testimony. Another lady standing next to the sobbing woman put her arms around her shoulders. "God bless Ms. Isis!" the woman wailed.

Monee was feeling very emotional and could feel that churning in her gut that she knew if she didn't say something, she would regret it later. Her heart was filled with empathy for these women and she felt an intense amount of love surrounding her. Monee slowly stood up.

"It is amazing the power and strength that God instills in His children to endure a tremendous amount of heartache and pain. It is the Devil's job to confuse, abuse, distort and cause us to abort our life purpose! But I know He is a liar and a thief and in John chapter 16, I can't remember the verse, but it was Jesus who said 'He who believed in me, the works that I do he will do also, and greater works than these he will do! I believe that the same divine power that caused Jesus to manifest miracles is within all of God's children. We just need to figure out how to access it. I know the first part of that is faith." Monee had to stop speaking because the woman began to clap and shout.

"The bible also says, 'beware because we may entertain angels unaware.' Ms. Isis was truly and angel. She was in my cell along with Precious, some of you may know who I am talking about. I am so grateful that God had sent her to us during this challenging time in our lives. Ms. Isis had wise words to share every day and she encouraged me and Precious to be strong and to rely on God for wisdom. It was very hard to watch her die, something that I will never forget. But I know she is with God now and is encouraging the folks in heaven!" Monee chuckled while a few tears fell from her eyes as she sat back down.

"Amen! Amen! Thank you, Jesus! I see we have some of God's warriors in here! God bless you all, especially the ladies who found it in their hearts the courage to stand up and share. Thank you! Well, I would love for us to be able to worship and praise all night but with Officer Tate standing at the door, I know it is time to close. So, ladies let us stand and bow our hears in prayer." Chaplin Bryant said in a hearty voice.

All the women stood and joined hands and Chaplin Bryant said a closing prayer. After the prayer, the inmates began hugging one another as they were leaving out of the sanctuary. Chaplin Bryant grabbed Monee's hand as she was getting ready to walk out of the sanctuary door.

"I would like to speak with you for a moment. Can you come with me please?" Chaplin Bryant said, still holding Monee's hand as she escorted Monee to her office in the back of the sanctuary.

"You can have a seat sweetheart." Chaplin Bryant said as she closed the office door.

"I remember you when you were first brought to this pod a couple of weeks ago. You stood out to me, there was something different about you. I asked the Lord what you were doing in here and today I have received His answer. What is your name sweetheart?" Chaplin Bryant asked with a look of sincere curiosity all over her face.

"Monee Green Ma'am." Monee answered wondering where the Chaplin was going with this conversation.

"Oh, you can call me Chaplin Debra, that's what all the ladies call me." Chaplin Bryant smiled.

"Monee, that is a very interesting name it sounds like money!" Chaplin Bryant smiled again.

"Yes, ma'am my mother said she named me Monee because she felt like I was going to be very rich. But I don't know now, maybe she had it wrong Maybe it was because I was costing her a lot of money." Monee said sadly then sighed.

"Well, I think she was right. You have a bright light inside of you Monee. Why are you so afraid to let it shine?" Chaplin Bryant looked very concerned and was looking into Monee's eyes as if she was trying to see her soul.

"That's funny you should say that because Ms. Isis said the same thing to me right before she died." Tears swelled up in Monee's eyes.

"Well, that is because that is what God wants you to realize that you are one of his chosen stars to shine brightly for His Glory. He showed me somethings about you when you were speaking. You have experienced much pain in your life at an early age, but it was all to help you grow into your divine purpose. You were born with the strength to move mountains and overcome many hardships."

"Maybe that is what my dream last night symbolizes...hardships."

"You had a dream, tell me about it." Chaplin Bryant leaned in toward Monee and folded her hands on her desk and waited. Monee shared her dream with Chaplin Bryant.

"You have the gift to interpret dreams?" Monee asked with hope emanating from her voice.

"I have many gifts, often God will reveal what needs to be revealed." Chaplin Bryant leaned back into her chair, closed her eyes, and took three deep long breaths. Monee waited and intensely watched the Chaplin. After her third exhale Chaplin Bryant sat up erect in her chair.

"The ship represents your spiritual journey. The ship also represents your ability to conquer problems that seem impossible to overcome. Water represents the spiritual realm, the unseen to the physical eye and your emotions. Are you following me?"

"Yes, I understand." Monee replied.

"The storm and the violent waves are your problems and trials during the first part of your life. Also, what you are going through right now is difficult and painful. You are having a rough time that is damaging you emotionally and mentally, but your spirit will not be broken. Once you learn to control your emotions and change how you feel about yourself the storm will calm and then sun will shine. You do know that you have the power within you to control your emotions, don't you?" The Chaplain asked. Monee answer yes with a quick nod.

"Once you tap into your power, your major storms will be over in your life and the sun, your true self will emerge, and you will prosper. Does that make sense to you?" Chaplin Bryant asked her, but before Monee could answer there was a knock at the door.

"Come in Officer Tate." Chaplin could tell who was at the door because the office door was glass. Officer Tate opened the door and walked in.

"Now Chaplin Bryant you know the rules and if you are going to offer counseling to one of the inmates it must get approve first and time must be allotted. I understand that Ms. Isis was in the same cell as inmate Green, so due to the extenuating circumstances I will let this go. Ms. Green, time to go." Officer Tate looked at Monee and nodded her head towards the door.

"Apologies Officer, I appreciate you understanding that God is on divine time and when the spirit moves me to comfort one of His chosen, I must do so. Monee God instructed me to give this too you. You are very familiar with His word, and He knows you need them now. God bless you and don't be afraid to shine." Chaplin Bryant handed Monee a bible, ink pen and a new legal pad of writing paper. Chaplin Bryant's face was beaming with encouragement and love. Her smile was big and wide, for the first time since Monee had been speaking with her, she could see every one of the Chaplin's big white teeth.

"God bless you too and thank you for your guidance." Monee smiled brightly back at the Chaplin and took the bible, pen and pad; clutched it to her chest and followed Officer Tate back to her pod.

Reflections

Discovering Your True Calling & Surrendering to the Process

When Monee was an adolescence and would attend different religious services with her mother, she learned about the Universal Law of Attraction. This troubled Monee deeply because she could not understand how at age five, she attracted a rapist into her life. This caused Monee to have more questions about God, Jesus, religion the Universal Laws and how she fit into the scheme of it all. She didn't realize that her questions are thoughts, and her thoughts are energy. When we send out thoughts the Universe will surely send us back answers. The biblical scripture Matthew chapter 7 v. 7 states:

"Ask, and it will be given to you; seek and you will find; knock, and it will be opened for you."

Monee began to receive her answers through challenges, experiences and synchronicities. She learned about the Universal Law of Magnetic Affinities. This law states, that human beings choose key attributes and circumstances about their life before entering this physical reality. We are souls having a human experience; before we have this experience, we exist in the spiritual realm. It is there that souls choose the time and location of their birth, who their parents will be, other souls who will interact and impact their life. The Astrological time of the soul's birth will determine personality traits, abilities, strengths, and weaknesses. Location and economic status of the parents all are divinely designed to assist the soul with what lesson and/or experience the soul wants to achieve during that lifetime.

Once Monee understood the law of Magnetic affinities, it was still hard for her to accept that she chose to be raped at five years old. So, she continued to ask questions to get a deeper understanding. Her primary question became "Why am I here and what is my divine purpose?" She began to have a reoccurring dream; that she was back in her home that she grew up in Cleveland. The house would sometime change; however the dream was always the same; she was trying to free children's souls that were trapped in the attic. After having the dream several times Monee realized that the dream was telling her what her calling was, to help children that suffered trauma just like she did!

Do you know what your calling or divine purpose is? If so, what ways did you receive messages or gain an inner knowing about your calling? If you do not know your calling or divine purpose in this lifetime; write down things you enjoyed doing as a child. Also write down the careers you wanted to pursue when you were a child:

_____

_____

_____

_____

_____

_____

_____

_____

_____

_____

_____

_____

_____

_____

_____

_____

_____

_____

_____

_____

_____

_____

_____

_____

_____

Now think about the challenges and traumas you experienced. Do you feel an inner calling in some way that you want to help people that have experienced something similar? Take some time to jot down a few thoughts or ideas that come to mind:

_____

_____

_____

_____

_____

_____

_____

_____

_____

_____

_____

_____

_____

Think about your passions; activities that you enjoy doing. What do you love to even if you didn't get paid doing it? Usually this is your true purpose; write it down:

_____

_____

_____

_____

_____

_____

_____

_____

_____

_____

_____

_____

The Universal Law of Free Will

All answers lie within. There are many different paths a soul can take on this human journey to connect with Source and gain spiritual enlightenment. If you are reading this book, it is not by accident; you have a desire to grow spiritually. Monee found herself incarcerated and during that time she was forced to be confined in that jail cell. However, it was her choice how she was going to respond to situation. She could have resisted and rebelled, and she would have never gained a new perspective about her life and the traumas she had been through.

Spirit beings having a human experience always have the power to choose how they react to major events that happen in their life. This is the Law of Free Will; the freedom to respond as you so please. This law operates in three distinct ways:

1. You have the power to regulate how a major event or crisis is going to impact you. You can choose your thoughts, feelings and actions when going through a challenge; you can transcend the challenge or minimize the impact of the disharmonious event, if one utilizes learned wisdom gained from previous events.

2. Once you achieve a "Master of Life Awareness," the ability to practice conscious detachment during a major life event, the less affected you will be by negativity. You will be able to allow the negativity to flow through you but not control you and your emotions.

3. No matter what you are going through, you always have the power to respond with positive emotions, compassion and with integrity. In doing so, your challenges will become less, and your positive manifestations will become more frequent.

The Universal Law of Conscious Detachment

Monee was able to detach from the outside world and go within. During her incarceration, she reflected on her past and discover how she ended up in jail. While in jail, she also learned how to surrender and stop resisting what she could not control. This is the Universal Law of Conscious Detachment. What we resist persists. Instead of Monee isolating herself, she shared her trials and truth with her cellmates. She extended Precious advice and showed Ms. Isis compassion and respect. There is an old adage that states, "when the student is ready the teacher appears." Ms. Isis was there in the same cell with Monee to share wisdom and encouragement. The chaplain gave Monee a bible to read. Monee opened her heart to receive answers and she got them.

What questions do you have about your life right now? Write them down:

_____

_____

_____

_____

_____

_____

_____

_____

_____

_____

_____

_____

_____

Did any answers to your questions pop into your mind? If not, know that your questions will be answered and pay attention to how the answers come to you.

If you did receive some of the answers from your own inner guidance, write them down:

_____

_____

_____

_____

_____

_____

_____

_____

_____

_____

_____

_____

_____

Affirmations to Connect with Your Higher Self and Discover Your Divine Purpose

I am connected to my true self.

I am a powerful spiritual being manifesting my divine purpose.

I am spreading love with my being.

I am open for new ways of communicating my wants needs and desires.

I am speaking and living my truth and I am grateful.

I am trusting my inner voice.

I am always guided by the energy of creation, and I choose to trust and allow.

I allow the whispers of the universe to speak to my heart.

I am allowing my inner voice to speak confidently and boldly.

I am open to new ideas and new ways of expression.

I am asking because I know that is the key to receiving.

I am living in alignment with my highest self.

I am passionate and boldly expressing my divinity.

I allow myself to love myself and that connects me to true freedom.

Clear as the clearest blue sky I am communicating my wants and needs.

I choose to take 100% responsibility for my life, and I am creating the life that I want to experience.

I am allowing my true self to shine through with more power and light than ever before.

Scriptures Regarding Spiritual Calling and Gifts

Matthew Chapter 22 v. 14
"For many are called, but few are chosen." (I recommend reading the entire chapter - Parable of the Marriage Feast)

Romans Chapter 8 v. 28
"And we know that all things work together for good to those who love God, to those who are the called according to His purpose."

Proverbs Chapter 18 v. 16
"A man's gift makes room for him and brings him before great men."

Everybody Has A Dream

While in these days of my youth
As I wander through the world
I search everywhere for a true love.
But it is more than just being loved,
If I need companionship or a comforting
thought to feel good,
I think about God.
I dream of becoming a success.
Everybody has a dream.
If I believe in myself and words from God
can inspire me,
then all I have to do is to keep hope burning
in my heart.
So let me dream and conquer my obstacles
and I will lose myself in determination and all my dreams
will become reality.
I know that everybody has a dream.
Everybody has a dream,
and this is my dream…
to love and be loved by someone special.

Chapter 7

Strongholds Are Broken

Monee returned to her cell to find Precious was still on the floor in the fetal position and sound asleep. Monee glanced over to the empty bottom bunk. It was difficult that the two inmates had to remain in the cell after Ms. Isis died in there. So, she understood that Precious couldn't bring herself to sleep on that bunk. Monee hopped onto her bunk with Bible in hand and laid there reflecting on the prayer service and her conversation with Chaplin Bryant. Monee was in awe; her mind was racing. There were hundreds of thoughts invading her mind simultaneously, and she couldn't focus on anything.

Before opening the Bible, she did what she always did at home; she said a small prayer. "God, give me the words of wisdom that I need most right now. Thank you!"

Monee opened the Bible to a random page. The Bible opened to the book of Proverbs, chapters one through three. Her technique when she opened the Bible to a random page to receive guidance was to start at the top of the left page, which was the beginning of Chapter one, The purpose of Proverbs. Then she would scan down the page to see if any scripture would jump out at her or catch her eye. She continued to scan chapter two on the right page, but nothing seemed to stand out. Then Monee scanned the last corner of the page, which was the beginning of chapter three; "The Benefits of Wisdom" was the title.

Monee continued to scan starting with verse one, and verse five seemed to lift off the page and pulsate like an open sign hanging in a store late at night, when all other stores are closed. Monee began to read verse 5,

"Trust in the Lord with all your heart,

and lean not on your own understanding;"

She continued to read verse 6, "In all your ways acknowledge Him,

And He shall direct your paths." Monee was astounded. She closed her eyes, took a deep breath, and heard that still small voice say, "Keep reading." Monee opened her eyes and looked at chapter three verse seven,

"Do not be wise in your own eyes;

Fear the LORD and depart from evil.

It will be health to your flesh,

And strength to your bones."

Monee stopped reading and grabbed the pen and writing pad that the Chaplin had given her from the end of her bed. She closed her eyes again and reflected on all the major decisions that she made in her life. She realized that most of the major decisions that she made in her past were either out of fear or lack of self-love. *"When did I ever actually trust God enough to give my problems and burdens to Him? When did I ever really surrender and allow God to work things out without me trying to make things happen?"*

Monee wrote down Proverbs chapter 3:5-6 on the writing pad. Then, she sat there for several minutes in deep thought. *"I can really only remember a few major decisions that I prayed about and waited on God to reveal the answer."* Monee thought about her childhood. She went back in her mind and scanned her memories.

She began to write, *Getting raped at five years old was not a decision, it wasn't my fault. It was a child that was left unprotected for the devil to take an opportunity to defile an innocent virgin child. I made the decision out of fear to not reveal what the devil had done to me. I was too young to understand what had just been done to me and how it would mentally, spiritually, and physically affect me for the rest of my life. I told my mother that I didn't need therapy and that was the end of the discussion. Children don't make decisions for themselves at least not when it comes to the welfare and mental health of the child! I was not even old enough to process accurately that I still had value and was spiritually a virgin, I never made the decision to give myself to a man.*

Unfortunately, that wisdom was not given to me, not by my mother and not by my father. I didn't have anyone growing up as a child to instill in me to love and respect Monee. Therefore, it was easy for me to have sex at the age of twelve and give myself to a sixteen-year-old boy who didn't even know my real name or my real age.

Tears began to quickly fall from Monee's eyes as if it was the first rain after a drought. Monee saw her beautiful son Nathan smiling at her when he was just an infant. She smiled as she remembered how she was going to get an abortion, until the day that a loving Angel came to her and promised her that she would have a son, and he would grow to be a great king. Monee was able to stop agonizing over her decision and trusted the Angel and God. It was then that Monee accepted that her pregnancy was not a mistake and that it was meant for her to have her son at eighteen.

Deciding to continue her education and go to college after she graduated from high school was a no-brainer for Monee. She was always very ambitious and knew she wanted and would need a college degree. However, when her mother told her it was time to move out and be on her own, deciding to go to college in a different city was divinely inspired and everything fell in place. Her transition to Columbus, Ohio, went smoothly. Monee knew that God was divinely guiding her steps. However, when she got to college, Monee began to stop listening to her inner guidance and began making decisions out of fear and lack of self-discipline. She was like a solider going to war with no training and no gun. The freedom she gained caused her to lose herself even more.

Monee kept writing, *In all your ways acknowledge Him, and He shall direct your paths. Wow! I always wrote my prayers out on paper because it was easier to keep my thoughts focused and clear that way. But I was always so driven and determined to make things happen for me that I didn't allow God to show me His way. I didn't know how to do things your way, Lord. I did what I wanted to do.*

Monee wiped her tears from her cheeks and wrote down verse seven on her writing pad. *Do not be wise in your own eyes;*

"*Hell, I was downright stupid at times,*" she thought. "*I don't know what person in their right mind decides to do drugs!*" She shook her head. Then, she heard that still small voice say, "You wasn't in your right mind, Monee."

"*You are right!*" Monee eyes got big, and her heart began beating fast as she finished writing down verses seven and eight, *Fear the LORD and depart from evil. It will be health to your flesh and strength to your bones. Whoa, this is deep! I was in evil environments interacting with dark spirits daily. The Devil is so cunning, I begin to tell myself that what I was doing was ok. I got to do what I got to do for me and my son. Even if that meant taking off all my clothes in front of strangers and having to be intoxicated and high to do it. What an oxymoron!*

How can someone stay healthy and strong in an environment that encourages sex, alcohol, and drugs? It is like putting a child in a toy store and telling that child not to touch anything, that's insanity! I was playing with fire, and I didn't know the rules of the game. However, now I know that no matter what route a child of God decides to take, it might take them longer, but they will get to their destination. I know it was meant for me to leave Columbus and move to Atlanta! The law of synchronicity was so obvious at that time in my life even Red couldn't deny it. Even though that was a very challenging time for me, I did utilize my gifts of intuition and claircognizance.

O   O   O

Monee's thoughts were interrupted when she heard Precious sitting on the toilet urinating. Monee sat up on her bunk. "Hey girl, you been sleeping a long time. Are you ok?" Monee asked.

"Yeah, Monee, but I am ready to get the hell out of here. I can't take this shit no more! I feel like I am about to go crazy. These walls are closing in on me, and I keep hearing Ms. Isis struggling to breathe in my head!" Precious groaned as she flushed the toilet. "It's amazing how in jail inmates become accustomed to doing things in public that we would never imagine doing in front of another when we are free. I guess that's the purpose to make an inmate as uncomfortable as possible to encourage them not to return. However, it is interesting how most first-time offenders usually become repeat offenders."

Monee turned to allow Precious some privacy to pull her pants up. "I know exactly how you feel, Precious. I find it strange that I have heard Ms. Isis struggling to breathe, too. I guess all we can do is continue to pray. Look what I got!" Monee said with excitement in her voice and held up the Bible that Chaplin Bryant gave her.

"A bible?" Precious said with distain. "I don't believe in God, Jehovah, Jesus, or whatever else you so-called God-fearing folk believe in!" Precious snapped as she turned her back to Monee to wash her hands in the sink.

Monee was in awe. She had always found it hard to believe that there were actually people in the world that didn't believe in a high power. Monee regarded atheists to be the eighth wonder of the world because she couldn't imagine going through all the hell she had been through without her strong faith and belief in God. Monee knew that she had witnessed too many miracles to not be a believer. However, Monee did consider that had she not had the supernatural experience she had at age twelve would it be so easy for her to believe in God? She wasn't sure. So, she tried her best not to judge people for their personal beliefs. God gave man with free choice, and that is how she let go of her anger with God when Nefarius initially left her back when they were living in Cleveland.

Monee realized that after Nefarius left her, she was angry with both God and Nefarius. Monee thought God had forsaken her. Why did you send me the God-fearing man who taught me the truth about God's true name encrypted in the tetra-grammaton and that Jesus wasn't the true name of the Messiah? But then Monee realized that she experienced the same revolt from Nefarius that God experienced from Lucifer. The ego is death to the soul. Lucifer and Nefarius both allowed the dark side of themselves to take over and was driven by ego and pride. Both made a conscious decision to destroy a beautiful relationship with another being that loved them unconditionally. Both deceived themselves into believing that they were inde-structible and did not need anyone.

Monee in her hurt anger and pain discarded all her positive tools that she had begun to use to create a new life with Nefarius and returned to her shadow self. Thinking that God was playing a cruel trick on her, Monee rebelled and went back to self-medicating and self-destructive behavior. Monee thought that the day she met Nefarius would be the last day that she would ever take her clothes off in front of another man, but that false wall of protection was torn down when he walked out on her and their children. Monee failed to realize that no human was ever her savior and that the Divine she was always seeking outside of herself or within a man was always within her and that she had to discover her true power and value.

"Precious, I understand why you don't acknowledge God right now. You have lost your mother and witnessed so much darkness that it is justifiable that you are angry with Him. However, He acknowledges you, and He loves you so much that He is patient, and His Lovingkindness and Grace are always there ready to be extended to you. All you have to do is ask for His help, and you shall receive it. I am a living witness to the Divine Power of God!" Monee said with a pureness in her heart that for a brief moment she could feel that she had touched a part of Precious's heart and a bit of healing to her soul.

Precious had opened her mouth to say something, but the loud intruding jail cell lock clicked open, and their cell door slowly slid open.

"Inmate Monee Green, pack up, you are getting released!" Officer Tate belted out over the intercom. "Released?" Monee was in a state of shock; she couldn't believe it. "I am going home? I'm going home to my babies!" Monee wanted to be sure that she understood what was happening. Monee stepped out of the jail cell and stood by the wall to see if Officer Tate would repeat herself.

"Inmate Green, what about pack up you don't understand?" Officer Tate snapped in a sarcastic tone. Monee began jumping up and down and ran back into the cell and looked at Precious. The two of them locked arms and were jumping up and down together. Monee shouted, "I'm going home!" a few more times, and then she began to frantically rip her mattress off the steel bunk and tossed her plastic cup, spork, toothbrush, and washcloth all inside the sheet and turned to walk out of the cell. Then she turned around and looked at Precious who sadly looked back at Monee. She ran to her and gave her another warm embrace and gave her the Bible the Chaplin Bryant gave her.

"Trust in the Lord with All thine Heart lean not to your own understanding. Seek Him and truth you shall find. God bless you!" Monee smiled and walked out, dragging the mattress down the steps with one hand and the sheet bundled up in the other.

It was thirty minutes later that Monee was being escorted back through the jail halls that she had walked down twenty-two days ago. Now, she was taking the same walk to freedom and to return to her life as a different woman. Monee knew now that she was no longer able to live her life as a human being but as a spiritual being having a human experience. Monee now realized that she attracted all the men into her life good and bad, and that every relationship she had was a reflection of how she was feeling on the inside at that time. Monee knew that her going backward and allowing Nefarius back into her life and in her personal space was out of lack of self-love and deceiving herself to believe that she could help someone else heal before healing herself. Monee now understood that it was finally time to start loving Monee and to make Monee's healing the top priority in her life. She didn't know where this new path of revelation was going to lead her, but one thing she did know was she was no longer a victim of her past but was the victor over her circumstances.

Monee walked out of the jail and embraced her mother who was standing there waiting for her. "Mom, take me home so I can put the devil out of my house," she said. "Thank you, Mother, for allowing God to use you to set me free, and thank you, God, for your Mercy and Grace! Hallelujah!"

Illusions

Trapped inside a spider's web
Fighting for freedom
Struggling to survive
Just don't want to stay alive
But want the ultimate goal in life
Thinking what I want is all I really need
Continuing to discover that the last
thing I need is a lover
That is passion sugar coated
You'll always be taking a chance
to a delusion you've devoted
Playing a game of Russian roulette
Believing you can pull the trigger
and there will never be any consequence.
Flabbergasted at the turn of events
How could all this confusion be heaven sent
I know the reality of the belief in duality
Will always hinder the possibility
of heaven on earth
To kill the devil what does it mean
I can't believe that my inner thoughts
stem from being such an evil thing
How is it that now I'm being used?
All this judgment is causing me to
become more confused
Always trusted in my intuition
Now I'm supposed to give it up because

I'm not in charge of the mission
Is this mission impossible with me
Or is this a stepping stone to eternity
I am definitely eager to see
how it is my inner me is so off beat
I can't proclaim to know God's plan
But one thing I will not do is put my trust in a man
Submission is all right, but humility is one
I can't seem to understand
There is something inside of me
Something I've had all my life
That something special is not going to change
because I'm some man's wife
I believe there is more to life than doing
what some man say
I pray you help me understand YAHWEH
So now I'm leaving you to you
There is nothing else that I can do
There is no justification
For our lack of communication
Other than the obvious implication
that we have no relation
Ship that is fine for me to sail on my own
Guess we can't share the same throne
I can't deceive myself to believe I'm always wrong
If that's the case I might as well sacrifice my life
What would be the use when in me there is no truth
On the straight and narrow I'll stay
I do believe in the one and only true living God YAHWEH
He loves me if no one else does and that is the only
love I need to make it to heaven above
To you I have nothing to offer
The book of my life God is the author

You can't explain or read me
You don't know my reality
The only one who can breathe for me is me
So stop trying to judge me as if
you created my destiny
What is going to be will be
Even if that is you without me

Faces of ME

Conceptualize as I mesmerize about accomplishing my dreams.
As I reflect, I now realize the world is not always as it seems.
Persons, places, and things can be the most frightening things when you don't
understand what they mean.

An innocence that I thought was stolen but the lie
had my potential frozen, captured, and now in captivity,
I fight to set my true self free!

My inner me is no longer my enemy because my soul has broken free!
Find out who you are before you decide what you are going to become,
shed light on the darkness and set your soul free!

www.ingramcontent.com/pod-product-compliance
Lightning Source LLC
Chambersburg PA
CBHW082054090726
47909CB00010B/3024